INEVITABLE

REACTION

A Mel Addison Mystery Series

A NOVEL

BY

ANGELA ABDERHALDEN

Seventh Wave Books, LLC

Book One
Questionable Ethics

Book Two
Unintentional Victim

Book Three
Inevitable Reaction

Inevitable Reaction
First Edition

Seventh Wave Books, LLC
2012

Seventh Wave Books, LLC
www.seventhwavebooks.com

First Paperback Edition: 2012

The characters, names, incidents, organizations, dialogue, and events portrayed in this book are fictitious. Any similarity to a real person, living or dead is coincidental and not intended by the author.

Inevitable Reaction: a novel/ by Angela Abderhalden

ISBN-13: 978-1938852046 (pbk)

Cover design by Jason Wilcox

Printed in the United States of America

Thanks to Jason for all his hard work and to Deb for the awesome editing job. You guys are great.

Congratulations to Amanda Goins the winner of the Name A Character After You Contest.

As always thanks to my family.

CHAPTER 1

What was that?

I bolted up in bed, heart pounding. The dark in my room enveloped me, and I knew, without a doubt, that something was wrong. Horribly wrong.

I concentrated hard but couldn't hear anything amiss. No noise. No movement. Nothing. Not convinced that this was just my imagination, I grabbed my three-cell Maglite from the nightstand and threw off the covers. Cautiously, I moved to the bedroom doorway. Again I concentrated hard, ignoring the thumping in my ear.

Nothing.

Clutching the flashlight even more defensively, I edged out of the doorway. The quiet was unnerving. I peered into every corner, in all directions, checking out the dimly lit room. The moonlight peeking through the window illuminated the rest of the apartment. My eyes paused momentarily on the two windows. Closed.

Nobody.

With the living room secured, I panned my eyes around the second bedroom located right next to my bedroom. Window closed. No one. Yet the hairs on the back of my neck were still up. My gut twisted. *Something is wrong here.*

Again I strained my ears so hard I heard the thundering of my heart beat. *A noise! On the edge of hearing. On the outside stairs.*

I dashed through the living room. As I rushed past my couch, I felt that the room was much cooler than it should have been. It hit me harder as I skidded to a stop in the kitchen, my legs and arms getting goose bumps from

1

the cold. With clammy hands grasping the heavy flashlight tighter, I glanced at the window, closed. My eyes snapped to the door. Closed. Bottom locked. Dead bolt, not.

In one fluid motion, I slid into my snow boots near the door and plucked my winter coat off the hook, slipping it on. Snatching open the door, I leaped onto the landing.

The cold hit me like a slap. My nose crinkled as I took a breath letting me know that the temperature had to be near zero. There was no noise or movement on the stairs. It hadn't snowed yet, so no foot prints.

Leaning over the top rail, I scanned the sidewalk below. Noone. My eyes flashed to the door leading to Dad's bar below me. Closed.

Taking a deep breath to ease my heart rate, I studied the surrounding area. Dead quiet. Not unexpected, it was the middle of the night. With a frown and starting to shiver, I examined the area one more time before moving back into the apartment.

As I leaned on the door, I turned the dead bolt, which gave a reassuring thunk and locked the bottom lock. *Did I imagine all of this? No.* I frowned. The room was definitely colder, and I did hear that noise. *I did.* Slowly I walked through my apartment again, checking every corner, looking to see if even a book was out of place. But it wasn't.

I slipped back into bed but couldn't fall asleep. Every mundane noise kept me awake.

Chapter Two

Turning to lock my door the next morning on my way to work, I paused. *Were those scratches at the keyhole there before?* I studied them. I couldn't remember if they had been there. I frowned as I locked the door. With a shake of my head I tried to convince myself that I had imagined the night before.

Didn't work.

Sitting in my Jeep, I stopped with my key in the ignition. Okay, now my imagination was running wild. The hair on my neck was up again. I looked around but saw no one unusual or suspicious.

I drove to work, my eyes continually panning to the rearview mirror to check if someone was following me. I didn't spot anyone.

Work today consisted of taking over for John Huddleston, whose job it was to watch a subject suspected of passing information to the competition about one of the electronic research businesses in town. Security Investigations, the business I work for, had been hired to see if we could find out who, when and where.

Boring.

Especially boring since it was a cold, grey, depressing day. Worse, we couldn't run the heater very often since we were trying to stay undetected. And it was going to snow. I could feel it in my bones. I waved at John who pulled away in his non-descript black Toyota pickup. His other car was a silver mustang, not a good car for surveillance. He was one of my bosses. Rich, my brother, was my other boss.

After a few minutes, I felt again that I was the one being watched. I looked around, including staring at my rearview mirror, but I didn't see anyone as I squirmed in my seat. *What is wrong with me? There's no reason for this feeling.*

Yet, I couldn't shake the feeling all day, even as I followed our mark to his job at Alliance Research in the late morning. I guess as a manager his hours were more flexible. I parked in the strip mall across from his building. At least now I could run the heater more often. As I waved my cold hands in front of the heater to warm them, I glanced around again. With a sigh, I settled back into my seat grabbing my hot chocolate in my thermos. Now I got to wait to see if he went anywhere during the day.

By the time Rich relieved me in the afternoon, I was sore from sitting in the car, tired of the rock station I was listening to and ready to give my nerves a break. They were tense from not only the constant watch of our subject but also from watching everything else, knowing that *I* was being watched too.

I locked up my Jeep at the office, glancing around. With a frown, I headed into Security Investigations. The biting wind whipped at me as I hurried inside. It hadn't snowed yet, but from the looks of the sky, it wouldn't be long.

I opened the door, greeted by the bell and the warmth of the office. It was quiet here today. Pam's desk looked lonely. Even the couch against the wall looked depressed. I suppressed a grin. *Gotta stop letting my feelings overshadow everything.* I heard scraping noises in one of the offices and knew that John was headed out. "It's just me."

"Come see me, Mel." It was not a friendly tone.

Just great! The boss is mad about something. I shrugged out of my winter coat and tossed it on the coat rack near the door. A glance at my watch, as I headed down the short hallway, showed it was three in the afternoon. I was dead tired and just wanted to go home.

"Yeah?" I asked the big, dark haired man seated behind his desk. His office was spartan and neat, everything in place, probably a left over from his military years. John was ex-Special Forces, still with the build and the attitude.

John raised his head, his eyes guarded. The air was thick with tension. Lately it had been this way between us, especially when we were alone in the office. "Anything?"

I shook my head. "I followed him all day, to get coffee on his way to work, then at work. Just his normal routine. I kept a log like you wanted. Rich has the evening slot, but I bet Mr. Langerhorn just sits tight at home tonight. It's gonna snow any minute."

John nodded and held out some phone messages. Pam, our regular secretary, was gone for a week on a family emergency. That meant that one of us had to answer the phones. I had suggested hiring a temp, but both John and Rich dismissed it since our business is based on confidentiality.

I'm Melissa 'Mel' Addison, and I work for Security Investigations, the only private detective agency in Quincy, Illinois. John and Rich are co-owners. They brought me on a short time ago to apprentice as a detective.

Quincy Illinois is a small town in middle America with small town problems. We sit on the western most side of Illinois on the Mississippi River across from Missouri, about fifteen miles upstream from Hannibal.

I grabbed the messages from John. "What's the schedule for tomorrow? Am I still taking over for you at seven a.m.?"

John leaned back in his chair. "I'll call first thing in the morning. Let's wait and see."

I nodded and headed across the hall to my office. My new desk was piled high with folders. Unlike John, I was a less organized person but still better organized than Rich my brother, whose office looked like a bomb hit it. I was doing employment screening for two clients. Since I was 'low man' here at the agency, I got all of the grunt jobs. As I sat, I thumbed through the call sheets.

One was from my Dad. The second was only a name. She was my travel agent, and I knew it was about tickets to Florida for next week that no one knew about. Another call sheet was from a former client's mother in Oregon. I sighed. I didn't want to call her back but I felt obligated. The next was from Tim Henkle. I frowned. *Who is this?* The last was from Jason Landry in Maryland.

I picked up the phone and dialed Jason first. Since it was already five in Maryland, I might have missed him. As I waited, I glanced at the Tim Henkle's number. *Did I know him?*

"Landry."

"Jason, I got your message."

"Oh hi, Mel. Yeah. I just wanted to let you know that we'll have to file papers to sue the two companies. I wanted to make sure that you're still on board with it."

"Absolutely. Whatever you think is right, Jason." I shook my head wishing everything about the accident was finished. I tried hard daily to move on with life. "So this means what, in terms of a settlement and restitution?" I heard him take a breath.

"Well, it depends on the courts. The earliest we could hope for is this summer, but I think the insurance company's lawyers are going to drag it out."

I frowned. Jason was a lawyer in my deceased husband's law firm. A year ago I had been in a car accident that took both my husband's life and that of our only child. I escaped with massive injuries to the chest and right leg. It took over six months before I even began to feel normal. The scars, emotional and physical, will be with me forever.

I saw movement at my door and noticed John looking in. He leaned on the door post, concern showed in his eyes. I held up my finger for him to wait. "What about our last offer?"

"It was no. It's up to you, but my advice is we might get even more with a jury trial. They were clearly in the wrong."

I sighed and rubbed my face. "Do whatever we need to do, Jason."

"Good. As you know, the system is sometimes slow."

"Yeah. This is so infuriating."

"I know. If you need anything from me in the next two weeks, talk to my secretary, Mary. Wendy and I are going on a vacation in the Caribbean. When I get back, I'll to try to light a fire under their butts."

"Okay."

"How are things going, Mel?"

I shook my head. "I'm fine. Enjoy the weather down there." I hung up the phone and looked at John. "Yeah?"

John studied me, the hard expression gone. "You got another call from Tim Henkle." He held out the paper to me. "Lawsuit in Maryland?"

I nodded taking the note. "The shipping company and the insurance company are dragging their feet." I leaned back in my chair and stared at my hands.

"Are you okay?"

I gave him a slight smile. "Next week will be hard. It'll be a year on Wednesday." I absentmindedly rubbed my right side where my scar was, then picked up the message from Tim Henkle. I looked at John. "Who is this?"

John frowned. "His voice sounded familiar."

I picked up the phone and dialed. "Tim Henkle, please." I looked up at John. "No. Thanks." I rested the phone back on its cradle slowly.

"Who was it?"

"Bart Hessor." A figure from my past and the local drug lord.

John's eyes hardened.

Chapter Three

"Hey, I didn't call him." I held up my hands, knowing what John was thinking.

"I didn't say anything to Rich about your last little adventure with Hessor, but if this continues, I will. Mark my word."

"John-"

"No. Hessor is bad news. I don't care what you have to do, make him understand that you are not interested in him."

"Look-" I started again. My anger rising quickly. We had had this argument just a few months ago.

I had met Hessor, an old boyfriend, on my first case with Rich and John. He indicated that he wanted to date me again. Then four months ago, I needed his 'services' to gather information. Being involved with the less than upstanding citizens, I had contacted him to help me. He made it clear at that time that he wanted to sleep with me. John caught me out on the information collecting 'date' with him. Yes, I was using Bart, but it was the only way to gather a piece of crucial evidence.

The argument between us was heated. John promised not to tell Rich or anyone else in my family, but he also made it clear that I was not to associate with Hessor again, even if it was the only way to get information. John was more of a big brother that night than an employer. He was right, but I wasn't about to admit that.

Bart's family and mine have been at odds for a long number of years. Bart's aunt and other members of his family are and were known members of the local drug cartel. If you can call the people who run the drugs in Quincy a cartel. My dad was a cop and brought Bart's aunt to justice but not before almost losing his life. Rich was also a cop, retired due to a disability and had tried time and time again to put Bart away. Mitch, my other brother still on the force, had taken up Rich's crusade.

During high school, right before dad arrested Bart's aunt, I had dated Bart. I was probably rebelling against my family, looking back on it. Bart was good looking, and I had been wild in my teenage years. No one in my family knew about the little two week affair. I think Rich suspected, but only John knows for sure.

"I will make an issue of it. Do not see Hessor again," he interrupted. Then he pointed at me. John never pointed.

I bunched up my fist and slammed it on the desk. As I stood, I looked John in the eyes. "I am not pursuing him, John. I told you the last time, I was using him. I don't want to sleep with him, so you can stop treating me like a teenager!"

John didn't blink or move a muscle. "You stay away from Hessor."

I took a deep breath to calm myself. My volcanic temper is legendary in my family. "Okay. I told him, like I promised you. I'll try again."

John shook his head. "Not try. Do."

"I will, I promise."

John's eyes held mine. "I'm heading home for some shut-eye. If it starts looking bad out, close up shop early." He stood staring at me. Then he moved back to his office. On his way out, he stopped in the hall to put on his coat. "Mel."

I looked up. That look returned to his eyes. "I get it."

John pointed again and left.

I sat back and tossed the paper I was holding onto the desk. I huffed. *Who cares if he tells Rich? It isn't my fault Bart doesn't get it. It isn't like I wanted to sleep with him.*

Shaking my head, I leaned forward and grabbed another call back sheet. I dialed the Oregon number. I knew why I didn't want John to tell Rich. I didn't want to disappoint my family. I was older and wiser now. And John knew that too.

"Olivia Trolowski, please," I paused. "It's Mel Addison from Illinois. Thanks."

She was the mother of Roma Trolowski, a former client that had been murdered in Oregon. We had been trying to help Roma deal with a stalker while she lived here in Quincy. Roma wanted to visit her family without Devon Miles, her stalker, knowing about it. So I faked being her at her house for several days in order to trick him and give Roma time alone with her family. But we hadn't fooled Miles for long. Later that week we got a call from the Oregon State Police that Roma had been murdered. We immediately turned over all of our evidence to them. So far, Devon Miles was still on the loose, although a warrant for his arrest on murder charges had been issued.

"Thank you for returning my phone call so fast," Olivia said.

"What can I do for you, Olivia?"

"I just wanted to thank you again for helping get Roma's stuff shipped back here. "I…" Olivia sniffled. "Have you heard anything about Miles?"

"No, I haven't. I don't think the Oregon State Police would call anyway. They received our research and paperwork. I hope it helped. Rich and I are still working our contacts to see if we can find him, but so far there's nothing."

"Thank you again for helping our daughter. She was so alive; there was a spark in her voice and a bounce to her step." Olivia sniffled again.

"I just wish we could have done more."

"Please stay in touch with us about, well, if you hear anything."

"I will, Olivia. I promised you that at Roma's funeral."

After several more reassurances to the grieving mother, I finally hung up. I called Dad next at the bar number. "Hey Dad, what's up?"

"Can I ask you to do me a big favor?"

"Sure. What?"

"Can you watch the bar tonight? I promised Dot that I'd go with her to do rounds of the old folk's homes and elderly shut-ins and forgot that Cam has to work. If the weather turns bad, it'll be a slow night anyway."

I smiled. Dad and my brother Cameron owned the bar together. Cam works on the fire department, and I had been helping them out doing odd jobs at the bar since I moved back to Illinois. I also lived upstairs from The Full Moon, renting the apartment from Dad. "Sure, Dad not a problem. I'll close up early here, say in about an hour. Is that good for you?"

"That would be great. Thanks. I'll see you then."

The night turned out just like he predicted. The snow started and people stayed home, except for the regulars. Two men were there every night regardless. Soon even they were gone.

A man walked into the bar and sat at the far end. Something about him made me suspicious, but I headed to wait on him anyway. "Can I get you something?"

"Soda."

"Just so you know, I'll be closing in about an hour. With it snowing this heavily, no one in their right mind would be out tonight."

He smiled as he watched me get the drink. As I got his change, he grabbed his cell and spoke softly into it. By the time I handed him his money, he was off the phone.

I returned to the stool located near the cash register near the middle of the bar. I could tell he wanted to be left alone, but I had a feeling that he was waiting for something. I didn't feel threatened, but I've always been one to trust my feelings. They were screaming right now.

Less than two minutes went by and the door opened again. This time the man who walked in carried himself with a familiar air of confidence. He shook the snow off his coat and smiled.

"What are you doing here?"

"Well, hello to you too Mel." Bart Hessor walked past the man at the bar. "Thanks, Sam. Stay with the car and let me know if anyone shows up." He patted Sam's back.

Sam slugged down his soda, nodded and headed out the same door he had walked through three minutes earlier.

Bart took a seat at the stool directly across from me. "Sorry about Sarah messing up your return call. When it started snowing, I figured your Dad would head home early. I drove by and didn't see any of your family's cars out back. I sent Sam in to see who was manning the bar." Bart's wry grin irked me.

I crossed my arms. "Are you dense?"

Bart responded with a puzzled look.

"I've never known you to be stupid."

Now he smiled. "What do you mean?"

"I said I didn't want to see you again. I do not want to date you. I will not sleep with you. Get it now?"

"Oh, I got it the last time. I just don't give up easily. You should know that, Mel. I've had the hots for you since high school. You were the only one in high school that I wanted and didn't get. Since you've returned, my feelings for you are even stronger. I know how you feel, but I intend to pursue you anyway." He winked. "One night with me is all I ask."

"No."

"I'll wear you down."

"No. Get the message now. No way, no how."

"If Huddleston hadn't pulled you away, like an errant school girl, I might have worn you down in St. Louis." His smile intensified. "You see, Mel, I think you're missing being held by a man. I have no doubt that soon you'll get so horny that you'll give into me."

"Listen…"

"I'll wait, but it won't be too much longer, if I remember you right." Bart stood up and tapped the bar with his gloves. "Call me. No one will find out about our affair. I promise." He winked one more time with a Cheshire grin, then walked out the door without looking back.

I waited until the door closed before I let go with a string of expletives. I kept muttering to myself as I washed up the few glasses I had and wiped down the bar. My thoughts were scathing towards Bart as I swept the floor, wiped down the tables, chairs, and bar stools. By the time I was turning chairs upside down on the tables and arranging the stools in their correct places, I had mostly gotten rid of all of the anger in me.

After locking up the bar, I went upstairs to my apartment. As I took off my coat, I rewound the answering machine. Ten messages. I must be getting popular.

The first three were hang ups. Stupid telemarketers. The next two were friends. The rest were more hang ups. I grabbed a drink out of the fridge as I dialed up Beth Majorham, an old girlfriend. Beth and I gossiped while I ate a late supper.

I walked into the living room with the portable phone and dialed the other message, Max Bauer from California. Max had been a cop in Quincy when I first returned here. We had clashed over territory on my first case. It was also then that he told me he wanted to get to know me better. He returned to California after we caught the murderers, but he called often and sent flowers occasionally. I liked him as a friend and if he still lived in town, I probably would be dating him.

Max wasn't home, so I left a message. *What to do with the rest of the evening?* The snow put me in a 'cuddle on the couch' kind of mood, so I put an old movie in the DVD player and snuggled into my old, comfy quilt.

An hour into the movie the phone rang. There was no one on the phone, so I hung up. Ten minutes later the phone rang again.

"Is it snowing there?"

My smile lit up the room as I muted the movie, letting it run silently. It was Max. "Yeah. We'll probably get several inches before midnight."

"Well, it's a blistering seventy-two here." The teasing tone in his voice was obvious.

"Shut up!"

"Just think, you could be here, sitting on my balcony, watching the sun set, drinking a margarita with me."

"Or you could be cuddled on the couch under my quilt with me, watching an old movie."

"Hmmm. Sounds tempting. What old movie?"

"*Gone With The Wind.*"

"I didn't know you liked the oldies."

"There's a lot about me you don't know."

"Yes and I'd like to change that. Come out and visit me. I'll go the extra mile to discover the real inner Mel."

I laughed. "Max, you do make my day."

He was laughing too. "So, have you found any more dead bodies in Quincy?"

"Nope. Right now we're following a guy suspected of giving out secret information." I took a sip of my drink and waited to see what he would say about that.

"In Quincy? Spies?"

I chuckled. "Believe it or not. One research company in town is snooping into another one. But man, is it boring. Give me a dead body any day."

Max chuckled too. My finding a dead body when he was still a cop here had pushed us into our friendship. "Speaking of dead bodies, are you trying to kill me?"

"The Maid Rites, uh? I just thought that you might be missing eating them." When he lived here, Rich and I had introduced him to Maid Rites, a sandwich at a local restaurant, Maid Rite. Everyone I knew ate there from tradition. They're a sloppy-joe type hamburger that are greasy and bad for you, but they taste so good. I had gotten him hooked on them. So I sent him some in a 'care package' several days ago.

"They were good. Not as good as getting them from the restaurant but still tasty. It's a good thing I live out here now. I think I'd have become addicted to them." He paused to take a drink.

We talked for well over an hour, then I decided I'd better get to bed since I might be doing surveillance at the ungodly hour of seven in the morning.

***

I woke to the alarm clock not very rested. Twice in the night someone called and by the time I answered the phone, they hung up. Consequently, I was not in the best of moods. Slowly I dragged myself to the shower.

At six-thirty John called. "There's no need to take over surveillance."

"Okay. Why?"

"Look outside."

I stood up and glanced out the kitchen window. "Wow!" There was several feet of snow covering everything. The busy road that I lived on hadn't even been plowed yet.

"I pulled the plug on surveillance at midnight."

"So, do you want me doing the employee checks at the office then?"

"When you can make it in," John paused. "Have you talked to Hessor?" His voice changed. It was back to that 'I'm going to watch out for you' tone.

"I did. He told me that he's going to pursue me anyway. So just stop. I can take care of myself."

"Did you know that he was arrested for rape once?"

I paused as I ate. It didn't surprise me. Once in our brief affair in high school, he'd put some moves on me. I left him lying on the ground, moaning, in obvious 'manly pain.' He has since even mentioned that we could have a replay of that night and that he would win this time.

"He got off on a technicality," John continued at my silence.

"Where are you going with this?"

"Watch yourself. I don't want you getting raped. He's bad news."

"I got the point the last time. Let it drop. I'll be extra careful. I promise. That's all I need, another big brother."

John chuckled. "Later."

I smiled as I hung up the phone. Maybe now John would stop being so brotherish. He was turning into a good friend, besides being a great mentor. I had learned a lot from him, but I still had a lot of learning to do.

I bundled up for the trek into work and stepped out onto my porch. I noticed that the snow was blowing slowly down my street, light drifts wafting along on top of the harder layer underneath. I turned to double check the door lock and saw a dead bird in my feeder. It wasn't covered in snow like the feeder itself. Poor thing must have tried to come out early this morning and died in the cold. I unlocked my door, grabbed a plastic bag out of my apartment and buried it in the garbage can.

The trip in took four times as long as usual with the roads being snowy and slick, not to mention stupid people driving like maniacs in the first really big snowfall of the year. We'd had smaller snow storms, but this was the first that had actually closed schools and some businesses. When I got to the office both Rich and John were there. John was on the phone, and Rich was standing in my office looking through the employee security check files. I had been working on them on and off for the past week.

"Good, you made it in," Rich said.

"Yeah. The Wrangler eats this stuff up." I smiled. "I'm almost done with them. Since I'm not watching Mr. Langerhorn, I should have them finished this morning."

Rich nodded. "I'll run them over on lunch, assuming the store opens." He handed me an envelope. "I found this stuffed in the door when I showed up this morning."

I looked at the standard business envelope. My name was on the outside. There was no other writing on it. I glanced up at Rich with a puzzled look. It turned into a frown as I opened the envelope and laid the note on the table. It read, 'Soon.'

"What is that?" Rich said, reading it upside down.

I shrugged. My mind immediately flashed to my conversation with Hessor, but then I dismissed it. Bart would never make so overt a move.

"John," Rich spoke louder looking towards John's office. His office was across the hall and down one door. The other conference/break/lunch room was next to my office on this side of the hall.

John put the phone back in its cradle and stood up. With a few steps he was at my door. He looked into my office and Rich, who had moved farther in, pointed at the note.

"I found it this morning stuffed in the door."

John quickly took in the note and his eyes locked with mine. I knew he was thinking the same thing that I had. "Mel?"

"I don't know." I was still looking at John. "I don't get it. Soon for what?" I glanced at Rich who was again looking at the note. "It sounds kind of like a threat."

Rich nodded as he grabbed the phone and dialed a number. "Detective Mitch Addison, please. Thanks." He looked at me then John. "Any ideas, John?"

John's eyes betrayed nothing as he shook his head.

Rich's attention went back to the phone.

As Rich talked to our brother, Mitch, asking him to come see us today, John looked at me again. He shook his head, then as he left the office, he pointed at me behind Rich's back. 'Be careful,' he mouthed.

I glanced at Rich then gave John a scrunched up face. I noticed Rich looking at me with a puzzled look. "What?" He looked at John's retreating back.

"Forget it." I sat down, seeing Rich shake his head.

"Mitch will be in this morning." Rich glanced out of his office into John's but apparently decided to let the matter rest.

"We have a new gig," John announced from his office. He reentered with his notes. "Doctor Winslow from Chicago is in California at a conference. She just arrived this morning. Several minutes ago she received a threat from the same group that was threatening her last year. She wants us to fly out and protect her during this conference."

Last year, on my second case with the guys, we were bodyguards for Dr. Winslow when she attended a conference and talk at Quincy University. She is a genetic biologist and was working on stem cell research. A group of activists threatened her before she arrived and then while she was in Quincy. We only had one close call in the women's bathroom, but I had disarmed the lady.

"How long?" Rich asked.

"Six days. She wants us there by tonight, actually the sooner the better she said." John smiled at me. "Busy?"

"Guess I'm heading to California. When do we leave?"

"I just arranged for flights out of St. Louis. If the airport is still running, we leave right after lunch."

Rich and I both glanced at our watches. Rich grabbed the remaining employee security check files off my desk. "Then you'd better get going, especially if the roads between here and St. Louis are snowy."

John nodded. "I'll pick you up at your place in thirty minutes, Mel."

I glanced at my desk then stood up. "I'll be waiting." I grabbed my coat off the rack in the front office and headed out the door.

As I reached my Jeep, I cursed. The two tires on the driver's side were flat. Looking closer, they had been slashed. Another curse escaped. I headed back to the office. John and Rich were discussing a matter in the front office when I opened the door. Both looked up surprised.

"My tires were slashed."

The two men exchanged looks. Rich held out his hand. "Give me your keys. I'll get them fixed and bring the car home. I want Mitch to see this."

John nodded in agreement. "I'll drive, Mel. It's a good thing we're leaving for California. Keep us up to date on what you find out, Rich."

Chapter 4

The flight was uneventful until we got to the hotel. The hotel was a sprawling complex with multiple interconnected buildings, including a three story parking garage and a grand front entrance. The trees and shrubs, strategically placed around the hotel were well tended and massive. A huge fountain splashed in a reoccurring pattern of jets of water. The fountain the centerpiece of the landscaping was surrounded by the large circular drive. The drive made the entrance look like a welcoming mansion. The front doors seemed small in comparison to the multiple storied hotel. The sign out front advertised and welcomed the Genetics International Symposium.

In addition to this, the grounds were a beehive of activity. A large group of people milled around the front entrance. The protestors were out in force. There were signs galore: 'Stop stem cell research', 'Save The Babies', 'Genetic Engineering is the Devil's Work.'

On the airport shuttle bus with us were four other people headed to the hotel. Three looked resigned to the protestors, as though they had been through this before. One female frowned and turned to a companion.

"This is my first conference in the United States. Is this normal activity?" she asked with a French accent.

The male who had obviously been traveling with her since they joked all the way from the airport, gave a resigned sigh. He spoke with a heavy southern accent. "Told you about 'em. Suckers are like leeches. Once they latch on… The blood suckers."

"Are they violent?"

I glanced at John as we listened to their conversation while watching the crowd as we drove up.

The male shrugged. "Probably not. At least they haven't been in the past. But this is a larger crowd than I've ever seen. Probably 'cause we're in California." He patted her arm. "Not to worry. Just hurry through them. Don't talk or make eye contact. Just ignore 'em." He winked at her. "Follow my lead."

I glanced again at John. He was frowning.

The other four people on the bus exited first. They were immediately identified as doctors and research specialists by the protesters. Insults were hurled at them, threats came next. John grabbed my arm and held me back at the door.

"Ugly."

I nodded as John motioned for the shuttle bus driver to wait with our bags.

Protestors were surrounding the others. We watched as they harassed people getting their bags and followed them all the way to the hotel, stopping short at the doors. Three security guards stood watch inside. Several protestors moved back toward the bus and us.

Finally John nodded his head toward the back. I followed him as the protestors glared at us. I could hear several of them asking each other who we were and if we had anything to do with the conference. I saw a couple checking papers and note pads with pictures on them. The protesters farther away continued their chants while thrusting signs in the air, but the ones near the bus, the ones that had been harassing our fellow travelers, seemed undecided about us.

We stepped out the back door amid murmurings of the protestors. They moved a few steps away and glared. John slung his garment bag over his shoulder, handed me my carry on and picked up my small suitcase. He put his arm around my shoulder, pulling me in tight. He had a 'dreamy smile' on his face. His smile changed to more of a natural one, and I could see humor in his eyes as he answered my obviously puzzled look. Leaning in, he whispered in my ear, "Subterfuge. Lovers."

I chuckled and gave him a peck on the cheek. With a chuckle of his own, he released my shoulder, switching his hold to around my waist. I took the cue and put my arm around his waist. The protestors were clearly puzzled. They left us alone and some even looked disappointed as they cleared a path for us to the entrance. A couple followed us to the doors, not saying anything, but the majority either went back to the curb to wait for another bus or joined in with the regular picketers.

We entered the lobby through a set of sliding glass doors. After the first ones shut, the sound from the protestors dropped to a murmur. After the second set closed, I could no longer hear them.

The lobby was a two story cavern with marble everywhere. Comfy looking leather high back chairs and couches lined the area. Tasteful carpet ran up to the check-in desk which looked to be made of cherry wood with a grayish marble counter top. There was a fireplace located in one of the corners, giving off an intimate and peaceful atmosphere in the secluded seating area.

I followed John after we parted and headed for the counter. My eyes panned the area to see signs directing guests to the business center, restaurant, pool area, fitness center, bar, gift shop, parking and conference center.

"Can you please contact Dr. Katherine Winslow in room 1018 for us?" John asked the rather plump clerk on duty. She immediately complied.

"Dr. Winslow will be down in a minute."

"Thank you." John turned to me and we waited.

It wasn't a long wait before Winslow came hurrying around the corner with a relieved smile on her face. "Thank you for getting here so fast. You don't know how relieved I am. Last night was scary." She gave a huge sigh as she shook our hands. "But more about that later. Right now let's get both of you rooms." She turned to the clerk. "Two rooms please. As close to my room, 1018, as possible."

The clerk shook her head. "We are fully booked, I'm sorry."

"Check please, anyway."

The clerk typed for several minutes before looking up. "Sorry. No one has cancelled and there are no no-shows. Sorry."

Winslow grimaced. "Look these people out there..." She thumbed over her shoulder out the doors. "...have threatened me. These are bodyguards I've hired to keep me safe. Someone tried to kill me several months ago. I need them to stay with me in the hotel."

The clerk didn't look happy but nodded. "Let me check with my manager." She picked up the phone and placed a call.

I smiled at John. I guess being one of the key-note speakers gave her a little pull. I turned and saw another transport bus pulling up to the hotel. The protesters were on the move. With a glance at John and Dr. Winslow, I headed to the plate glass windows near the doors to watch.

The protesters were getting bolder. They physically bumped several of the people getting off this bus. One of the men getting off the bus drew all of their attention. They moved fast but so did the security guards, who headed outside to help him into the building.

Suddenly John was standing next to me. "Getting uglier."

I nodded and tried to decide who was in charge of the protesters. There seemed to be three people guiding the group.

"Memorize the leaders' faces," John spoke even softer than normal, almost at a whisper.

"Already am. Looks like there are three. Bullhorn over there." I inclined my head to the man with the instrument, unused. He was short with a dark receding hairline, pasty white. He reminded me of a nerd all grown up.

"Blond Poofy near the bus." She was a blonde headed woman who looked more like a trophy wife than a hard line protestor. "And Carrothead right smack in the middle." This guy was very skinny, anorexic skinny. Almost clown like, he had a full head of curly red hair. His mouth seemed overly large as he yelled at the man being escorted by the security guards.

John chuckled. "Good names. Don't forget Jabba the Hut near the car down by the road."

I looked a little farther down the street. Sure enough, there was a large black man leaning on a car, arms crossed, with a brooding look, as his eyes intently watched the action. He pointed at one woman who had parked her car and was trying to sneak undetected into the hotel. Bullhorn called out to a couple of people who immediately turned and verbally harassed her. "Ah. Missed him. Anymore?"

"Not that I see." He glanced back at Winslow. "Looks like she was successful. I'll talk to in-house security as the two of you get settled. Stay in your rooms until I come and get you."

"Got it, Kemosabe."

***

I set my bag on the luggage holder in the bedroom and smiled at her. "It's okay, really."

"They said they didn't have any more rooms. I had to bribe the manager to get a room for John. Since I have two beds here, I figured you wouldn't mind." The older lady swept graying hair out of her eyes.

It was a huge hotel room, suite actually. It had a living room area with a sinfully comfortable looking couch, two side chairs, a desk with an office chair that rivaled mine back home and an armoire with a TV. The kitchenette area had a small refrigerator next to a marble counter with a microwave and coffee maker on it. The bathroom was to the left of the kitchenette, and looked larger than a normal hotel bathroom. The bedroom area, separated from the living room area by a three quarter high room divider, had two double beds, a flat screen wall mounted TV and its own little seating area near a balcony that over-looked the pool. The entire suite was tastefully decorated.

"Thank you for being so understanding," Winslow said, leaning on the dividing wall.

I nodded, pulling out my dress clothes to hang up. I glanced at her. She was in great shape for being in her fifties. I knew that she was extremely active when she wasn't in her lab working on whatever she did there. Something to do with stem cells, DNA something, and genetics in general. Even after sitting in on several lectures last year, I still couldn't tell what she did. But I knew she ran every day and worked out. I'm sure she could kick my butt any day, and I'm not that out of shape.

I smiled again. "Stop, Doctor. Besides, this way you'll have around the clock protection." I really didn't think she needed us in the hotel, not with the security guys around, but who was I to argue with a paying client.

Winslow smiled back. "Like I said last year, call me Kate. I never thought of it that way. I'm just glad I could get the two of you here so fast. After last year, I know I'm in good hands."

"And like I told you last year, I was just in the right place at the right time." I finished and we moved back into the living room part of the suite.

"And didn't hesitate." Winslow sat down at the table and opened her laptop.

"Instinct."

"Either way, I was glad you were there." She worked the mouse and looked up at me. "I have a welcoming mixer in half an hour. John said he'd be back after he put his bags away, right?"

"Yeah. And he also wants to see the threatening letter you got before we head down."

"What?" Winslow looked at me for a couple of seconds with a blank look. "Oh yeah, right. I've got it here somewhere." She moved some papers. "Where did I put it? Here it is." She pulled it out and handed it to me. "It was shoved under my door about ten minutes after I got into the room. They must have followed me after I checked in."

The note was printed on ordinary white paper. It was short and to the point.

'Dr. Katherine Winslow,

This is fair warning that you need to cease and desist from all experiments dealing with stem cell research, cloning, and genetic recombinant DNA research. The people of this country find what you and the others do an abomination. Stop now or bad things will happen to you and your business. You will regret sharing information with others that will lead to more genetic abominations.

Signed 'Coalition to Stop Genetic Experiments'

While I had been reading, Winslow had been working on her computer. Under her breath she muttered, "Damn."

"Problem?"

"Uh? What? Oh, no. Just something unexpected at the lab." She grabbed her cell phone.

I watched her rifle through papers on the desk. One slid to the floor. I picked it up and handed it back to her. From habit, I glanced at it. It was a list of businesses or government agencies or something. I handed it to her. Now that I had a few minutes, I grabbed my cell phone out of my pocket and dialed a number. Still no answer, but I got his machine. "Hi Max, we're here. Give me a call."

She was talking to an assistant or someone about money. She didn't seem happy but hung up. "Your conversation seemed happier than mine."

I smiled. "I have a friend that lives here in Mayfield."

"Boyfriend?"

"Yeah maybe. I guess."

"You guess?"

I shrugged. "I guess you could call him that. He left Quincy before we reached the boyfriend level. Since we came out here, I thought I'd call and see where we stand, how about you? Did you ever get back together with the man you were dating?"

She shook her head. As a divorcee with no children, I knew she spent a huge amount of her time at the lab. She claimed that research was her child. From what I learned last time, she spent every waking minute working and thinking about it. So I figured that they hadn't gotten back together.

I put my cell on the end table and headed to the bathroom. I hoped I could squeeze one night away from the conference to see Max, or he could come here if he wasn't involved with a case.

I took my time in the bathroom, knowing that John would be several minutes himself. Besides checking in with security, he also wanted to check in with Rich. On the plane he explained that once again I would be acting as her assistant so someone would always be at her side. John would guard her the rest of the time.

We entered the large conference room/ball room for the mixer. The room was ornate with chandeliers and fancy tables. The biggest area in the middle had no tables but was already full of people standing in smaller groups talking. Along the walls, to the left and right, were small bars with two servers, filling glasses with what could only be alcohol. On the back wall was a small buffet which from this distance looked like finger foods.

Winslow stopped short with a frown on her face. "I forgot my business cards." She turned to head back.

"I'll go and get them. Where are they?" I offered, pulling the key card out of my pocket.

"Thanks. They're sitting on the desk near my computer."

I turned to leave as John moved with Winslow toward the buffet tables. I didn't hurry but took a leisurely walk back to the room, which was on the other side of the hotel complex, getting used to the area.

I was returning to the conference center via a different route, which lead me past the hallway leading from the kitchen, when I saw Carrotthead sneak out of the kitchen door. I immediately stopped and backtracked to the hallway. He was no longer there, so I headed down the hallway, which seemed to head back toward the hotel rooms, to see if I could find him. I saw him as he turned the corner. Breaking into a run, I turned the same corner. I soon saw him verbally harassing an Asian lady who stood stock still staring at him. Suddenly he gave her a shove.

"Hey!"

Carrothead paused and turned to look at me, so I took off running again. A strange look crossed his face. He growled something at the lady and took off running.

I stopped by the lady's side. "Are you okay?" The lady said something in another language; I assumed it was Japanese. "Sorry I don't speak your language." I smiled and she returned the same smile as though she didn't understand me either.

At that moment, another Asian lady appeared from nearby elevators and seeing us, hurried to our sides. "So sorry. She does not speak English. Can I help you?"

The first Asian lady whose name tag read Pho Haung, said something to the newcomer whose name was Tran Le. They conversed for a few seconds.

"Ms. Haung wants to thank you for making screaming guy run away." Both ladies gave me a slight bow.

"Is Ms. Haung okay? The guy pushed her."

Le turned and asked Haung. "She say he did not hurt her only… uh… surprise her. Again, thank you."

I smiled. "Not a problem. Are you two ladies heading to the mixer?"

Le nodded and we began walking in that direction. As we neared the ballroom, I turned to them. "If that guy or any of the protesters harass you again, let security know. I'll tell them about today. I doubt the protesters are allowed in the hotel."

"Thank you. Thank you very much," Haung said obviously struggling with the words.

I gave her a slight bow and we parted ways. I headed to where John and Winslow were standing. When I got there, I pulled John a step away and explained what happened. He told me he would let security know and excused himself. I stood near Winslow nodding and making nice with the other scientists. Finally John reappeared and had me step off to the side.

"Security is checking things out in the kitchen to see how he got in. Management was not happy with them." John's lips quirked up at the corners. "I'll escort Dr. Winslow. Why don't you just hang out and watch. I doubt any protestors get in here."

After getting a bit to eat, I moved to the bar and ordered a beer. People watching is one of my favorite sports.

I used to attend legal conferences with Craig, my dead husband, and we'd bet on who was sleeping with whom. Apparently science conferences were the same with flirting going on. I smiled as a mousy, shabbily dressed lady made overt sexual gestures to a male. Yes, conferences must be alike no matter the topic.

"Enjoying the show?" A soft, sexy woman's voice sounded next to me.

I turned in surprise to see a very thin, almost anorexic, red headed lady in her mid-forties. I greeted her smile with one of my own. "I enjoy people watching."

"There's a lot to see. My name is Cynthia Vernon. Call me Cyn." She held out her hand to shake.

"Mel," I said with a little trepidation. The look in her eyes was one I usually associated with men trying to pick me up.

"I noticed that you arrived with Dr. Winslow."

I took a drink of my beer, noticing that she was watching me intently. "I'm one of her assistants."

"Lab Assistant?"

I shook my head, going with the same story we had cooked up the last time we had been her body guards. "No, I'm her Executive Assistant."

"Ah yes. Kate and her paperwork. Sloppy."

I nodded in fake agreement. "You know her?"

"I worked in her lab for a couple of years. Now I run my own lab."

"Doctor?"

Cyn nodded at me with a small smile. "PHD. Same field as Kate, slightly different twist. I see Kate came with a man. Do you know him?"

"John Huddleston. I believe they're just friends." I glanced with her at the couple. John was standing near the professor but not close enough for intimacy.

"Yes, I could tell." The lady paused to take a drink of what looked like wine. "Did you bring a boyfriend?"

My gut was telling me that this was wrong. Cyn was hitting on me. "No."

"I see. You have the look of someone who knows what they like." She watched me over her glass. Her eyes held a wealth of sexual innuendo.

I chuckled. "I do, but not what you're implying. I'm heterosexual."

"Confirmed?"

"Beyond all doubt."

"So you've experimented?"

I laughed this time. "Not at all. I just know what I like, and it's not the same equipment that I carry." I winked. "Sorry." I nodded with my head at the other wall. "Try the blond over there. If I'm not mistaken, she's in your league." I had watched her hit on a brunette waitress earlier, successfully, it looked like.

"I know. She's my partner. We're always on the lookout for... new experiences." Cyn leaned in closer. "If you change your mind, let me know."

"Not a chance of that. Enjoy the fishing tonight."

"Trolling is half the fun." Cyn chuckled as she moved on.

I shook my head and headed over to John and Winslow. When I reached them, the people they had been talking with walked away. I must have still been smiling because John had a puzzled look on his face.

"See the red head with the blond by the wall?"

John's eye panned over to the two ladies, so did Winslow's. John looked back at me waiting.

"The red head, Cynthia Vernon, just hit on me."

John's eyes jumped to the two of them again. He looked back at me with lifted eyebrows.

I laughed at John taking a drink of my beer. "Just stop." I punched him gently on the arm, a sibling type hit.

Winslow looked closely at me. "She's a lesbian?"

"Oh yeah. She told me that she and her partner always look for 'new experiences' at these conventions." I smiled at Winslow's astonished look. "She also told me that she used to work for you."

"She was a lab tech. She finished her grad studies and went on to run her own lab. The blond is Marsha Dodington, another PhD. How do you feel about her hitting on you?"

I shrugged. "I turned her down in no uncertain terms. I disagree with the lifestyle philosophically, but it's her life. Live and let live."

Winslow nodded at me as several people approached us to talk shop with her.

John moved me slightly away from the group but kept his eyes on them. "I didn't get a chance to tell you what Rich found out about the situation back home. Your tires were indeed slashed with a knife. Mitch also took the note. Nothing new."

I frowned.

"I haven't mentioned yet about Hessor to Rich." John's expression was once more hard to read.

"I told you on the plane, Bart doesn't want it known to anyone that he's pursuing me. He went so far as to make sure no one was at the bar last time we spoke," I said, then immediately regretted it.

His eye's hardened even more. "Tell me."

With a sigh and a look around, I quickly told John of the incident. "Trust me, Bart will chase me, but he wouldn't come out and antagonize Rich like this. He knows Rich still has some pull on the force, besides Mitch and he wouldn't expose his 'business' like that."

"Men do funny things when chasing a woman."

I inclined my head in agreement. "True, but I don't think so in this case." I looked John in the eyes. "Are you going to tell Rich?"

"Not yet." With that, he moved back to Winslow's side and joined in the conversation.

I shook my head. *What is going on back home?* I pulled my cell out of my pocket. *And why hasn't Max called me back yet?* It was unlike him to not return calls— usually it was only a couple of hours. I had expected a quick response from him knowing that I was in his neck of the woods. *Hmmm.*

***

A loud whisper woke me up. As I tried to figure out where I was and what was happening, someone leaned against our door. It rattled lightly against the door jam.

I shook my head trying to clear it. For some reason I seemed fuzzy, like I wasn't fully there or there was fog in my brain. I slid out of bed, almost lost my footing and stood up. The room seemed to spin for a second when I noticed Winslow coming out of the bathroom drying her hands and hair.

"What?" she asked softly. "I thought you were sleeping. I couldn't sleep. I thought a nice, warm shower might make me sleepy. Sorry for…"

I waved my hand, grabbed for the bed. "Someone at the door."

She looked that way and with a puzzled frown stepped quickly over there. "There's a piece of paper here."

I stumbled over to the paper, still in a fog, as she picked it up.

"More threats." She held it out for me.

I shook my head, undid the door locks and peeked out. A man entered the elevator down the hall. The other way was clear. I closed the door and leaned on it. I was so tired. "I need to call John."

"I'll call John. You look horrible. Go back to bed."

I shook my head as I rechecked the locks. "My job." I took several deep breaths which helped clear my head a little. After grabbing my cell phone and stumbling back to bed, I dialed John. While we waited, I looked closer at the note.

This one was not a personal threat to Dr. Winslow but a general condemnation of the whole group at the conference and that God would exact revenge on all of them.

Within minutes, John was at the door. After explaining what happened, he said he'd do a check of the floor and other areas. We were to stay locked in the room and meet downstairs the next morning.

I don't remember going back to sleep.

Chapter 5

I accompanied Kate downstairs the next morning. I had a notebook in hand as though I was going to take notes for her. I knew this would be boring, but we were getting a great deal of money from her, so I was willing to fake it. John met us as we stepped out of the elevator.

"So far everything is clear," he said with another glance around. "I spoke with House Security. The group harassing you is begin watched. There's only a small group of protestors out front. The only leader I can see is Blond Poofy who is in charge this morning. If the others show up, they won't be allowed in the hotel, and the police will be called."

"What about last night?" Winslow asked.

John shrugged. "Security told me that the man was chased off before the police arrived. And except for the threatening note left under all of the doors, they haven't been seen again."

Winslow nodded at John with a look of relief on her face. "Mel will be with me, but where will you be?"

"I'll wander around. When does the first panel finish up?"

"Oh right!" Winslow said and quickly fumbled through paperwork in her barely opened briefcase. She had kept it at her side all morning. "I was going to give you a schedule of events yesterday. It's here somewhere..." She continued to paw through it.

John looked around at the people gathering.

I glanced around too but for a different reason. The glass of tea I had with breakfast this morning was starting to work on me. And, I had awakened with a massive headache. I didn't know why, two beers usually didn't affect me like that, but the Tylenol I took was only now cutting the pain. "John, I need to go to the bathroom. Do you know which way it is?"

John pointed down a corridor.

With a nod, I headed that way. Around the next corner I found the women's bathroom, but it looked like there was a line formed already. I stepped up to the last lady who turned to me with a disgusted look.

"Only two toilets in this bathroom. And the other one down the other hall is the same. This will be very bad in a couple of hours." She smiled. "I can't believe the bathrooms in this part of the center are so small, not like the ones on the other side." We were in the oldest looking part of the conference center. It was also the closest to the hotel.

I chuckled. "I wonder if there are any more around?"

She shrugged. "Let me know if you find any. Coffee goes right through me."

I smiled and headed down the corridor. I quickly left the general area of the conference center and found what looked to be a deserted corridor. This was definitely a less used part of the hotel. The carpet in this section was the most worn, the walls looked scuffed, and the lighting was dimmer. Maybe this was an employee access corridor or something.

As I rounded the corner, I came face to face with Carrothead. He hesitated, then took off running back the way he came. I immediately followed but he was fast. When I turned the corner some distance away, there was no one. However, I had found more bathrooms. I waited several seconds, hoping he would return, but he didn't. I considered calling John, but nature called first. At least these weren't too far away, and it looked like no one else had found them.

As I pushed open the door, the first thing I noticed was that there were no lights on. And from the way the door opened, no light from the corridor made it into the bathroom. Odd but maybe it was because they weren't used often. There was something else too, an odd sense of something not being right. I wasn't sure why, but something was wrong.

I felt near the door for the light switch. My hand contacted a sticky substance. *Yuck!* I pulled my hand away and tried again. This time I found a light switch. As I turned it on, I wondered what I had touched. I was definitely going to report this to housekeeping.

The light flashed on and I froze. My eyes roamed the room. I couldn't move.

Blood was everywhere, on the wall, on the floor and as I looked down, on my hand. "What the...?"

My eyes took in the gore again. Then I saw the legs sticking out from under one of the stalls. I looked around again, still in shock. Blood was splattered on the walls, the mirrors and even the ceiling. The person lying in the bathroom was most assuredly dead.

I looked closer at my hand. The blood was sticky, almost completely dried on the wall where I had smeared it. My eyes panned down to the floor to see that I had also stepped in a small smear of blood. Man! I had contaminated the crime scene.

I cursed softly. My right shoe was still sticking partially in the pool of blood. I slipped off the shoe, leaving it where it was and stepped back.

"This is bad. This is really bad."

The door swung closed. I took a deep breath and with my left hand dug into my right pocket and dialed John's cell. I held my right hand away from my body like a doctor. *Eeeeyew!* I wanted to shake it off. I wanted to wash my hand a hundred times, but I knew I couldn't, at least not until the cops got there. I stared at my hand as I listened to John's phone ring. *Yuck!*

"Yes?"

"I'm in the corridor that leads away from the conference. It looks like an older part of the building. I was looking for more bathrooms, but I found a dead body. Get security please."

"Stay right there. I'll find you." John's phone went dead.

"Why does this always happen to me?" I asked the dark phone. I moved to the far wall and leaned against it, prepared to wait. But the impulse to shake my hand was getting harder and harder to fight. I shuddered as my eyes panned to the closed bathroom door.

Someone was dead. Murdered. And I had found the body, again.

Chapter 6

The female detective walked into the room where I was seated and sat next to me. When the first cops arrived, I was taken to a small office several doors from the bathroom and asked to stay there so they could get my statement. It seemed like forever before anyone got back to me.

"My name is Detective Amanda Goins. The officer in charge of the scene said that you found the body."

I nodded.

Her eyes were watching me in a detached way, studying me closely. I almost smiled. I felt like I was once more being scrutinized by my father for doing something wrong. I looked her over too. She was taller than me by about an inch, and her blond hair, dyed I might add, made her look like a model. But the way she carried herself dispelled the illusion. She was most definitely a cop and probably a very successful one.

"We would like you to accompany us to the station where we can get a better statement."

I opened my mouth to say that wasn't true but just nodded instead. "Sure, but I need to let my associate know where I'm going."

"And that would be who?"

"John Huddleston. We were hired by Dr. Kate Winslow as bodyguards."

There was a momentary pause before Goins answered, "I'll have one of the patrol men do that. Please follow me, Ms. Addison."

I stood up, then glanced at my hand. "Can I wash my hand before we go? This is creeping me out." I held out my hand so she could see.

The detective almost smiled. "I'll get a Tech."

About twenty minutes later, after pictures, getting swabbed and a thorough hand washing, I settled into the passenger side of the unmarked blue sedan police car. She motioned to a uniformed cop and spoke with him for a few minutes. Finally, she moved back to the car and we drove away. She didn't speak the entire time in the car. *Odd. I would think she would ask me questions.*

So far the only questions I had received had been from the initial officers at the scene. They had been routine questions of why I had been there and what I'd done when I discovered the body, along with general information about me.

When we reached the police station, Detective Goins didn't speak except to tell me which way to go. The room looked like any you might see on TV, more so because it had a one way glass window in it. I knew that most interrogation rooms no longer used them, they used video equipment which made me think this might be their 'hard' interrogation room. 'Soft' interrogation rooms looked more like a very small meeting room with a comfy chair or two, a table, maybe even a couch. This room had a square table and uncomfortable looking hard chairs. *Maybe all the other rooms are in use.*

I sat where she indicated, facing the mirrored glass. As I glanced around the stark room, I saw the video camera in the corner near the ceiling. It wasn't until we were in the room that she spoke any meaningful words.

"Would you like something to drink while I gather the paperwork to take your statement?"

I paused wondering what was going on. *Why treat me like a criminal?* "No, but I'd like to go to the bathroom. I didn't get to at the hotel."

The detective just looked at me with a neutral expression. "It'll be a minute." She left the room.

I waited. It seemed like a long time with my bladder sending increasingly urgent signals. I knew I should have gone when we were still at the hotel, but she had hurried me. Finally she opened the door and motioned for me to follow her.

We both went into a nearby ladies bathroom and she indicated a stall. When I exited, she was leaning against the wall waiting for me. She escorted me back to the interrogation room. "Sit down. I'll be just a minute."

I stood looking at the observation window. It felt as though someone was watching me. Suddenly the imp in me emerged. With a big grin, I moved the chair near the table and sat down with my back to the observation window. I almost chuckled. It would be fun to see if she would make me move to face the window and camera.

When she walked back into the room a good ten minutes later, she didn't look happy. Grabbing the chair from the wall, she placed it next to mine so that her side was to the window. The file she carried was still closed. The look she gave me could cut diamonds.

"Yes?"

"Would you mind moving your chair to this side of the table?" She pointed at the place where the chair had been originally. "That chair always stays in that position."

I smiled. "Makes it so the suspect is facing the observation window and video camera. I'm not comfortable with that. How about you just take my statement and let me get back to the conference?"

Goins scrutinized me. She looked like she was deciding how nasty to get.

I sighed. No need to antagonize the cops too much, no matter how much I liked doing it. "If it will make it 'easier' on you." I moved the chair back to its original position. I turned the smile on the window and waggled my fingers at the window and camera. "Hi, if anyone is watching."

"Why would someone be watching?"

"I don't know. I just have never like interrogation rooms. It makes me feel like I've done something wrong."

"Have you?"

"Not recently." I gave her a large smile.

She never cracked a smile but merely continued to stare.

I stared right back. I knew this game, although I didn't understand why she was playing it with me.

The detective cleared her throat. "Tell me about the incident this morning."

I relayed what had happened in a clinical fashion, very detached, very formal. When I finished, I waited for her to ask more questions. It would be a fun exercise to see how far I could push her, and maybe then I could determine why she was being so cold. Possibly it was just her personality, but it would have made more sense to act friendly.

She opened the file and scribbled a few words in it. It was obviously not enough words for my statement. She flipped a couple of papers which I didn't get a good look at, then she closed the file.

"You told the officers at the scene that you stopped just inside the door. How far did you go in?"

I almost sighed. "I stopped at one step. Knowing that I had contaminated the crime scene with my shoe, I took it off and left it." I swung my leg out from under the table to show her my sock. Then I wiggled my toes for the window and camera.

"Why did you leave the shoe?"

"My father and brother were both cops in Quincy, Illinois. I have a brother still on the police force, a detective. Between all of the stories from them, I know not to mess with a crime scene." I scratched the back of my hand. "By stepping into the blood on the floor, I might have smeared a footprint. I remember once that a forensic specialist said that it was better to leave the object that smears in place so they can account for the object. So, I slipped off the shoe and backed off." I smiled. "Would you like this one for comparison? Trust me, I don't want that one back and one shoe is useless to me."

"We'll see," Amanda said. "So, you're familiar with police procedure?"

"I know a bit about it."

A man stuck his head into the room and motioned for Goins. I glanced at my watch. It was getting close to lunch. I just wondered how much longer this would take. I smiled at the window again and slouched in the chair.

Twenty minutes later, Goins reentered the room with a male detective. The man was older than Goins by a few years and had a classic cop look. Square face, tough look, and he obviously didn't like to wear ties since it was loose around his neck and the top button undone.

"This is Detective Ben Hambrick," Goins introduced us.

I held out my hand. "I'm sure you already know, but I'm Melissa Addison. Call me Mel."

"Mel." Hambrick smiled a friendly smile at me as the two sat down opposite each other.

"Can I ask you a couple of questions?"

"Sure. Ask away," Hambrick said. He was obviously the 'good cop' in this partnership.

"When can I go?"

"Soon. We have a few more things we want to ask you, then we'll arrange to have you taken back to the hotel conference center. Was that all of your questions?"

I smiled back. He was going to make this fun. "Actually no. Since the Mayfield police are investigating the murder, is the hotel in Mayfield's jurisdiction?" The cities of Mayfield and Plainville sat side by side each other.

"Yes. Why?"

"It's just that I know a detective that works here and since he hasn't returned my phone calls, I was wondering if you could track him down for me."

Hambrick gave me a slight frown. "Did you call him after you found the body?"

"No. I didn't know what jurisdiction I was in since the hotel sits on the edge of the city. I called my boss and had him get a hold of hotel security. I already told the officer at the scene and Detective Goins that." I paused, then smiled at Hambrick. "I called Max Bauer twice yesterday to inform him that we were going to be in town and asked if he would like to get together. We're friends. I called again this morning after breakfast. Yesterday all I got was his machine. This morning it just rang. Ask Max. I was just wondering why he hasn't returned my calls is all." I noticed Hambrick's eyes changed a bit and flicked to Goins. "Or not. I'll track him down later." I glanced between the two. "Lastly, who was the body?"

"You don't know?" Hambrick asked.

I shook my head. "Again, as I've said twice, I only saw the legs. The rest of the body was in a heap, so to speak, and I couldn't make out a face. Besides, it's not like I wanted to go any farther into the bathroom."

Hambrick nodded. "Cynthia Vernon."

I know my face showed surprise.

"Do you know her?" Hambrick asked, leaning toward the table a bit.

Goins just studied me.

"I met her last night at the mixer," I paused then clarified. "The International Genetics Conference held a mixer last night."

"Go on." Hambrick motioned for me to continue.

I looked from one to the other. *What is going on here?* "I was at the bar. She, Cynthia Vernon, approached and propositioned me. I turned her down, and she informed me that she used to work for Dr. Winslow."

"The lady you were hired to protect?"

"That's right."

"And?"

"And nothing. We parted."

"You said you were at the bar. Had you been drinking?"

"Yes. Two beers."

Hambrick looked at Goins who opened her file and made a note of that. "How did she leave?"

"She walked away."

Hambrick smirked. "I meant, was she mad?"

"No. As a matter of fact, we joked about the fact that she was fishing for a 'new experience,' as she termed it."

"She thought you were a lesbian."

"I assume that's why she hit on me."

"Are you?"

I laughed. "Not hardly. If you need proof, ask Bauer."

Goins looked up at Hambrick. Their eyes met but neither said anything. She continued to write.

"So, it didn't bother you that she assumed you were a lesbian?"

"No."

"What did you do after that?"

"After she asked me?" I saw his nod. "I informed John Huddleston and Dr. Winslow of it."

"Why?"

"I don't know. I guess because I knew John would get a kick out of it."

"What about the rest of the evening?"

"What about it?" I asked back. I folded my hands on the table in front of me.

Hambrick leaned back in his chair. "What did you do after you talked with your associate and the doctor?"

"We stayed for a while because Dr. Winslow was schmoozing. Then we called it a night. John escorted us to our room. I went to bed."

"You're sharing a room with Dr. Winslow?" His eyebrows arched.

I smirked again. "Separate beds, Detective. She couldn't get another room and had a hard time getting one for John."

"Did you leave the room at any point that night?" Goins chimed in.

"Nope. I did poke my head out of the room once. That was when one of the protesters slid a threatening note under our door. I called John and he came to our room. He talked to hotel security about it. I went back to sleep."

Hambrick glanced at Goins. "Here's what we'd like you to do" he paused as Goins put a legal pad in front of me. "In your own words, write down everything that happened since arriving at the hotel. Finish with when the first police arrived at the scene. Okay?" He took a pen out of his pocket and laid it on the pad.

I sighed as I picked up the pen. This was going to take a while.

Chapter 7

Once more I glanced at my watch. I had been finished with the 'report' for over half an hour now. Goins had retrieved it and brought me a soda since it was lunch time. I wasn't really all that hungry now, but I was totally bored. For the first ten minutes I had walked around the room. I returned to the table and finished off the soda. I laid my head down and closed my eyes. I wasn't sleeping, but I figured if someone was watching me, they might as well be as bored as I was.

I looked around the room now and focused on the window. *Is someone watching me?* It almost felt like someone was staring at me. I was probably wrong, but I smiled and waggled my fingers. Then I sobered. A sudden thought struck me as I went over all of the questions that they had asked me. *Do they think I killed Cynthia Vernon?* I leaned back, put my hands in my pockets and thought about that.

Ten minutes later, Goins walked back into the room. I didn't move an inch but waited until she seated herself next to me. She looked like a cobra eyeing a mouse. I could almost see her tongue getting ready to flick out. I stared back.

"I've given my statement. Can I go now?"

"In a little bit," Goins said in a soft, low tone. There was a hint of still having more questions for me.

"Okay. Let me put it another way. I'm leaving."

Goins's hazel eyes locked with mine.

I could feel myself getting angry. My voice lowered and the tone hardened. "If you think I did something, tell me. I hate this cat and mouse stuff."

"We just have a couple more questions for you."

"No. I'm done answering questions. I've given you my statement." I stood up.

She didn't say I couldn't go, but she still acted as though she didn't want me to. I knew that the only way they could keep me from leaving was to charge me with a crime. I leaned down to the table and moved in closer to her face. "Either charge me, or I'm leaving."

Still she didn't answer.

"Last chance. Charge me and let me call my lawyer, or I'm walking out that door." I could feel my volcanic anger rising.

Our eyes locked.

"Good." I took two steps to the door. I desperately needed to get out of there before I blew my top. Not good if they were thinking I killed Vernon.

Goins stood. "Mel."

I stopped and turned. "I've cooperated more than I needed too. Are you charging me with a crime?"

Goins hesitated.

The door opened. Max Bauer strolled in. His smile beamed like a bright sunrise. "Hi, Mel."

I turned on him and my anger hit full blast even as my eyes panned over him, taking in his deep blue shirt with darker blue tie. He made my heart flutter even as the anger erupted. "Don't 'Hi Mel' me."

His smile grew. "Calm down. Amanda let me talk to Mel alone, please."

Goins glanced from Max to me and back again. "Sure." She left with a dark look.

I swiveled back to face Max. "Are you charging me?"

Max motioned to the chair. He sat down where Hambrick had been. I stayed standing.

"Sit."

"Bite me." I put my hands on my hips.

Max laughed. He motioned to the chair again. "Calm down, Tiger. Take a deep breath. I just want to talk to you."

"Why didn't you return my phone calls?" I was still standing but calmer.

He grimaced. "My answering machine messed up yesterday. I left a glass of water near the machine on my counter, and the cat I'm babysitting must have knocked it over. All I heard on the tape was, 'Max it's Mel, we are...' I called your house twice last night and once this morning. Every time I tried your cell, the call was dropped. Sorry."

I took another deep breath. I sat down in the chair with a glance at the window with a 'I told you so' look at Goins who I knew was watching. Max laughed again. I turned a sober look at Max. "They think I did it, don't they?"

Max hesitated. "They're suspicious." He leaned on the table with a smile. "How do you do it?"

"Do what?" I leaned back in my chair, arms crossed.

"Find dead bodies."

I smirked. "What evidence do they have? Outside of the fact that I found the body."

"I can't tell you that."

"Here we go again." I threw my arms up. "They have to have something other than that. I don't understand what it might be, try as hard as I can. Can you at least give me a hint, so that I can refute it?"

Max didn't say anything.

I smiled. "At least I didn't contaminate their crime scene. They have to give me credit for that."

Max nodded. "You did real well. Hambrick and Goins were impressed. I told them your history and that of your family." He smiled again. "Level with me, Mel, are you leaving anything out of your statement?"

I shook my head immediately, looking him right in the eyes. "I have no reason to. I found a dead body and reported it immediately. I called John, he got the cops."

"Yeah. I spoke with him."

There was a knock on the door and it opened. Hambrick showed in a man dressed in an expensive suit. "Max, this is Charles Degrad, an attorney. Mr. Degrad, Detective Max Bauer."

Max's face clearly showed his surprise and puzzlement.

Degrad ignored Max. "Melissa Addison?"

"Yes?" I was just as puzzled as Max.

Degrad sat next to me and handed me his card. "Sorry it's taken so long for me to get here. I was asked by Vincent Viking in Quincy, Illinois to represent you, should any charges be filed."

Max glanced from me to him and back. "Mel?"

"Got me." I looked at the card then turned a smile at Max. "Are you charging me?"

Max glanced at Hambrick. "No." He paused. "Are you retaining counsel?"

I looked the lawyer in the eye then looked back at Max. "Not yet. I don't need to. However, I would like him present the next time Detective Goins decides to piss me off. Look, you know me. You know where I am. I'm hungry. Maybe Mr. Degrad can drop me back at the hotel. If you have any other questions, call me or come by. I'm not going anywhere until Saturday. I don't mind answering questions, just tell Goins not to do it in an accusing fashion. Okay?"

Max smiled with a glance at the lawyer.

The lawyer shook his head at me and my apparent foolishness. He addressed Max and the still standing Hambrick. "Call me if you are going to speak with her again. In that case, she will retain counsel. Now please allow

Ms. Addison to leave. I believe that you have detained her long enough." He stood and motioned for me to get up too. Despite the fact that I hadn't actually retained him, all of us knew I had. Both Max and I stood up. I tossed my empty soda can into the trash.

"Max, do you want to…" Hambrick's voice trailed off as he handed Max a sheet of paper.

With an almost grimace, Max took the paper. He handed it to Degrad but looked at me. "Sorry Mel."

"What?" I asked Degrad. Max's eyes had a strange look in them.

Degrad quickly read the paper. "And this is for what purpose?"

"Evidence," Hambrick answered.

"What?" I stood up, glancing between Degrad and Max.

Max sighed. "It's a property voucher."

"For?"

"Your cell phone."

"Evidence? Why? I didn't…"

Degrad touched my arm. "It's legal. Give it to them." I pulled my cell out of my pocket, looked at it, then handed it to Hambrick. Degrad folded the paper and stuck it in his pocket. "Let's go Ms. Addison." He motioned to the door.

I glanced at Max.

He looked sheepish. "Mel, if you can stick around for a few minutes, I'll take you back." He held up his hands. "No questions. Mel and I are friends, Mr. Degrad. I promise I won't interrogate her without you present."

"Ms. Addison?" Degrad asked.

I glanced at him then looked at Max. I knew better. He would pump me for all the information he could get. But I didn't have anything to hide, and I would rather ride with Max than someone I didn't know. I turned back to Degrad. "It's okay. I'll watch him closely, but I don't want to wait in this box any more. I'm sick of this room."

Degrad stopped in his tracks in the hallway after all of us exited the room. He turned to the cops as Goins exited the observation room to join Max and Hambrick. "Do not question my client." This was directed at Max. "She has retained me as her attorney, and you will call me first before you question her again. Do you understand?"

The cops nodded silently.

"Good." Degrad turned to me. "Are you sure you don't want to ride with me?"

I smiled at Degrad. "It's fine. I can be very tight lipped and stubborn."

Max laughed out loud. "That's for sure."

Degrad actually smiled. "Okay. It's against my better judgment, but Vincent said you were smart. Do not answer any questions about the case. Have a good day and call me any time." He departed.

Max shook his head, still chuckling as he headed me away from the interrogation room. Hambrick joined in his chuckles and followed. Goins stood still, not even smiling. I glanced back as we turned the corner. Goins opened the interrogation room door. Max opened a set of double doors in front of me and held it open.

Inside the room, the noise level was a low murmur of voices. There were at least fifteen people, either at desks or milling around the room. Several were on phones. Four were gathered around one desk concentrating on several pictures. Two phones rang, one right after another.

Hambrick moved past me with a smile and a nod. He headed to a nearby desk covered with paperwork. He placed my cell on the desk.

Max tapped me on the arm to get my attention and headed to the opposite side of the room to a relatively organized desk. As I got closer, I saw a photo of me framed on his desk.

"Really?" I pointed at it.

He blushed as he sat. "When I'm having a bad day, you cheer me up."

"Ah." I sat down and glanced again at Hambrick. He was slipping my phone into an evidence bag.

"Do you want a soda or something while I finish up some paperwork?"

I shook my head, still watching Hambrick. The detective was now typing on his computer.

"Mel?"

I turned. "Yeah?"

"Sorry about that. I wanted to do it differently."

I shrugged. "I've got nothing to hide. By the way, tell Detective Goins that if she wanted my prints that badly, all she had to do was ask. I saw her going into the interrogation room after we left. It could only be to retrieve my soda from the trash. Besides, my prints are on record in Illinois." I smirked at him.

Max laughed loudly. "I'll tell her."

I got comfortable at his desk. I browsed the paper work then turned my attention to the others in the room. I noticed that Hambrick left with my cell phone. I was bored in about three minutes.

It wasn't much longer and Max finished with what he had been typing on the computer. He actually typed at an impressive speed, as opposed to Hambrick's two finger hunt and peck style. "I'm almost done, then I'll take you to lunch."

"Can I call John while you work?"

He pointed at his phone. "Dial nine to get out."

I picked up his phone and dialed. "John, thanks for calling back home."

"Sure," John was whispering so he must have been in a meeting or nearby. "I figured since they wouldn't let me talk to you and kept you that long, that they had suspicions. Rich agreed and called Viking. Were you charged?"

I looked at Max, who was seemingly occupied with paperwork, but kept noticing his eyes flicking to me. And he shuffled papers when he wasn't really ready for them. "No, I haven't been charged. Max is here and bringing me back after we stop for lunch. Or do you need me sooner?"

"That's fine. When you get here, I want you to call Viking. Then detail everything for me."

"When did Max talk to you?" I now was intently watching Max.

"Shortly after the female detective took you away. I hoped he'd make it here before you left. He said he'd find out what was going on," John paused. "I know you didn't do it Mel, but watch what you say to Bauer."

"Trust me, Bauer is completely out of luck if he thinks he can get anything more out of me." I smiled a big smug smile at Max, who now looked up.

John chuckled.

"See ya." I hung up the phone. My smile at Bauer turned more smug. "Don't even try it. I won the last time. Remember?"

"Oh, I remember." He finished his paperwork, then added it to the pile in the tray. "I brought the BMW bike to work today, so I found an extra helmet here. Can you ride with one shoe off?"

"Actually," I slipped off the shoe and handed it to him. "Give this to Goins and tell her to use it as a suppository."

Max laughed and tossed it on his desk. "I saw that the two of you didn't get along. She's really not that bad a person. I'll be right back." He touched my chin as he left.

Before long we were tooling along on his bike. It was an awesome bike. I had driven it once. The metallic blue BMW R1150RS, a cross between a touring bike and suicide bike, accelerated like a smooth cloud. *Sweet.* He told me at a stop light that he needed to head home to feed the cat he was watching, then we'd head out to eat. I asked him if we could stop somewhere so I could pick up another pair of shoes.

After a stop at a discount shoe store, Max pulled up to a square, bland looking building that housed four apartments, two on the bottom, two on top. I got off the bike and handed Max the extra helmet, looking around.

"Where's the balcony?"

Max shrugged. "I lied. I can't afford a balcony. I thought it might entice you to come out here." He kissed me lightly on the cheek and headed up the stairs.

I followed him. *Did I really want this? Is this what I want?* My body was saying 'yes' in no uncertain terms, but my heart was not necessarily in agreement.

Max lived in the upstairs apartment on the right. He opened the apartment door and motioned me in. I raised one eyebrow at him and walked in.

His apartment was obviously a one bedroom. I could see into the kitchen from the door. It was separated by a breakfast bar. The living room had a sofa, a recliner and an entertainment center with flat screen TV and what looked like a kick-ass stereo. A blue recliner with cream speckles faced the TV. The nearby light beige sofa matched the carpet and walls. Normally it would have been boring and bland, but he had light blue accent pillows on the sofa that matched the throw blanket draped on the back of the sofa. The pictures on the wall and several abstract artsy pictures tastefully complimented the living room. In one corner stood a small desk and his computer.

The kitchen had white, boring appliances, typical of most rentals. There were two doors leading off of the living room on the left side. One was for the bathroom, the other one, presumably for his bedroom, was closed.

I headed farther into the living room, heading to the kitchen bar. As I passed the sofa, a huge white cat pounced from between the recliner and the sofa to land inches from me. I took a step back in surprise to find myself up against Max. The cat bounded up to the sofa then onto the back.

He caught me by the waist and chuckled. "Meet Tada."

I stood up and looked closer at the big, white fur-ball. The cat's expression looked like it was enjoying itself. Then it stretched, and I swear it was laughing at me. "Tada?"

"Yeah, as in ta-da, surprise," Max said moving into the kitchen. He pulled out a can of cat food, and Tada followed him in.

I brought up the rear, still watching the cat.

"Tada belongs to an old girlfriend of mine. I actually gave her Tada on one of our anniversaries. Tada got the name when she was a kitten. She enjoyed jumping at people." Max looked at me over the cat which jumped onto the counter. "Get down." He picked her up and dumped her to the ground.

I sat at the breakfast bar in front of him. "An old girlfriend?"

Max stopped and looked at me. "Clare doesn't like to leave Tada at a vet. She's in Europe right now for another week." His eyes got a strange look in them as he stared off to the side of me into space. "We were high school sweethearts. We broke up a while ago after a long on again, off again relationship. She's recently married. Actually, this is their honeymoon."

I leaned my head on my hand, amused at this information. Max was usually so mysterious about his past. "Really? And how do you feel about her getting married? Sounds like you still carry the preverbal torch for her."

"No. We were close though. I actually proposed once. Right before we broke up for good." He looked down at the can of cat food he was holding over the bowl. He seemed to be debating with himself. "It's over." Max smiled, but the strange look was still in his eyes. "Trust me. I've moved on."

"Doesn't sound like it. Want to talk about it?"

"No. It's over. I'm over her."

"You're a horrible liar, Detective Bauer." I smiled to take the sting out of my words. There was something that still bothered Max about this woman.

"Really. I am. There were things…history." Max smirked.

I laughed. "Bauer, you are one strange man."

He reached out and tapped my nose. "You're the strange one. Always finding dead bodies."

I looked around his room. "I don't see Degrad here."

Max sighed. "Sorry."

I smiled.

"I have left over lasagna in the fridge or do you want to go out?"

"You said you were taking me out. What, are you getting cheap on me?"

Max blushed. "Actually, I'm a little low on money right now, if you want to know the truth."

"Lasagna is fine."

Max put the cat food on the floor near the water bowl and got lasagna out of the fridge. He shoved it in the microwave and handed me a plate. "What do you want to drink? I don't have Kool-Aid."

I chuckled. When we first met, I still drank it in honor of my son. It was a habit I was only just breaking. "That's okay. I'm trying to get myself clean of the stuff. Anything you have is fine."

Soon we were eating. The lasagna seemed to be home made and tasted delicious. I was glad we stayed here to eat. Max sat next to me at the breakfast bar. He was great company as always, and the time passed quickly. We were laughing at Tada jumping at the front door to scare off a bird. I turned to see Max staring at me.

"Yes?"

"I have two questions. One personal, one not."

"I knew you couldn't stand not to question me. Go on, ask the impersonal one first."

"Who do you think did it?"

"I have no idea."

"Mel, I saw that crafty little brain of yours working while you were sitting in there. I was watching you for a while. The Snooping Sneak strikes again." He smiled a large smile. He stood up and took both of our empty plates to his sink. Max turned around and leaned on the counter to stare at me.

"I honestly don't know." I looked deeply into his blue eyes. "Do you think I did it?"

"Absolutely not. But I know you. The others don't."

The silence stretched out as our eyes stayed locked. I tried to determine if he was serious.

"Well, at least one cop thinks I'm innocent."

"Innocent? Hardly. Not guilty of murder, absolutely." He grinned. "No, Mel. I know you didn't do it."

"What's the evidence that would lead them to think that I did?"

Max shook his head.

"You can't tell me," I said with a tone.

"I will tell you that I was asked, since I know you, to hang out at the conference with you." Max crossed his arms. "Will that be a problem for you?"

"Your job is to watch me?"

"Officially, yes. But since I know you didn't do it, I'm actually going to try and find out who did it. And knowing you, all I have to do is tag along and let you be you." A lopsided grin appeared on his face. "Do you have a problem with pretending I'm your boyfriend to allow me access to the conference?"

"Boyfriend?"

He nodded. "Which leads to the personal question."

"Yeah?"

"Are we going to be just friends or can I flirt with you now?" The blue eyes were sparkling with amusement, but there was also something that I couldn't identify.

"I guess you can flirt, but I'm not agreeing to anything else. Understand that. I don't know exactly where I stand yet." I watched as his eyes got hopeful.

"One other question."

"You said two."

"I lied."

"Go on."

"How can you be here less than one day and manage to find a dead body?"

Max always made me laugh.

Chapter 8

We found John and Dr. Winslow walking out of a meeting. I introduced Max as a local friend and gave John a look to play along. Max shook Winslow's hand, and since they were headed up to the room, we accompanied them.

As we walked, Winslow quizzed me about what had happened. I gave her the line that Max had given me, that I was released pending further investigation. Winslow was appalled at the thought. She mentioned that the cops had spoken to her at length and that a lady detective wanted to talk with her again that evening.

After getting into the room, Winslow disappeared into the bathroom still toting her briefcase. I turned to John who was sitting across the table from me. We leaned toward each other and in whispered tones, I told him everything. I included the fact that Max was 'undercover' to watch me and find the killer.

John looked at Max, and some sort of male communication flashed between them. I had no idea what it meant. He leaned back as we heard the toilet flush. "I still want you to call Vincent Viking. By the way…" John glanced up as Winslow walked out. "Rich caught Langerhorn passing information back home. It was done through his wife."

I raised both eyebrows. "Really? How did he find out?"

"Rich's car wouldn't start. He was parked near the alley to Langerhorn's house." John smiled, which for him was something. "As he was checking out the problem, a new car showed up. The competitor's manager walked up to the house, received an envelope and handed one back."

"In plain daylight?"

"Yes. Rich even managed to catch it on tape."

Max wasn't joining the conversation but he was smiling and shaking his head. His chair was pulled up close to mine.

I called back to Quincy and spoke with Vincent Viking about my situation. He told me that Degrad had been a college roommate and that he was very good. He stressed that I shouldn't talk to the police without Degrad present. I thanked Vincent and hung up. It was time to go back to the meetings.

In the meantime, Winslow asked Max what he did for a living. Max replied that he worked for a road crew trimming trees. He was off work right now due to a back injury. I smiled at him from behind Winslow's back, he had come up with that story awfully fast.

As we were leaving, Max stopped me. He looked at John. "Mel will be right out, okay?"

"We'll be downstairs. Conference room F."

The door closed behind them and Max turned to me. I leaned against the wall near the door. Max and I were only about a foot apart.

"Point out the blond, Marsha Dodington, who was with Cynthia Vernon last night. And anyone else that you know might be connected to her. Okay?"

I nodded.

A twinkle appeared in his eyes. "If I kiss you right now, will you haul off and hit me?" We had had this conversation the last time we had been in a similar situation in Quincy.

I gave him a flirty smile. "Live life on the edge."

He seemed indecisive.

I opened the door and moved past him. "You took too long to decide." I walked down the hall without looking back, my heart beating a mile a minute.

With a quick jog, he caught up with me. He glanced at me but said nothing. We stood there waiting for the elevator in silence. I smiled at him as I entered.

Max stood at the entrance to the elevator, waiting. His eyes staring into mine. Intent eyes, deep blue that pierced me. As it started to close, he hopped in. He kept moving toward me and pushed me up against the wall. His lips contacted mine and we kissed, his lips asking and mine responding, tongues caressing, heat rising rapidly. His hands held my head as he pressed my body against the wall, his body rubbing gently against mine.

At the forth ding, he pulled away and looked into my eyes. There was definitely a yearning in the blue orbs and the sexy, gorgeous smile. "Dangerous."

I smiled back. My heart rate competed with the second hand on my watch and my lips tingled as I licked them. My body yearned for more. "Life on the edge."

Max laughed.

Chapter 9

Max was sitting in the lobby of the convention center when we exited from the lecture. The club chairs were clustered in small groups, making several intimate conversation areas. I started to move over to him but noticed Marsha Dodington standing by herself near the door of conference room D. "John, I'll meet you at the restaurant."

John glanced at me, then his eyes flicked to Dodington. His eyes swiveled to Max who was watching from his chair. "Tread lightly." He winked, knowing that I was going to talk to the dead lady's lover. "Keep me informed." He moved Winslow toward the elevators.

I nodded and with a hand motion, stopped Max's rise from his chair. I headed over to Marsha. "I'm Mel Addison. Sorry for your loss, Marsha."

The blond sniffled once but held back tears. "I heard you found her."

I nodded.

"The cops said she was... she was bludgeoned to death."

"Yeah." I glanced around, but no one was within hearing distance.

Max caught my eye and with his chin pointed at her in question.

I glanced quickly at her. She was wiping her nose, so I gave a quick head nod back. I turned my attention to Dodington. "I know the cops probably already asked you this, but do you have any idea who would want Cynthia dead?"

"I don't know of anyone. I mean, we have gotten our share of protestors and all, threats and such. But the lab is not as controversial as say Winslow's. We don't actually do genetic experiments, DNA sequencing and other controversial testing there." Marsha shook her head, pulling out a Kleenex. "That guy that got into the hotel last night banged on our door. He said nasty things to us through the door but..." She shook her head. "He knew it was our room. We've had dealings with him before." She sniffled and wiped at the tears again.

"Who was he?"

"I didn't know his name. He was Caucasian. Short. Dark receding hair." Bullhorn. "Cyn... Cyn called him James something. She's dealt with him before." She wiped her nose again.

"I was surprised to see you still here. I don't think I could have stayed." I touched her arm in sympathy.

"I have to. We're in competition for several grants and not only do we need to stay abreast of the latest developments, but I need to present what we're doing. It's hard, but I have to tough it out. Cyn would want me to." She set her briefcase on the floor to pull out more Kleenex and blow her nose.

"What else have the police questioned you about?"

"Everything." She looked me in the eyes. "I heard that they've been inquiring about Cyn trying to pick you up. Sorry about that. We didn't mean anything by it."

I nodded in understanding. "Was there anything unusual happening last night after the mixer?"

"Cyn and I headed back to the room. I took a shower, and I heard Cyn's phone ring. She was arguing with someone on her cell. When I got out, she was gone. She left me a note that said she'd be right back. I fell asleep after I took my allergy medicine. It really knocked me out. When I woke this morning, she still hadn't come back." Marsha shrugged and wiped at her nose. "I got ready and came down for the meeting. It wasn't long after that, that..." Marsha stopped barely able to contain a sob.

"Any idea who she was arguing with or about what?"

Marsha shook her head, blotting tears again. "The shower was running."

I looked around and saw Max watching us intently. "Marsha, this may sound strange, but why weren't you upset about her note and her not returning last night?"

Marsha blushed a light pink. "At conferences we give... we used to give each other permission to experiment with other women. Then if everything went according to plan, we'd all get together another night for, well, you know."

"Actually I don't know." I gave her a slight smile. I was hoping that she would continue to talk. The last thing I wanted was for her to think I had killed Cynthia.

Marsha gave a little look around the area near us. "Cyn was very open about her sexuality. I, well, I still get embarrassed about it. I've only recently come out. I'm still not very open...well, we get all the girls together for a big romp."

"Like an orgy?"

"Sort of." Marsha gave me an embarrassed grin. "Cyn, well, Cyn saw you earlier when you first arrived. And then when you showed up at the mixer. She's... she was like a savant about picking out other lesbians. With you, she said she couldn't tell really if you were or not. You puzzled her. She felt that you were sexually repressed in some way. She thought maybe it was because you hadn't come out yet or only recently or were still in the closet. She was sure she could get you to join us. She's... was really good with newbies."

Now I almost blushed, almost. "Not at all. I just haven't had sexual relations in a while. I lost my husband and son just a year ago in a car accident."

"I'm sorry. That must have been what Cyn was picking up on."

I made a motion with my hand to forget it. Time to bring the subject back to more comfortable subjects, at least for me. "Was Cyn having any problems at work?"

"No. All of our people are well paid. I make sure of it as the accounts executive. It's the best way to keep people loyal. We're actually very successful. Although not cutting edge genetic, we're working on trying to find the DNA sequence for several genetically linked diseases, just like part of Winslow's lab as a matter of fact. Cyn was to present her paper tomorrow on one aspect of it. I guess I'll have to do it now." Marsha glanced at her watch. "I need to head up to my room. I have several calls I need to make before I collapse. Thank you for being so kind. Most people won't talk to me for fear of what to say."

I patted her arm. I knew the feeling. "Take it easy, Marsha."

She hurried away with a sniffle.

I turned to find Max at my elbow.

"Well?" His eyes followed Marsha's path.

"Well, what?"

"What did you find out?"

"Nothing." I started to move away from him.

Max grabbed me by the elbow and moved me around the corner of the hallway and into a slight recess made by two walls. His head swiveling back and forth checking for people near us, he lowered his voice more, "Tell me."

"Let go of my elbow."

He immediately dropped his hand. "Mel, this isn't a game. We're running out of time. You're this close to being arrested for murder." His fingertips were only millimeters apart.

I rubbed my elbow. "I didn't find out anything that she didn't tell the cops. A dark haired man named James somebody, Marsha thinks, harassed them through the door. She said Cynthia had dealings with him before. Anyway, Cynthia had an argument on her cell phone last night. Marsha was in the shower. She can't even guess who it might have been. When she got out of the shower, Cynthia was gone and didn't return. This morning she found out what happened."

"We didn't hear about the harassment. I'll let Goins and Hambrick know." Max looked down the hallway in thought. "What did she blush about?"

"It was nothing."

"Just tell me."

"Why?" I cocked my hip.

"Because it might be important."

"It's not. Trust me."

Max sighed. "Tell me anyway."

I hesitated, staring into Max's deep blue eyes. He glanced around again and I followed suit. Still no one was around. "Fine. She was telling me of her and Vernon's sexual permissiveness at conferences."

Max's head attention snapped back to me. "Go on."

I shook my head with a smile. "Pervert." He gave me a smirk. "She and Cynthia gave each other permission to experiment at conferences, meaning try new women. Then they'd get together for an orgy before it was over."

Max's eyebrows flew up into his brown hair. A smile flashed on his face. "Really?!"

"Pervert." My smile increased at his heightened eyebrows. "She was also apologizing for them hitting on me."

"I was wondering about that," Max said, his voice lowered and got a sexy tone.

"Stop. You know me better than that."

"I've only heard stories. I have no firsthand experience." His voice got even huskier.

I smirked.

"You drive me insane." He leaned over and kissed me lightly on the lips.

"Did you check in with your fellow cops?"

Max nodded, leaning closer for another kiss.

I ducked out from between him and the wall. "What did you find out?"

"I can't tell you that."

"How am I supposed to clear my name if I have no idea what evidence they have on me?" I jammed my hands on my hips.

"Calm down. It's purely circumstantial or they'd have already put you in cuffs. Just keep telling me what you've found out, and I'll go from there." He looked me in the eyes. "Deal?"

"That seems a bit one sided."

"It has to be. I can't reveal things to you." He paused. "Tell you what, I'll confirm information if you guess it."

I studied him. "Sure, Bauer. Like I believe you." I headed away.

Max grabbed me and stopped my progress. "I promise," he paused looking me square in the eyes. "Do we have a deal?"

"Deal." I walked away from him with a huff. I wiped the frown off my face as he caught up with me. "Do you have a home computer?"

"Yeah. Why?"

"I need to do some surfing. Do you mind if I use yours tonight?"

Max hesitated.

"Or I'll go and buy a laptop. I've been wanting one anyway."

Max shook his head. "No, you can use mine."

"Good. I'll talk to John and see if I can get the night off to go database surfing."

"About?"

"Stuff."

"What?"

I sighed and stopped. We were standing near the entrance to the restaurant. I could see through the plate glass window and saw John and Winslow already at a table waiting for us. "It's not anything yet. Just a remark Marsha made. I want to check it out." I saw Max's eyes harden. "You'll be there, after all it's your computer. I'll even let you sit and look over my shoulder. If you don't drool."

Max shook his head with a chuckle and let go of my elbow. "Call me when you're done eating."

"Aren't you eating with us?"

"Can't afford it."

"I'm going to quiz Winslow about the ladies. Don't you want to hear it?" I watched him glance into the restaurant then down at the floor. "I'll buy." I walked away muttering loud enough for him to hear, "And all I could find was a cheap date. He better be good in bed."

Max laughed and followed me into the restaurant.

John readily agreed to give me the night off. I explained it to him when Winslow went to the bathroom. We were almost to dessert when John steered the conversation to the deceased.

"Mel said that Vernon worked for you," John asked as he finished off his plate.

Winslow nodded. "Yeah. When she was a grad student and then for some time after that."

"Was she a good worker?"

"Absolutely. And she always went the extra mile when we were deep in research." Winslow smiled. She looked at Max but he was deeply engrossed in his steak. "Why do you ask?"

"Mel and I are just wondering who would want to kill her? We need to help the police come up with other suspects." John leaned back, watching her.

"Of course, that makes sense. The only one that I can think of would be Marsha, if the protestors have been ruled out. Personally I think it was them. I heard Marsha telling someone that a guy was banging on their door. All of us have had them disturb us, and we've had our share of death threats. A couple of other presenters mentioned to me that they saw protesters sneaking in and around the hotel. And the night before I arrived, I heard one of them was arrested for assault." Winslow shrugged and looked out the windows from the restaurant into the hallway. "Like that one." She pointed.

All of us looked. "Blond Puffy," I said looking at John, but the next words were for Max. "Wasn't she one of the leaders that we saw yesterday when we arrived? You know, the one leading the protestors in harassing people as they walked into the hotel."

John nodded. His eyes flicked to Max.

That suddenly reminded me of Carrothead in the hallway right before I found Vernon. I wondered why I hadn't remembered him before. I snapped my fingers. "That reminds me John, I ran into Carrothead. You know that protester with the bright red hair that we saw yesterday, about my height and thin with red curly hair. Anyway, I chased him right before I found the bathroom with Vernon." I saw Max look up, his fork half way to his mouth with his last bite of steak.

"Exactly when and where?"

Max resumed eating but kept glancing at me.

"I turned the corner and chased him down the hall. That's how I found the bathroom."

"Blood?"

I thought before answering. "I couldn't tell, but he sure took off in a big hurry. Can you call the police and tell them during the next session?" John immediately nodded, knowing that I was using him to let Max know.

I mentally shook myself to get back to the line of thought before I interrupted with my story. "Why Marsha? Why would you think she would kill Cynthia?" I asked leaning forward.

"She was jealous of her from what I've heard. She and Cynthia started V & D Clinical Laboratory after leaving me. Cyn was more into the research aspect, while Marsha wanted to do more clinical testing. I hear they've had some mighty loud and righteous fights about it."

"V & D?" I asked.

"Vernon and Dodington, I would guess," Winslow said with a smile. "I also hear that Cynthia was cheating on Marsha. The research world here is so small after all."

I met John's brown eyes.

"Enough that she might want to kill her?" John asked leaning forward.

Winslow shrugged.

"Can I ask you a question?" Max interjected.

Winslow looked at him with a condescending look. "Sure."

"What do you do? I mean I've been listening while I was waiting for Mel, and from what I heard, you do some sort of work in genetics. Are you the people making sheep and cows and such?"

I glanced at Max. He had worded it so that he sounded rather uneducated.

Winslow gave him a smile. "No. One thing my lab is working on is genetic tests for specific diseases. It has to do with the genome and gene placement on the DNA strand. It's really too complicated to explain here. Although we do work in stem cell research. It's only a small section and not cutting edge research. But, I'd like to expand in that direction, especially if I get this grant I'm working on"

Max scratched his head. "So you take apart DNA?"

"Sort of."

"And do what with it?"

"The biggest sections of my lab work to find the genes connected to several diseases so that we can cure people or provide better drugs to help combat the diseases. We're still a ways off of doing that, curing the diseases that is. The drug part is much closer. Other divisions in my lab do other things, like I said, some controversial and secret."

"Like secret government stuff?"

"Not at all." Winslow smiled broadly. "Although, some of what we do we try to keep secret. There are things we're working on that we don't want other labs to see. They might use our research and get there before us. Also, we compete with other labs for grants and foundation money and such. Despite the image of a doctor working long hours in a closed up dark and dank lab, I spend almost as much time trying to drum up money to keep us open."

Max still looked puzzled. "And this lady, the dead one, worked at a similar lab?"

"Owned it and worked there. Yes."

"So most everyone here is competing for money from everyone else?" Max laid his fork down and pushed his plate away.

"A good number." Winslow motioned to the waitress. She looked around the table. "Does anyone want dessert?"

I shook my head, as did the guys.

"Check, please," Winslow told the waitress.

"Let me pay for Max." I reached for my wallet.

"Nonsense," Winslow said. "I can write this off of my taxes." She winked at me then turned to Max. "Are you sticking around tonight?"

I was the one who answered. "Actually, John gave me the night off, so I'm heading out with Max. I'll be back later tonight. Can I get you anything from town?"

Winslow's face brightened. "Could you pick me up a couple of candy bars? My favorite is York Peppermint Patties."

Chapter 10

Max motioned me to the sofa as he unplugged the laptop on his desk and handed it to me. He bent and extracted the cord from under the desk, then headed to the kitchen. "Soda? Water?"

"Water's fine." I found the on button and energized the laptop. It had a fairly large screen, about seventeen inches. Even being this big, it was thin and light. "Cool laptop. How old is it?"

"Bought it right after I moved out here. Got a great deal on it, a little over nine hundred. It was a display, and the store was no longer carrying that model." He walked out with a soda for him and a glass of ice water for me. After handing me my glass, he put two coasters on the coffee table and set his soda down. He sat next to me, reached over his end of the sofa and picked up a remote. He turned on the stereo and flipped stations until he located a classic rock station then turned it low. "And fast."

"I see that." It was already booted up. The background on his desktop was a picture of me in my cutoff jeans, t-shirt and carrying my shoes. My hair was blown back and uncombed from the boat trip on the Mississippi. We had barely known each other when he tracked me down. I had been out on the river with Mitch and his friends. I didn't ski that day due to my leg, but I had a great time anyway. "When did you take this picture?"

Max grinned. "Don't you remember the day at the river?"

I nodded my head. "I mean--yes, I remember that day. I mean, how did you take that picture? You didn't have a camera."

"Phone."

"No way. The quality is too good for a camera phone."

Max's grin got even bigger. "A friend of mine enhanced it."

I huffed and clicked onto the internet. In reality, it felt good to be wanted by someone. A warm feeling spread through my whole being.

Max slouched on the sofa and leaned his head back as I typed in a website that we used for tracking people. It usually gave us information that was hard to get from other sources. I typed in the office username and password, but it denied me access. I grabbed Max's cordless phone extension off the coffee table.

"Rich, hey. Got a minute?"

"Sure, Sis. How's it going with Max and the cops?"

I glanced at Max. "They're like cops everywhere. Suspicious." Max made a face at me but Rich laughed. Max stood and headed to the bathroom. "John said you were headed out here."

"Yeah, can't have my baby sister in trouble with the law."

"Ha ha. Look, I'm trying to get into the main database to check a name, but it's not allowing me access."

"Yeah, we don't have it set up as a remote access. What did you need? I'll look it up and bring it with me tomorrow." I heard Rich take a bite of something.

"Marsha Dodington." I spelled it for him. "She's Cynthia Vernon's partner. They own a lab called V & D Clinical Laboratory. I'm not sure where it's located. They do genetic testing and such, similar in nature as what Winslow's lab does."

"Just a minute, Mel." I could hear him scribbling on a piece of paper. "Okay, go ahead."

"Rumor has it, they've been arguing over the running of the business. Can you see if it's a privately held company and if company reports are available? Also see what their rating is with Standard and Poor." Max walked back in and sat down next to me.

"Why?"

"Just to see if they're financially solvent."

"Good thinking, Mel."

"I have my moments. Lastly see what sort of grants they're competing for. Winslow told us that most everyone here is competing for money. If they're in a tiff over money with someone else, that might be another avenue of conflict, adding more suspects. In addition, see if they've filed any police reports or restraining orders on any of the protestors or any one recently." I turned to Max. "Do you know the names of any of the protestors?"

"Who are you talking to, Mel?" Rich asked.

"I'm at Max's apartment on his computer."

Max was still frowning. "James Daniels. He assaulted a doctor at the conference center two nights ago."

"Short nerdy-looking guy. Black receding hairline?"

Max nodded.

"Bullhorn."

"What?" Max and Rich stereo-ed in my ears.

I smiled at Max. "John and I gave nicknames to the leaders that we noticed with the protestors the other day. Bullhorn, because he carried one. There's also Blond Puffy, Jabba the Hut, and Carrothead. Do you know the names of any of the others?" I gave description of them to Max.

"Carrothead's real name is Jason Tonia." Max shrugged. "I'll ask Ben and Amanda about the other two."

"Rich, did you hear Max?"

"Yeah. I'll run their names too." There was a pause. "You've really been thinking about this."

"I had a lot of time to think while I was being held in that stupid interrogation room." I smiled at Max.

"Viking called me after you spoke with him. Watch what you say to Max. I know he likes you and you like him, but he's still the law."

"Spoken like a true cop, Rich."

"I'll take that as a complement."

I tapped my finger on the table. "Have you found out anything else from Mitch or about my Jeep?"

Rich hesitated. "I was going to wait until I was out there, but your apartment was broken into."

My stomach clenched in a familiar way as my blood pressure increased. I hesitated before speaking to make sure that my voice didn't have the angry edge I knew it would otherwise. "Okay… When and why?"

"It happened the day you left. We don't know why. Nothing was taken that we could tell. Mitch filed a report. Dad and I scoured the place. It looked like some paperwork was moved around but that was all."

"Which papers?"

"Bills, legal papers dealing with the law suit, birth and death certificates. Your whole strong box was riffled through."

I crossed my arms and huffed. I was breathing fast. Max rubbed my back.

"Calm down, Mel." Max rubbed my back more.

"Call John and tell him. I'll be back at the hotel by ten if you come up with anything else."

"Okay. See you tomorrow."

I hung up. Max was staring at me.

"What was that about?"

"The day we left to come out here, someone broke into my house and went through all my stuff. Right before we left that morning, someone slashed my tires and left a note at work. It said 'Soon.'" I took a deep breath to calm myself, then turned back to the computer. I switched tactics and Googled government grants for genetic research.

"What does that mean?"

"I don't know." I took another deep breath and put the thought aside. Nothing I could do about it. Rich, Dad and Mitch obviously had it covered back home. I had more to concentrate on here. I was still the major suspect in a homicide.

***

Two hours later, I was still at it. So far, the search hadn't revealed much of anything. There were several government grants out there, and I even found a few private grant foundations giving money for specific disease research, but mostly it added up to a big zero.

Max had been intently watching me for the first half hour, then he laid his head back and got comfortable with his feet on the coffee table. He just monitored my activity. He had a phone call during that time, but all he had done was answer yes and no to questions. We spoke little. Usually the only sound was me typing.

I stretched and rubbed my eyes.

"Done yet?" Max asked, amusement in his tone.

"Yeah. For tonight. If I was at the office, I think the main database we use would have coughed up better information."

Max leaned over closer to me. "I was thinking…"

"I thought I heard some grinding noises over there."

He laughed silently. "When you turned Vernon down, where did she go?"

"You know I shouldn't be talking to you. Everyone has warned me, Degrad, Viking, John, Rich…"

Max nodded. "Tell me anyway."

I sat back and thought. "She moved over to the wall near Marsha."

"What did they do?"

"I didn't pay that much attention."

"Try. You usually have an awesome memory."

"Let's see." I stared at one of his abstract paintings on the wall. "When I spoke with John and Winslow, the ladies were talking with their heads together. You know, like whispering or talking in a serious conversation."

"And then?"

"They only stayed a short time after that, if I remember correctly."

"Did you notice them at all during that time?"

I focused on the painting again. "Yeah. Once. Sort of."

"Sort of?" Max's face took on a puzzled look.

"Cynthia was staring intently at me. I looked across the room and she turned away. She left after that, I think."

"Hmmm." Max leaned back and rubbed his chin. "Was Marsha with her?"

"No." I shook my head. "Wait a minute, yes. Marsha followed behind her, now that I'm thinking about it." I smiled at Max. "I wonder if they ever got the waitress to join them or if she turned them down too."

"They hit on a waitress? Why didn't you say anything to us about that?" Max sat up. "Describe her to me."

"First of all, I didn't think it was important, and I still don't see the relevance. Second, you didn't ask." I thought about the brief glimpse I had of the waitress. "Brunette. Same hair color as me. Shorter and younger. Maybe twenty two or three. Short hair." I touched at the top part of my neck.

"Name?"

"I wasn't that close."

"Would you recognize her if you saw her?"

"Maybe."

We sat in silence for a minute or two, both of us thinking. "Max?"

"Yeah?"

"Just how was Cynthia killed?" I saw him hesitate. "Marsha said the cops told her it was blunt force trauma to the head. That makes sense because of all the blood everywhere, but something about it sounds fishy."

"You didn't hear this from me."

I nodded.

"She was knifed several times."

"Where did all the blood come from? I mean, it was on the walls, the mirrors, I think I even saw some on the ceiling."

"There was. They think, and since I haven't seen the autopsy report yet, it's still speculation, that she was knifed then had her head beaten against the wall, the stall, and several other places."

"After she was dead?"

"That's the thought."

"Must've been strong, so, we're talking a man here."

Max shrugged. "Or a really pissed off woman."

"Were there any footprints found?"

"Besides yours?"

I gave him a dirty look.

"Only one bloody one besides yours. But several others were taken from the scene. I haven't heard yet on the outcome from the lab or what type of shoe might have made any of them. Amanda has them working overtime on it."

"Fingerprints?"

Max nodded. "Several have already checked out to be employees, besides the ones of yours by the light switch. Two so far are unidentified; they're still working on them." Max leaned over and kissed me on the lips. "I'll pass along the information on the waitress to Ben. They were interrogating Carrothead last time I talked with them."

Neither of us spoke for a few seconds, but our eyes were locked in a mutual intensity. I knew our thoughts were running in the same direction. My blood was beginning to boil as his blue eyes delved deeply into mine. I moved into his arms and we kissed. A breath-stopping, heart beating, make the panties wet kind of kiss.

After several minutes of making out, I pulled away from him and licked my lips. "I've got go back to the hotel."

"No you don't." His voice was low. Husky.

"Yes, I do. I'm on night duty."

Max sighed. "Okay, Tiger. But I want a rain check."

"What am I? A department store?" I smiled as we stood up. After exiting his apartment, Max grabbed my hand and held it as we walked to his Trooper. "Don't forget, we have to get Winslow a couple of candy bars."

Max nodded and held open the door for me to get in. He leaned in and kissed me again. "You're a great kisser." His eyes turned sexy again. "I can only imagine what the rest is like." He winked as he closed the door.

I laughed. When he slid in behind the wheel, I chuckled. "Maybe, you'll find out. Someday. Maybe."

Max smiled back as he pulled out of his parking lot. We stopped at a nearby convenience store then headed back to the hotel. When we reached the main entrance, we both looked around, but the place was empty. Max leaned over and kissed me again. "Be careful until you get to your room. There's a killer out there, and this person knows you didn't do it."

I nodded in agreement.

"I won't be around first thing in the morning, but I should see you at the lunch break." With a final light kiss, I hopped out of his truck and walked inside.

I headed to the elevators, noticing that many of the couches and chairs were filled with conference people, either in serious conversations or laughing and having a good time. The restaurant was still doing a fairly brisk business, and the bar was packed. The wait for the elevators gave me time to think.

The case was forefront of course, but I drew no new conclusions. I felt there had to be something I was missing. With a shrug, I let those thoughts go.

Next, my mind went to Max. *Man, can he kiss.* The thought of his lips on mine sent explosions though my body again. I touched my lips and could almost feel his lips on them again. *Am I ready for this?* I could feel my body screaming 'Yes!' but my heart was still wavering. I liked Max, to be sure but... It seemed my brain also put the 'but' in the way. *Why? Why am I hesitating? This never happened in the past. If I saw a guy I liked, I pursued him.* Craig had been the last. The rat bastard.

I realized I was standing in the elevator. As it continued to rise, I clenched a fist around the bag that held Winslow's candy bars and my sodas.

It was cheaper to buy the sodas at the store than out of the soda machine near the ice maker.

I couldn't understand why I wasn't trusting my body and heart. Okay, so not all of my choices in men had been winners, Bart Hessor for one, but still. Max was a cut above all of them. Just the thought of Max always made things brighter, even with a murder investigation hanging over me. Max was special. I could feel a warmth creeping into my heart. No other man affected me like this, ever. Including the rat bastard. At least not to this degree.

The elevator doors opened.

So why didn't I take my usual tactic and jump in with both feet?

I could feel a frown on my face as I exited the elevator and turned right toward the hotel room. My eyes were focused on the floor as I walked, still thinking of Max. When I looked up, Blond Puffy was just bending over to slide a note under a hotel door. And I realized that it was my hotel door.

"Hey! Hey lady!" I called, increasing my speed to a very fast walk.

She turned and fell against the door.

"You... Stop."

Blond Puffy stared at me for all of two seconds, then took off running. A bag that had been hanging in front of her, swung to her back.

I took off running after her. Before I reached my hotel room, John stepped out. As I passed him at a full run, I said, "Blond Puffy." I dropped my bag at his feet without hesitating or slowing.

I heard behind me John speaking to Winslow. "Take this. Lock the door. Stay in the room." Then I was out of ear shot.

I was slowly catching up to her. She kept turning her head to look at me. We turned another corner, and I had a feeling she was heading to one of two stairways. The first was closer to my hotel room and we had already passed it. So, she was running the circuit to get to the other stairs by the second set of elevators. The hotel was a square tower with elevators on opposite ends of the floor.

When we turned the last corner, I slowed. She was still running fast, but I recognized the man coming down the corridor up ahead who had just passed the other stairs—John. Finally she must have recognized him too because she also stopped.

"You will go to hell, both of you. You are working against God," she said between breaths.

John just smiled at her as he dialed a number on his cell.

Blond Puffy looked my way as I stopped. "You create abominations in your labs. You will die a painful death."

"Okay. Thanks for the warning." I smiled at her too.

Her face scrunched into an ugly troll-like face. She launched herself at me. I stood my ground, automatically going into a ready stance. As she grabbed at me, I used her momentum and twisted her to the ground. The arm lock I placed on her stopped all of her resistance.

A chuckle came from down the hall. I looked up to see John closing his phone. "Good throw."

"Good thing I started back at the dojo."

He walked up and extracted a pamphlet from her green and white messenger bag. More threats and propaganda. "Hotel security is on the way. They've already alerted the local cops. One of the other attendees called them a minute or two ago."

"Good," I said, tightening my hold by twisting just a little as she struggled. Not that it really mattered with John there. With his background in Special Forces, he probably knew more ways to detain or hold someone than I would ever know. "Should I let her up?"

John looked intently at her. "Nah, let her sweat."

She cursed at us. The words were filthy, obscene and some new combinations I had never heard before. And I knew a lot of curse words.

"Wow." I stared down at her. "I never expected those sorts of words out of her. She looks like a soccer mom." I looked up as hotel security hurried down the hall to us.

"Are you okay?" the first security guard asked as his eyes took in the situation.

"Fine." I let her up, and the larger guard took her by the arm.

John spoke at the same time. "This lady assaulted my associate."

"Okay. Come with us and we'll let the cops deal with her. You can file a report with them."

I sighed. More cops. "I guess. Winslow's candy bars are in the bag I dropped by the door." John nodded as I followed the guards down the hall to the elevators.

Chapter 11

I sat near Winslow listening to another presenter the next morning. As she droned on, I desperately tried to stay awake. I hadn't gotten back to the room until after one in the morning. My eyes lids started drooping again when suddenly the hair on the back of my neck rose. I sat up slowly, not drowsy at all now. I felt like someone was watching me, staring at me. But, when I looked around, I didn't see anyone focusing in my direction. Still I couldn't shake the feeling. I tried tuning back into the speaker, but the feeling grew deeper. Looking around, this time I saw a conference worker intent on me as she headed my direction. She handed me a note. I thanked her silently and opened it. It was from John.

'Come outside. Tell Winslow I'll be back here.'

With a puzzled look, I leaned over, tapped her on the arm and showed her the message. "It's from John," I whispered. Collecting my notebook, I quickly and quietly made my way toward the back of the room.

John had been standing inside the big double doors and as I got closer, he left. I found him waiting for me just outside.

"What's up?"

"Max called. Goins and Hambrick are coming to pick you up. They have a couple more questions for you."

I frowned even as my stomach did a flip flop.

"I've already contacted Degrad for you. He said he'll meet you at the police station. Say nothing to the cops until then."

"Did Max say they were arresting me?" My heart beat faster.

John shook his head. "He said questions."

"Everyone is telling me not to talk to them, but since I didn't do anything, why shouldn't I help them with as much information as I can?"

John looked off in the distance thinking. "My understanding from Viking is that the evidence is circumstantial. We know you didn't do it, but anything you say could be added to that evidence. We'd rather have you appear uncooperative than have to defend you in court. Let Degrad do his job."

I just looked at him.

John smiled and touched my shoulder. "I've got a lot invested in you. I don't want to have to start over with a new employee because you're in the pokey."

I gave him a half-hearted chuckle. As we were standing there, Goins and Hambrick walked down the hall.

"John Huddleston, Detective Amanda Goins," Hambrick introduced her. John had already told me that he had been interviewed by Hambrick. They shook hands. Hambrick turned to me. "Ready to go?"

"If I must." I faked a smile. I handed John my notebook and saw Goins giving me a strange look. "The good cop, bad cop routine doesn't work with me. My Dad used it so much that it has no effect." I gave her a sugary sweet smile and walked away with both John and Hambrick chuckling.

I noticed that neither of the cops were following me. I stopped and turned. "Are you giving me a ride or do I have to take a cab to the police station?"

Goins shook her head and started walking. Hambrick continued chuckling as he followed. Soon they were walking on either side of me.

"Max said you had a great sense of humor," Hambrick said.

"Just so you know, Degrad is already on his way."

"We figured as much," Goins said. It was the last thing said for the entire ride.

***

While I waited for the arrival of Degrad, I sat in the interrogation room alone. The cops had already informed me that they wouldn't be in until he arrived and that the reason we were in this room again was because it was the biggest. I tried to sit still, but the time and silence weighed on me. There was a pen and legal pad on the table. I picked up the pen and began clicking it. After a couple of seconds, I realized what I was doing and stopped. I set the pen down. I drummed my fingers on the table. When I realized I was doing that, I stopped. With an effort, I placed one hand on top of the other to keep the jitters quiet. Within seconds my foot started bouncing. Finally the door opened and he walked in.

"Thanks for calling me. You wouldn't believe how many people won't take my advice."

I smiled in relief. "I actually considered it. Since I did nothing wrong, but Vincent Viking suggested that I have you present. I trust Vincent."

Degrad nodded. "Good." He unbuttoned his suit and sat. He laid his briefcase on the table, extracted a legal pad and pen, closed it, and sat the briefcase at his feet. He smoothed his tie. "I'll jump in during the questioning if I think it will compromise you in any way. Otherwise cooperate as much as possible. Ready?" At my nod, he stood up and stuck his head out the door.

In walked Goins, Hambrick and Bauer. I smiled. Goins appeared unfriendly. Hambrick smiled back. Both sat at the table. Bauer stood off to the side. I couldn't read the expression on his face. Goins and Hambrick were dressed in the usual similar clothes, but Max had on a pair of jeans and a light green polo shirt. Both looked well-worn and comfortable.

"Ask away."

Hambrick pulled out a stack of photos and placed them in front of me. "Can you pick out the waitress that the two ladies propositioned?"

Degrad's head went from Hambrick to me and back. "What is this about? What waitress?"

"Mel mentioned..." Hambrick started.

"I let it slip..." I interrupted him, "...to Max that I saw Marsha Dodington, Cynthia Vernon's partner, proposition a waitress at the mixer. I only remembered it later when I was talking about something else with Max."

Degrad frowned. "Detective Bauer didn't question you, did he?"

I kept my eyes on my attorney. I knew how to lie. "No. We were talking about something else. He was a good little cop and never mentioned the case at all."

It didn't look like Degrad believed me, but he motioned to the photos anyway.

I glanced up at Max. He was staring at the floor. Picking up the pile of photos, I slowly paged through them, comparing them with my shady memory. I picked out two women, then studied them closely. I shook my head at the detectives intently watching me. "I only saw her from the side. I couldn't testify that it's either of these two ladies. If I could see them from the side, I'd be able to, maybe. Sorry." I handed the photos back.

Goins spoke as Hambrick picked up the photos. "We figured as much. The photos were a shot in the dark. Tonight, there's a wedding reception in the east wing of the hotel. The manager assures me that all of the wait staff who were at the mixer will be working the reception. Would you be willing to walk with us through the kitchen and reception area to pick her out?"

"I will be called and be present," Degrad stated. The cops both nodded and looked at me.

"Sure."

Degrad made notes on his legal pad. I glanced at them, but I couldn't read his scribbles. Looked like kiddie writing to me.

Goins glanced at Hambrick then flicked her eyes to Max before continuing. "How many phone calls did you make yesterday on your cell phone?"

I noticed Degrad's head come up, but he said nothing. Something about my cell phone was raising an alert. "Uh, two maybe three. I called my Dad, Max and…" I paused looking at nothing while I thought. "Maybe a friend, Beth Majorham, before I called my Dad. Yeah, Beth before Dad. Why?" I looked from one cop to another at the table. I suddenly narrowed my eyes and flicked them at Max. I looked back at Goins. "There was a call on my cell that I can't account for, isn't there?"

She betrayed nothing, but I saw Max flinch slightly. She cleared her throat. "Did you make any other calls that night?"

"Don't answer," Degrad said.

I looked around the room and my eyes landed on Max who was now staring at his shoes, hands shoved into his pockets. Deep. The muscles in his arms were tight. His lips were pressed into a thin line. There was a scowl on his face. I frowned.

"Here's the warrant to pull your phone records." Goins laid it in front of me. "This is for both your cell and home phone as the warrant states." Goins pulled a stack of papers from her file.

Degrad pulled the warrant over and quickly scanned it.

I could feel my own muscles tightening, especially in my stomach. My blood pressure was climbing the scale like a squirrel up a tree. I took a deep breath to calm myself. I had nothing to hide.

Goins laid them in front of me. "Please explain the ones highlighted. The others have been accounted for."

I flashed a look at Max, who was now staring at me. Glaring. I tried to keep the puzzled look off my face. *What does that look mean?* Degrad leaned over and looked at the numbers.

"I'd like to talk with my client alone please."

The cops moved out of the room, with Max giving me another scathing look as he left. *Why is he mad at me? What does that look mean?*

"Quickly run through them. Tell me if any of them are suspicious," Degrad said.

I looked over the list. The only ones I didn't recognize were a bunch on my home phone caller ID. "Only these. They must have been the hang ups I had been getting before I left. They showed up on my unit as unidentified." I paused. "What was that about my cell?" I shuffled through and pulled out the paper with my cell numbers. "Here. See I called Beth, a friend of mine." My eyes jumped ahead. "What number is this?" I pointed at a call made the night I arrived at the hotel.

Degrad grabbed the paper underneath it. He frowned. "It shows that the number is registered to Cynthia Vernon."

"What? I didn't call her." I know my mouth must have been hanging open.

"Can you explain it?"

I shook my head.

"Just keep it together and don't answer any questions. Let me deal with it," Degrad said, then he called the cops back in.

"Let's run through them, Mel," Hambrick said after they were seated again.

I picked up the papers again, stunned. Someone must have stolen my cell, used it, then returned it without me knowing it, and incriminated me in the crime. And Max knew it! I glanced up at him, and he was once more glaring at me with those hard eyes. Silently I cleared my throat as Goins motioned to the papers. I looked down at the highlighted numbers. "This is to an old client of the firm's. Roma Tronolski." I pointed at the first one.

"Where can we reach her?" Goins asked.

"She's dead. A stalker killed her. You can contact the Oregon State Police for confirmation." I paused to pull his name out of my memory. "Detective Yardley is in charge on that case."

"Okay. Go on." She scribbled notes.

I grimaced at the next number highlighted. "This number is to Bart Hessor in Quincy, Illinois."

"And he is?"

"An old friend." I looked up at Max. Now I knew why he was mad.

"Why so many calls to Hessor?" Max spit out, his eyes boring into mine.

"It's a private matter."

"Tell me anyway." Max's tone was harsher than I had ever heard it.

Degrad leaned over and whispered in my ear, "Will this incriminate you in any way?"

I shook my head, whispering back, "Just embarrassing."

"I think you should answer it, but if you don't want to, then don't."

I swallowed and looked at each cop in the room ending with Max. "Bart Hessor is an old boyfriend that I ran into a while ago. He made it known that he wants to sleep with me. I have continually turned him down. On a case, just a couple of months ago, I… I needed information, and he was the fastest way to get it. So I called him." My eyes locked with Max's. "After that he has been, well, very persistent." I looked away from Max and flipped to the caller ID sheet. "These numbers here are also from him. This is his business phone. And this is to his dance club, Rascals, in St. Louis, Missouri."

"Do Rich and John know about this?" Max asked.

"John does. He can confirm my story, if you need to get the full scoop on it." My tone took on a bite. I noticed Goins and Hambrick glance at Max, then they glanced at each other and exchanged smiles.

"Moving on," Goins said with a motion to the paper.

I brought my attention back to the paperwork. "This is to another old client, Earl Boden. This number is no longer his. He's not at his house."

"And where is he?" Hambrick asked.

"In a nursing home. He tried to kill himself and didn't succeed. He botched it good and now can't communicate."

Goins handed me a pen. "Write down the name of the nursing home please."

I did.

"And the rest of the numbers?" She made the motion again.

"This is to my lawyer in Maryland, Jason Landry of Landry, Blakemoor and Brooks. Oops, sorry they changed names. Landry, Brooks and Associates." I quickly added their names to the list.

"Why do you have a lawyer in Maryland?" Hambrick asked, leaning back in his chair.

"I lost my husband and five year old son in a car accident a year ago. I still have a law suit pending with the trucking company and also with the hospital that treated my husband and myself."

Hambrick swallowed. "Sorry."

I nodded, not even looking at Max, but out of my peripheral I saw him shift on his feet. I picked up the list again. "These calls on my caller ID, I have no idea about. I'd been getting several hang-ups a night right before I left. On my unit it came up as 'unidentified.' I think it's a telemarketer, but I don't know for certain."

"There are six different numbers here on the caller ID list." Goins pointed to them, the skepticism lost on no one.

"I can only tell you what I know, detective. I've not lied to you about anything." I looked her right in the eye.

Goins looked down writing notes. "Off the subject of the calls, we understand that you're proficient at Judo."

My gaze shifted to Max. There was no way they got that information from anyone else. He wouldn't meet my eyes. "I was. I recently started back at my old dojo again."

"What rank did you hold?"

"Second degree black belt. Although my skills are very rusty, so actually I'd put myself at a much lower rank."

"That includes training in various other instruments, like nunchucks and such?" Hambrick asked.

"No. I think you are confusing Karate, Aikido, and several other martial arts with Judo."

The cops just stared at me. Goins spoke up, "So you have not learned the use of them?"

I smiled. "Judo is a 'throwing' marital arts. We don't use weapons. There are a few choke holds but no weapons. Nunchucks and throwing knives, swords, etcetera, are used in other martial arts." I paused. "And as I said, my skills are rusty. Up until three weeks ago, the last time I went to class was right before I learned that I was pregnant."

Hambrick looked at Goins. They both looked at Max. Some sort of communication passed between them.

Max stood up from the wall and walked to the table. He cleared his throat and looked me in the eyes. "About the call on your cell to Vernon…"

"She will not answer that question. Unless you are charging her…" Degrad looked pointedly at each detective. "This interview is over," Degrad said and stood up. He had already put his notes in his briefcase. "If you're going to charge her, since I'm now representing her, I *will* receive a phone call first. Given the fact that she has cooperated, I ask that if you're going to charge her, please allow me to bring her to the station. There's no need to embarrass her at the hotel." He nodded at the cops and motioned me out the door.

I walked out with a quick look back at Max. He cocked his head with that hard to read look. I didn't speak until I was in Degrad's car. "From the way you were speaking, it sounds like I'm going to be charged."

"Maybe, maybe not." Degrad smiled. "I also like to try to intimidate cops if I can."

I chuckled. "How can I prove that I didn't make that call?"

"Was the cell phone ever out of your possession?"

"No."

"Where do you carry it?"

"My pocket."

"Doable. Easy enough to pick your pocket and return it without your knowledge. Shouldn't be too hard to make that case in court." He glanced at me as he drove. "The thing with this Hessor guy?"

"I dated Bart in high school. When I first met Max, they, the Quincy police, were investigating Bart not only for drug dealing but for murder." I relayed how the two guys met and about my first case with Security Investigations. By that time I finished, we were nearing the hotel.

"Is Bauer an old boyfriend also? Was that the reason he was so upset?"

"Max was interested in me too while he lived in Quincy. I'm only now getting to where I might date him." I looked out the window for a few seconds. *What do I want?* When I looked back, Degrad was still studying me from the corner of his eye. "Can you get a copy of those phone calls?"

Degrad smiled confidently. "I copied them down as they questioned you." He motioned to the briefcase. "Even made a copy for you. Hope you can read my penmanship. Vincent said that the three of you were excellent investigators. I thought since you didn't know who they were, you might want to look into it."

I smiled back. "You bet. Good thinking." I pulled out a sheet of legal paper with his scribble on it. Not extremely legible but not the worst I've ever had to decipher. He pulled into the hotel as I shut his case.

Chapter 12

We were standing in one of the seating areas with Winslow who was answering questions before the lunch break, when John nudged me with his elbow. After getting back from the police station, I had been conscious that someone was watching me. It was unnerving. I continually tried to find out who it was. *Is it the cops?* There were plenty of people to be suspicious about since most were just walking around, but they all seemed to be connected to the conference. It was frustrating. I mentioned it to John, and he said he'd keep an eye out too. This time, when I followed John's gaze, I saw Max slowly walking down the hall. He immediately stopped and waited, watching me.

"So? He knew about Vernon's number and didn't tell me." I glanced once more at Max. He had that little boy guilty look.

He jerked his head back toward the door and mouthed, "Please."

I ignored him.

"Pump him for information. Pam will call soon with the phone trace. Be back here in two hours." John nudged me with his elbow.

"What if I don't want to?"

John did a double take. "Not curious?" Then he gave me a crafty smile. "Find out about the autopsy. No one can do that much damage and not leave some trace."

I grunted. He was right. Max would be feeling guilty, and I could use that against him. I scrunched up my face at John, then headed toward Max.

Max cocked his hip and stuck one hand in his pocket. There was no smile in his eyes.

I walked past him with just a single word. "Coming?" I didn't even look at him but hurried across the conference center and exited. I headed directly for his Trooper. Getting in, I shut the door and waited.

Several steps behind me, Max finally climbed in. We sat in silence for several seconds.

"Drive."

"Where?"

"I don't care. Just drive."

Max took off. Silence still ruled. Shortly we stopped at a park. It wasn't very big, maybe two square blocks. I got out and walked away from the truck and passed the playground area. I spotted a fountain with deserted benches near it. Max followed me. He stood in front of me for a split second, then joined me reluctantly. Again we sat in silence.

Max cleared his throat. "I'm sorry, Mel. I couldn't tell you. The only reason they have me on this case is because of my connection to you."

I still didn't look at him. "What other evidence do they have against me?"

"None. But they're digging hard."

"Am I their only suspect?"

"From what they've told me, yes."

"What about Carrothead?"

"They're still looking into him and the other protesters, but... well, you're still their priority."

"And your job?"

Max sighed. "To watch you. I'm supposed to find a way to search your room."

"Just ask."

"May I search your room?"

"Absolutely not."

"Why?"

"Because I don't trust you." I finally turned to him. "The deal is off, Bauer. It's every man for himself, and I'm real good at taking care of myself."

Max looked down at his feet. "I'm sorry, Mel. I hate this. You don't know how hard it was not to tell you. I can't do this. I can't spy on you anymore." He stood up. "Let's go back to the hotel. I'll get myself taken off the case. You won't hear from me again."

He slowly walked back to the Trooper, head down, hands in pockets. Sitting in the car, he stared at his hands. Grimacing at what my heart was telling me, I stood up and joined him. I gently slid into the SUV.

"Okay, here's the new deal Bauer. You spy on me for Goins and Hambrick, but you tell me everything they have on me. Everything. If you promise not to lie to me again, I'll keep you informed of anything I find out." I waited until he looked at me. "But you have to be totally honest with me."

Max raised his blue eyes to mine. "So, you forgive me?"

"Not yet. It'll depend on if you continue to be honest with me."

"Deal. I don't want to see you in jail. I know you didn't do it."

"I know." I gave him a small smile. "Now let's go grab a burger and then you can search my room."

"I'm sorry for deceiving you."

I nodded, accepting his apology. "So, has the autopsy come back yet?"

Max chuckled. "I knew that would be your first question. Are you sure you weren't a cop in a former life? Yeah, it has."

"Anything I need to know?"

"They believe the knife blade was about six inches long. The perp is right handed and about five ten or so."

"Great."

Max nodded. So far, I fit that description. "The kill stab was in the chest, the first blow. The second and third were just to let off steam. After that, the head was caved in by various objects in the bathroom—the counter, the wall, the hand dryer, and the stall. Someone was definitely pissed off with the damage done to her after death."

"The fingerprints found in the bathroom so far have all checked out to be employees. That was apparently an employee bathroom. They do have a fingerprint on the door of one of the stalls which is not an employee's or yours. The foot print was from a tennis shoe. The forensic specialist is, even as we speak, eliminating all of the employee's shoes. So far there's no match. Another point in your favor, it also doesn't match your shoe."

I grunted, unconvinced.

"And, although you're the only suspect so far, I think Hambrick is becoming convinced it's not you," Max informed me as we pulled into a fast food restaurant. "What do you want?"

"Chicken sandwich, fries, shake." I looked at him as he pulled up to the speaker. "You're eating too right? Because I'm not letting you have part of mine."

Max smiled, embarrassed. "Well…"

I sighed. "This is becoming a habit of yours. I'll buy. I thought cops got paid on a regular basis." I dug out my wallet.

"I'm trying to pay off my credit card bill."

"If you would stop sending me those expensive flower arrangements, you might be able to afford to eat." I shook my head.

"I'm glad you aren't mad at me anymore."

"Who said that?" I gave him a Cheshire grin. "Keep up with the news. Anything else?"

"The big stumbling block in your case is the cell call."

"I know." I sat thinking about it after I handed Max the money. We drove away both eating. Right before we got to the hotel I looked at Max. "Were there any fingerprints on my cell besides mine?"

Max shook his head, finishing off his soda. "The phone was almost wiped clean. There were only a couple of your prints on it. I told Goins that you wouldn't be dumb enough to call the deceased on your own cell if you planned to kill her."

"So, what do they think is my motive?"

"They really don't have one. I can tell you what was initially thrown out as possible, but most of their theories have fallen by the wayside."

I motioned for Max to go on as I sipped my shake.

"First, it was thought that it was connected to Dr. Winslow, since they thought you were working for her. When I told them that you were a snooping sneak, not the terms I told them mind you, and it was confirmed with John, they dropped that idea fast. The next theory was that you were upset that the lesbian propositioned you, especially when they learned you had been drinking and knew Judo."

"Thanks for telling them that."

Max's head snapped to me in surprise. "I didn't tell them that. Dr. Winslow did."

"Oh."

"I informed them that two beers were not enough to get you drunk enough to come unglued like that. Luckily, they haven't found out about your anger yet." Max lifted his eyebrows. "The fact that you've been cooperating with us in everything is winning Hambrick over."

"What about Goins?"

Max shrugged. "The trick with the shoe at the crime scene played heavily in your favor too." He paused, "Mel, about the cell call?"

"Yeah?"

"Level with me. Did you leave your phone anywhere at any point?"

I shook my head. "John and I have been puzzling over that all morning. It was in my pocket where I always keep it. Except when I'm sleeping, then it's on the night stand." I shook my head. "I just don't get it. Degrad said that it wouldn't be hard to discredit that in court. He could prove it might have been snitched then put back."

"True. But when?" Max tossed the empty bag into the back, behind our seats. "It was before the mixer. Where were you?"

"In my room or with the others. John doesn't remember seeing anyone near me except at the bar, but he wasn't really watching me either."

"Was Marsha near you at any point?"

I thought about it. "No, although when I was in the bathroom with Winslow one time, it was wall to wall standing room only. She could have been there. I didn't know about Marsha then." I shrugged again. "Can they convict me on just that?"

"Arrest? I doubt the DA would file charges to be honest, the evidence is pretty flimsy in my opinion, but I'm not lead detective." Max looked at me before exiting the car. "I'm going to actually have to search your stuff."

"I have nothing to hide."

"But what about Degrad?"

"Let me deal with him. You and I both know I didn't kill Vernon. This way you can tell Goins and Hambrick that you searched and found nothing without having to lie to them." I hopped out of the Trooper, and we headed into the hotel.

After getting into the room, I motioned for Max to do his thing. I sat on my bed and watched as he went through my one piece of luggage.

Max smiled as he held up a pair of my bikini underwear. "Cute." They were white bikinis with little, yellow and blue ducks on them.

I smirked. "For when I'm feeling especially lucky."

Max laughed and tossed them back into the suitcase. He searched my winter coat and all the drawers in the room. Finally, he stood up and looked around.

"See. Nothing."

He frowned. "I'm only doing this as a precaution. I knew I wouldn't find anything." He sat across from me on the other bed. His eyes surveyed the room again, stopping on Winslow's luggage on the chair in the corner by her bed.

Max grabbed it and looked through it too. He glanced at me and my up lifted eyebrows. "I know technically this isn't your stuff, but hey, I didn't know that. I might as well be thorough." He smiled. Finished, he was just setting it back in its place when the door opened.

I threw a look at the door, grabbed Max and laid him back on Winslow's bed, lying on top of him. A stunned looked crossed his face as I stuck my face in his and began kissing him deeply and with lots of feeling.

John chuckled from the doorway.

I stopped kissing and turned to see John standing with Winslow poking her head in from the doorway. Her expression was mildly amused. "Hi!" I moved off of Max. He laid there, stunned.

Winslow moved in and set her briefcase on the dresser. "We didn't mean to interrupt. I spilled some coffee on my blouse, and I needed to change it." She moved to the suitcase as Max sat up on the bed.

John nodded his head toward Max with raised eyebrows.

I smiled and gave a slight shrug.

Winslow grabbed a new blouse and after grabbing her briefcase, headed to the bathroom to change.

"Sorry," I said to Max.

"Don't be." He sat up with a huge smile on his face. "You can provide a cover for me any day." He grinned at John.

John sat next to me on the bed, glanced at the bathroom door and looked at me. I knew that look. It was the command, 'Tell me.'

"Max wanted to search the room."

John frowned then glanced at Max. "No offense, Max, but that was wrong. Degrad should've been informed beforehand."

"John, I've got nothing to hide," I said.

"Remember what I told you."

"John," Max said with a side glance at the bathroom, "I'm actually trying to clear Mel. I know she didn't to it."

John gave a slight shake of his head. "Pam called on the phone trace."

Max narrowed his eyes but didn't say anything.

John continued, "All six are pay phones. One is only a block from the bar."

"Why? Who?"

John shrugged. He glanced at his watch. "Rich should be here this afternoon. We'll see if he came up with any information from the databases."

"Rich is coming out?" Max asked.

Both of us nodded.

"By the way John..." Max glanced at me. "On the phone call warrant, there was a good number of calls from Mel to Hessor and the other way around. She said you knew about it." Max held up his hand to stop my protest.

John's face twitched; someone else probably would have rolled their eyes. "Hessor gave Mel some information on a case that she should have obtained another way." He paused, giving me one of his knowing looks. "Hessor has been a pest since."

"And Rich doesn't know this? Or her family?"

"Not yet," John spoke to Max, but he was still looking at me. "Unless she does something stupid again."

I rolled my eyes.

Winslow walked out and stood watching us.

I leaned back in the chair. "Hessor's more persistent than viral diarrhea."

Everyone paused at the image. Max broke the silence, "I don't like it, Mel. I'll call and talk to him if you want me too."

"Please!" I said, standing up. I walked past Winslow to the refrigerator to get a drink. "Men."

Winslow chuckled. "John, I need to find one of the committee members to make sure that the audio visual equipment is set up for my presentation. Are you with me, or should I take Mel?"

John glanced at Max then at me. "Me. Mel, you're with her during the presentation. Twenty minutes. Conference Room B."

"Yes sir, Bossman." I fake saluted him as they left. John shook his head with a smile and closed the door behind him. I sat in the chair at the table and looked at Max. "What now?"

Max rubbed his chin. "I'm not sure. While you're at your meeting, I'll check in with Goins and Hambrick and let them know I made the search. Can you arrange to talk to Marsha again with me around? I'd like to see her reaction up close as you talk to her."

"You think she did it?"

Max shrugged. "Statistics say Vernon knew the murderer. A family member or close associate. Maybe a friend. Since Marsha was her partner, that actually puts her in the first position in my book. Up to this point, I've been trying to come up with ways to get you off the hook. I think we've reached that point."

"Really?"

"I think it would be hard to make a case against you. Not that we couldn't get enough to arrest and hold you, but I think Degrad would have an easy time getting you off."

"Thanks."

"For what?"

"Believing in me."

"I never doubted you." His blue eyes sparkled and the lines around his eyes softened. "From the minute John informed me of what was going on, I've been campaigning for you. I've staunchly defended you to Amanda and Ben."

"Then, thanks again."

"I know a way you can make it up to me."

"I think we're just about even. Not quite, but close."

"Even?"

"You're lying and deceiving. Remember?"

Max blushed.

I smiled. "Just for the record though, how could I make it up to you?"

"Kiss me again. Like that." He motioned to the bed.

I laughed and stood up. "Dream on Bauer, that was a cover. Come on, let's go see if we can find Marsha Dodington in the short time I have."

Chapter 13

We were walking around the main conference area looking for Marsha when I spotted the brunette waitress. I nudged Bauer and followed her. She headed to the kitchen on some errand. She hurried as though she were late for something, then exited the building out a door next to the kitchen.

I opened the door to see her across the parking lot, leaning on the wall, inhaling on a cigarette.

Max whispered. "The waitress?"

I nodded. "Me or you?"

"You. I'm just the boyfriend, remember?" He walked past me, sauntering up to her with a smile. "I hate all these laws. Can I bum a smoke?"

I hid the smile and followed Max. I watched his butt in those tight jeans. *Nice!* I moved closer as Max lit the cigarette, closing his eyes as he inhaled deeply. As he blew out, it sounded more like a sigh. I suppressed the astonished look on my face. I wouldn't have pegged him as a smoker. I turned to the waitress, a plan popping suddenly into my brain. "Hi. Teresa, right?"

Her eyes widened. "How did you know?"

I smiled. "I'm psychic."

"No way!" Her jaw dropped slightly and a smile formed on her face.

I chuckled. Max snorted.

"I'm kidding. I read your name tag." I pointed at her chest.

"Oh!" Teresa laughed a silly laugh. "Yeah. Good one though."

"And, you were pointed out to me."

"Yeah?" Her smile faded as she shifted on her feet.

"A mutual friend of ours said you were a lot of fun and that I should approach you." I glanced at Max who was flicking his eyes between us. He raised his eyebrows at me in question.

"Oh?"

"Yeah. Marsha Dodington."

Teresa blushed bright red as she glanced around the area. She lowered her voice. "Look, if the manager ever finds out I was in the room…"

I waved a hand at her, stopping her mid-sentence. What I wanted to do was dance up and down with joy. I saw Max suppress a quick grin as he took another hit on the cigarette. "I understand. And it's not exactly like you think."

She glanced at Max, then back at me.

I glanced around myself, acting as though I didn't want anyone to hear us. I even lowered my voice and moved closer. "Marsha mentioned a few things and I, well, we were wondering if you might, well, swing both ways? If you get my meaning." I raised my eyebrows.

Teresa panned my body, then did the same for Max. She gave me a sly grin. "Well, I'm actually bi."

Max's eyes got wide, but he hid the rest of his surprise well as he turned his head to spit. When he turned his head back toward us, he was once more the picture of innocence.

"I was wondering, um, see my boyfriend and I want a third." I looked around again. "But you'll have to be gone by morning. I don't want to sound blunt, but how long did you spend with Marsha?"

"All night." Teresa tossed her butt in the grass with many others. "Although, we slept part of the time."

"When we get another for a 'party,' we like to make it last." I slipped my hands into my pockets and cocked a hip.

She grinned. "I can outlast the best. Marsha was a piece of cake. I wore her out fast. We were waiting for her roommate, but she never returned." Teresa looked down. "I heard about it. It's all that's been talked about." She looked around again. "Now Cynthia, she was a hotty."

"The three of you?" Max asked. He flicked the ashes off.

"Yeah, for a while. She hit the shower as a refresher, then Marsha and I did. When we got out, Cyn was gone. She left a note that she'd be back. Marsha was hoping that Cyn was bringing back a forth, something about another lover of Cyn's was here at the conference." Teresa shrugged at us. "We played a bit, then fell asleep. I was actually going to leave after Marsha fell asleep, but I wanted to see Cyn again. What a body!"

"Okay, let us talk it over, Teresa and if we decide to 'play,' I'll contact you. Okay?"

Teresa looked us up and down again. "I work straight for the next three days, during the day. Just track me down. Could be a lot of fun." With a sexy look at me, she headed back through the door.

Max tossed the cigarette away and coughed once. "Now I remember why I stopped smoking. Ugh, that was horrible."

I laughed. "Good play though."

Max shook his head. "If I didn't know better, I'd have thought you actually had done something like that before. You lie well."

I kissed my finger and touched his lips. "Who said I was lying?" I winked and walked back into hotel without looking back. I so much wanted to burst out laughing. The look on Max's face had been, well, priceless.

The door actually closed behind me before Max opened it and hurried next to me. The look on his face was still priceless. It was astonishment, excitement and disgust all rolled into one. I couldn't hold it in any longer. I started laughing.

Max continued to stare at me as we walked. He faked a stumble and grabbed his heart, then he started singing the song "Wild Thing" by the Trogs. "Wild Thing, you make my heart sing. But I wanna know for sure…"

I laughed even louder at his rendition of the song. It had been the nickname in my wild teen years given to me by Mitch, my other big brother. With a shake of my head, I leaned over and kissed him on the cheek. "Grab some gum, Bauer. Your breath smells."

Chapter 14

We caught up with John and Winslow who were standing in the hallway before the next presentations. Dr. Winslow was speaking with several conference attendees. Max walked half-way down the hall when his phone rang. He stopped and back-tracked farther away to answer it. John and I kept a look out as Winslow schmoozed. Finally, I noticed that Max motioned for me. I tapped John on the arm and headed to Max.

"Yeah? I've got to get going." I glanced at my watch. "Next session is about to start." I noticed a large number of people drifting into the room.

"That was Ben. The lady who assaulted you last night, Sonia Kelper, a.k.a. Blond Puffy, has a record." He smiled. "Cute name by the way."

"Did she kill Vernon?"

"No. She has a good alibi, but she has a warrant out for another incident in Massachusetts. They're trying to flip her about the other guys." Max's attention drifted to the door. "John's motioning for you." He leaned in for a quick kiss. "Get going."

He left quickly, and I headed into the room. I slid into a seat next to Winslow. The speaker at this session had her back turned as she fiddled with some equipment near the podium. I leaned over to Winslow and whispered softly, "Did you know Cynthia Vernon very well?"

Winslow's look was guarded. "Why?" she whispered back.

"I heard that another of Cynthia's lovers was here at the conference. I was wondering if you knew who it was?" I glanced up to the podium. Marsha Dodington turned around ready to present Cynthia's paper. *How ironic!*

"I didn't even really know she was a lesbian." Winslow looked at me. "I had my suspicions, but I didn't care what people did in their outside lives as long as it didn't interfere with the lab work." She paused and looked at Marsha too. "I seem to recall another female friend right before she got hooked up with Marsha, but I don't recall who."

I frowned, hoping that she could point out another person for the cops to investigate.

"Why? Is that who she was meeting in the bathroom?"

I shrugged. "From what two people are telling me, she received a call on her cell and had an argument with someone. One person mentioned it might be a former lover." I looked around the room. "I just wonder who it was."

Winslow shrugged back as Marsha began. I looked around again. *Why do I feel as though someone is still watching me?*

   ***

Right before supper, Winslow and I returned to our room to 'freshen up' before meeting John downstairs. I used the bathroom first and changed into a comfortable shirt, since I didn't need to be in business attire. After Winslow came out of the bathroom dressed in casual clothes too, we gathered our stuff to head to the restaurant.

"I've just got to ask you a question, Kate." I turned to make sure the door was closed as we left.

"Yes?"

"How come you just left your briefcase in the room? You've carried it everywhere before." We headed down the hall.

"What? Uh, I never let it out of sight until the presentations are over." She brushed at her lint free shirt. "I have too many papers to protect. But since all of my main competitors have now presented, I don't need it with me all the time."

We got on the elevator. The door opened two floors later. Jabba the Hut blocked the door until it closed. I was already pulling John's extra cell phone out of my pocket.

"Ah, Doctor Winslow," the tone indicated that he had planned it.

I stepped between the two.

"Stop the experimenting. What you are doing is wrong. Bad things will happen to you like Dr. Vernon."

I hit John's speed dial number. "Jabba is in the elevator with us."

Jabba looked at me. "And you, what are you defending this baby killer for? You are no better..."

"I don't kill babies. You people should get your facts..." Winslow began.

"Both of you are going to hell. You are abominations and this is..."

"What floor?" John asked.

I swiveled my head back and forth between them, then glanced at the indicator on the elevator. "Seven." Both took a step toward each other. I stepped back, pushing into Winslow as I slid John's phone into my pocket. I put my hands up in a half surrender gesture but it was also a defensive stance. "Easy. We don't want any…"

"Whoever killed Dr. Vernon, should kill again…"

"I am trying to better the world, you fool…" Winslow pushed up against me.

"…so that your experiments can't lead to genetically perfect…"

"We can conquer diseases and maybe cure cancer…"

Instinctively, I got into a ready stance as Jabba took another half step toward me. There was no way he was getting nearer Winslow.

The elevator stopped and the door dinged open. He glared at both of us and slipped out. I closed the door quickly. As the elevator moved, I took a deep breath.

Again I dialed John. "He got off at fourth floor."

"Security is covering the exits. Everyone okay?"

"Yeah. Just verbal harassing…" I glanced at Winslow who was brushing her shirt down in mock humility. "On both sides."

John chuckled as the phone died.

When the doors opened on the first floor, John, Rich and Max were waiting. Rich and Max were off to the side deep in conversation, while John was right at the doors. He glared at someone who moved to get into the elevator. They immediately backed up. He motioned us out.

"No report from security yet."

I nodded. "They're getting bolder. I swear Jabba planned that."

"James Packetson," John informed us as we headed over to Rich and Max. "Yes, I agree he probably did. Carrothead was seen just a few minutes ago near the pool. Security told me the police are on their way."

"I hope they stay locked up," Winslow said as we came to a stop near Max and Rich.

"Not that I'm criticizing or anything, but maybe next time arguing with him might not be the best idea." I caught Winslow's eyes.

"You're probably right, but I'm tired of them getting their facts wrong. And I'm tired of being scared." Winslow halted by the two men. "Ready to eat?"

Rich and Max stopped talking. Rich smiled at me and leaned in for a hug. "Hey sis. Doing okay?"

"Yeah. Fine. Did you bring the information?"

"Yeah right here. I don't think it will help. Everything seems normal." He hefted some paper-clipped documents. "Ready anytime you are." He motioned for Winslow to enter the restaurant.

I glanced at Max who hadn't said anything but smiled at me.

John stopped me. "She argued back?"

"Gave as good as he did."

He grunted.

"Mel will be in in a minute." Max and John exchanged a look. John inclined his head and entered the restaurant behind Rich.

"I won't see you until morning. I've got a development on another case." He smiled. "But I wanted to let you know that they found residue of a foreign substance under Cynthia's fingernails, and they're still checking on it. She also had chocolate in her mouth when she died."

I puzzled over that. "So? What does that mean? What do Goins and Hambrick make of it?"

"They don't know either. I just wanted you to know." He looked me in the eyes. "Be extra careful now, Mel. Especially with these two guys being spotted here."

I glanced past him. Marsha was rushing to the elevator. Grabbing his shirt, I headed toward Marsha. *Please let the elevators be slow!* Max took in the situation and followed. "Marsha!" I called softly.

She turned to me and then to Max.

"Oh, this is Max, my boyfriend. He flew out to see me and some friends that live in the area. I was wondering if I could ask you a couple more questions."

Marsha shifted her weight. "I don't know. I heard a rumor that the police think you did it."

"I didn't, Marsha. Believe me. If the cops had any sort of evidence, I'd be in jail." I tried a friendly smile for her. "I just wanted to ask if you were having trouble with any other labs over money?"

"No," she said quickly. Too quickly. "It's always tense as we all compete for the same money, but not any trouble over it."

Max looked toward the outer doors and a group of people gathered there, and to his credit, he looked bored beyond words. I glanced at him then back to Marsha.

"I also heard that Cynthia had another lover here. You wouldn't happen to know who that would be?"

"No." Marsha brushed at her dress and then smoothed her skirt as the elevator doors opened. "I really need to be going."

Max turned to me after the elevator doors shut. His voice was soft, just above a whisper. "She lied about the lover."

"Yeah, I know." I glanced around the area to see Winslow watching us from the restaurant. I looked at Max. His back was to the restaurant. I leaned over and gave him a barely touching kiss on the lips. "Don't you want to see the information that Rich brought with him?"

"Can't right now. Gotta go."

"Okay. Come by early tomorrow. Are your fellow detectives going to pull me away to find Teresa tonight?"

Max smiled as he lightly ran his finger along my jaw line. "No. Amanda said she'd just pull her aside and wouldn't blow our cover."

"Good." I glanced around again. The hair was up again on my neck. I knew someone was watching me.

Max pulled me close and gave me another kiss. Another quick, barely touching kiss. "I need to go. Take care, Mel."

With another look around to find the watcher, I headed into the restaurant. Even during the meal, I couldn't shake the feeling of being watched. I tried my best to ignore it. I finished supper faster than everyone else, so I pulled out Rich's file.

The information on Marsha Dodington and V & D Clinical Laboratory didn't help much, just like Rich said. I read through the information twice. Something was there, but I wasn't putting two and two together. Rich had gotten her personal information, along with Cynthia's. He had also pulled their Standard and Poor rating, which was excellent, and other corporate literature that he could find. The last thing in the file was a list of previous grants and loans they'd had and those they were currently applying for. I read it during supper while the guys were talking with Winslow. Rich was staying in John's room for the three remaining nights, then we were all flying home.

Winslow and I retired to our room after supper. She said she wanted to work on paperwork for the next day. I wanted to sit and think, away from prying eyes.

I was lying on the bed, looking up at the ceiling, when someone pounded on our door. Thinking immediately that it was a protester, even though the police had cleared them out by now, I headed to the door, motioning for Winslow to stay seated at the desk. "My job. Just in case," I told Winslow with a smile. As I walked to the door, John's spare cell in my pocket rang. I pulled it out but didn't look at it right away.

I glanced out the peep hole to see a disturbing sight. Goins was standing with Hambrick behind her. I glanced at my watch to see that it was after eight. I took a breath and opened the door. "Yes?" I shoved the phone in my pocket as it stopped ringing.

Goins held up a piece of paper. "We have a warrant to search your belongings." She moved past me, handing me the paper.

I stepped back stunned. *What is going on? Max already did this. He said he told them.* I glanced at Hambrick, but he moved just inside the door, next to me. He watched me, not Goins. I turned back to Goins who was searching my suitcase. Next she moved to my winter coat hanging in the closet.

Goins turned to Hambrick and nodded. As she did so, she extracted an evidence bag from her pocket and began reaching for something in my coat.

I opened my mouth to speak, but Hambrick interrupted me.

"Melissa Addison, you're under arrest for the murder of Cynthia Vernon."

Chapter 15

Hambrick grabbed my arm and moved me toward the door.

"What the…?" I glanced back to see Goins putting a bloody knife in the evidence bag. "Where did that come from?"

"Quiet," Hambrick said softly as he moved me out the door.

I ignored him. "Dr. Winslow, call John and Rich. Tell them…"

That was all I got out as Hambrick hustled me down the hall. Goins followed us carrying my winter coat and stuffing the evidence bag into a large envelope. Neither spoke to me.

On the elevator, I turned to them. "I want to call my lawyer."

"When we get to the station," Hambrick said. He never looked at me. Neither did Goins. They exchanged a look between them. Goins nodded and pulled out a cell phone. Hambrick tightened his hold on my arm. I jerked it out of his grasp.

"It's me. Meet us at the station. We need to talk to you. Thanks." Goins hung up the phone with a slight nod at Hambrick.

I seethed, barely staying in control. *How did the knife get in my coat? Who planted it? And did the same person call it in to the cops?* Max could verify that it hadn't been there earlier. I frowned. I knew better than to talk to the two arresting officers. I knew my rights.

The trip to the police station was tense. No one spoke. The two hustled me into the same interrogation room and disappeared. I sat back, arms crossed, frowning. The only thing they said to me was that Degrad would be called. Now I waited, again.

A short time later the two detectives appeared in the room. Goins carried a file folder. As they took seats on either side of me, a strange thought occurred. *I was never mirandized. I hadn't been frisked or cuffed. What is that about? And why were they in here without Degrad? They can't question me without him.* I almost smiled. This would blow their case wide open.

Goins smiled.

I know I looked shocked. Then it hit me. I wasn't really under arrest. "You didn't mirandize me."

Goins smiled bigger. She reached into her pocket and laid my cell phone in front of me. "Here's your phone back. And true, we didn't."

I glanced at Hambrick, who chuckled.

"No frisking, no cuffs."

"Max said you were quick. When did you figure it out?" Hambrick said leaning back in his chair.

"Just now. I was too mad up to this point." I relaxed and let out a deep breath. "Why?" I stuck the cell phone in my pocket.

Goins slid to a more comfortable position in her chair. "Your information and stories have checked out. We officially ruled you out as a suspect this morning. Late this afternoon, we received an anonymous tip that the murder weapon was in your possession. Specifically, we should check your coat. Since Max had already informed us of his search with negative results, we were extremely suspicious. However, in order to keep up the pretense for the murderer, we decided to 'arrest' you in order to get the evidence here."

"The search warrant?"

"Did you read the paperwork?" Goins asked me.

"Honestly? I was too stunned."

She smiled again. "Hambrick's emission tests on his car."

"But, then the knife is not admissible in court."

Hambrick nodded. "You do know your stuff. However, if we have your permission to search your coat..." He left it hanging in the air.

"If you don't mind, I'd like to talk with Degrad before I say yes," I said. "Why the fake arrest?"

"You already said you were familiar with police procedure. By not following it, we figured you would know it was fake. Sorry for scaring you," Hambrick said with another grin. "We contacted Degrad before we entered the hotel. Amanda called Max. He should be here any minute."

"I'd like to call John and Rich."

"In a bit. We'd like to keep the illusion that you're under arrest for the sake of the murderer. How about we let Degrad call them?" Goins asked.

"I guess." I tapped my finger on the table thinking about everything that just happened in less than thirty minutes. I glanced at the two cops. "Do you know who the murderer is?"

The two exchanged a look between them. Goins spoke, "No, but we know it's not you."

The door flew open. Max burst in. "What's going on, Amanda?" he asked with a quick look at me. I could tell he was pissed. "Did you arrest Mel?"

I smiled at him, as did the other cops. "Max, they did a poor job of it, too. No mirandizing, no frisking, no cuffs. Just what do they teach you people out here about law enforcement?"

Max looked from me to Goins, who was smiling, then to Hambrick, who was trying to contain a chuckle. Max's confused eyes came back to me. "What?"

Amanda held her hand out to Hambrick. "Pay up, Ben. Told you he'd freak." She looked up to find Max staring at her. "You've got it bad."

"So, you didn't arrest her?" He let out a breath.

"And you're so fast, too. No," Goins said. "We faked it. Have a seat. When Degrad gets here, we'll lay the whole thing on the table."

Within a minute, Degrad entered. "I'd like to speak to my client alone please." The cops left and Degrad turned to me. "Sorry. I tried to warn you about them, but apparently I wasn't fast enough."

"That's okay. This way my reaction was natural, so if the murderer was watching he'd see a true reaction."

Degrad nodded. "I understand they want permission to search your possessions? Have you given them your permission?"

"Nope. I said I wanted to speak to you first."

"Excellent. I think it's best to allow permission. Did they return your cell phone?"

"Yep." I tapped my jean pocket. "Can you call Rich and John and let them know. I know Rich is probably coming unglued."

"Let's see what the cops want to do first, then I'll call John. Okay?" When I nodded, he stood and brought the cops back in. He sat with Hambrick and Goins at the table, while Max stood off to the side. Degrad spoke, "We agree to the search. What was taken?"

Goins extracted a piece of paper and handed it to Degrad. "Preliminary paperwork. I'll send you the regular paperwork as soon as we get a chance to log it in."

Degrad scanned the paper then handed it to me. "Fine. Now what's the game plan?"

Hambrick leaned forward. "We'd like Mel to 'spend the night' in jail," he quoted into the air. "In reality, we're willing to put her up for the night in a different hotel. Then in the morning, Max can take her back to the conference center having been 'let out on bail,' " He looked at me. "We'd like to play along. We'd like to use you to force the murderer into making another mistake."

"Who do you think it is?" I asked.

Hambrick sighed. "We have no clue. All we have is the unidentified finger print, a shoe print, and now this phone call telling us about the knife from a disguised female voice. We're leaning toward Marsha Dodington. Forensics is checking to see if it could have been a male voice disguised to be a female. If so, then possibly James Packetson." He shrugged. "The problem is that we only have two days before everyone starts to leave."

"If that happens," Goins interjected, "the possibility of solving the case drastically drops."

Degrad turned to me. "Well?"

I shrugged. "I guess. Whatever I can do to help. I still want Rich and John to know what's going on though."

"Absolutely." Hambrick leaned back in his chair. "Max tells us that both are very experienced. And they can help keep an eye out for you, besides Max."

I glanced at Max when he spoke. "I've got a suggestion. Instead of putting Mel up in a hotel, how about having her stay at my place?" Our eyes met.

I chuckled as I noticed Goins and Hambrick exchange knowing glances. "Sure. Why not?" I handed the paper back to Degrad.

Degrad folded the paper and stuck it into his pocket. "And how about I bring Mel to the hotel in the morning?" After everyone agreed, Degrad dialed John's cell.

***

It was after ten by the time we made it to Max's place. I gave out a big sigh and sat down at his counter while he fed Tada. "Hey, I forgot to ask where the tip about the knife came from."

Max filled the cat's water bowl. "I asked Amanda that," Max said before he looked up at me. "It was from the pay phone near the restaurant. She said they're still looking at hotel security tapes and talking with people to find out who made the call. However, she did say it was a female voice, badly disguised. The techs told her that if we get a suspect, it shouldn't be hard to match voice prints."

He leaned on the counter. "I about had a heart attack. I wish they would have called and told me what they were doing ahead of time."

I chuckled. "I about wet myself when Hambrick announced that I was under arrest." I gave Max a conspiratorial look. "I've worked hard never to hear those words."

Max laughed. As he shook his head his blue eyes took on a mischievous, sexy look. "Gonna be fun having you here tonight."

"Don't get any ideas, Mister."

Max extracted his cuffs from behind his back. He held them up. "I have to make sure the prisoner doesn't get away." He swung them around on his finger.

"You wouldn't!"

Max grinned evilly. "I've been waiting a long time to get you under my influence." Then he tossed the cuffs on the counter. He moved up to face me across it. Slowly he leaned forward and kissed me. Just a quick, lips only kiss. "You can have the bed. I'll sleep on the couch," he whispered to me.

I chuckled. "Wow. You aren't even going to make a play for me?"

"Disappointed?" He leaned closer over the counter.

"Maybe a little."

"Flirt."

I leaned up and kissed him on the lips. At first, the kiss was just lips again. Then I gave into my feelings and added more. I caressed his cheek and lightly brushed his ear. He captured my head in his hands and pulled me closer, almost over the counter.

Max stood up part way and in order to keep kissing him, I crawled onto the counter. Again he moved and within seconds, I was sitting on his side of the counter, still kissing him. He pushed my legs apart so that he could pull me to the edge of the counter. Finally he let up on the kiss.

"I like flirts," he said softly in my ear.

I smiled at him and leaned forward for another kiss.

Max pulled back. He shook his head with a sexy grin, his eyes twinkling. He whispered, "No, I don't think I will kiss you. Although you need kissing, badly. And that's what's wrong with you. You should be kissed and often. And by someone who knows how.'"

I started laughing. "How long have you been waiting to use that line?" My hands dropped off his shoulders.

Max grinned, still holding me close. "Since I heard that you were watching *Gone With The Wind*. It was my Grandma's favorite movie when I was little. That was my favorite scene."

I chuckled again. "Let's see... "Oh!" I tried to put a southern accent into my voice. "'...and I suppose you think you are the proper person?'"

Max smiled. "'I might be. If the right moment ever came.'"

I focused my eyes on his shirt and tried to remember the scene. "I think it goes... 'You are a conceited varmint...'"

Max shook his head. "Scarlett says..." Max's voice took on a falsetto sound. "'You are a conceited, black-hearted varmint, Rhett Bulter. I don't know why I let you come and see me.'"

I cracked up laughing. "Bauer, you are something."

With a sexy look into my eyes, he leaned in and kissed me. His lips expressed his need and possession. His hand held my head again under my jaw. I threaded my right hand into his hair. I touched his chest with my left hand, running light circles with my fingers. One of his hands traveled down my side and pulled my hips tighter into him. He wiggled tighter into me. I crossed my legs behind him.

I felt emotions resurface that had lain dormant for a long time, feelings and wants that I had buried along with my husband.

Max's right hand held my lower back while his left hand moved to the nape of my neck. His mouth let up and he kissed my cheek in soft butterfly kisses moving toward my ear. As he reached my ear, he breathed ever so softly. I shivered. He grabbed my earlobe with his teeth. Then his tongue flicked it gently.

His soft, warm breath cascading down my neck sent even more shivers down my spine. His lips caressed my earlobe. His breathing in my ear was driving me insane. I moaned and tightened my legs on him. This was heaven.

The phone rang.

Max groaned in regret and slowly let go of my earlobe. He looked me in the eye. "I'm on call this week." His eyes betrayed how much he didn't want to answer the phone. Still holding me tightly, he grabbed the phone off the wall. "Bauer."

I released my leg hold on him, leaned back and took a deep breath. This was moving way too fast for me. I glanced down. My hands shook. I rubbed them on my legs.

"Clara!" Max shook his head, his eyes staring off into space. "Yes, you are interrupting something. No, Tada is fine. You don't have to check in every day. I said I would call if anything went wrong." He blew out his breath. "I know, I know."

I scooted out of Max's embrace and got off the counter. Quickly, to get out of his reach, I headed to the living room. I noticed that his eyes followed my every move. I walked over to the screen door, pretending to concentrate on the parking lot.

What did I want? Did I want a relationship with Max? What if he...

A car pulling up down the street caught my eye. I think the odd thing was that the person didn't get out, but my thoughts returned to the room. *What did I want? Did I want to sleep with Max? And if so, what is this major reluctance going on in my head?* While I had been kissing him, my heart was doing the cha cha, but that little voice in my head tisked, tisked me. Silence crept into my head, and I realized that Max was off the phone.

I glanced back to the kitchen to find Max watching me from the counter. He was leaning on this side of the counter, watching me with crossed arms. I turned around to face him.

"Moving too fast?"

"I..." I swallowed and looked down at my feet. "I don't know what I want, Max. I... It's..."

"Saved by the proverbial bell?"

"I'm sorry." I nodded slightly.

Max smiled as he moved in close. He held out his arms for a hug, then pulled me into a bear hug. "I said I would wait. I still hold true to that." He released me and held me at arm's length. "Yes, I want to throw you down on the floor and ravage you, but…" The twinkle in his eyes returned. "I think the wait will be worth it."

I leaned my head on his chest. *It did feel good to have arms around me again.* He gave me a light hug.

"Bed time. If we aren't going to make love, then I need to sleep. Some of us aren't in 'jail' and need to go to work in the morning." He held me by the waist and led me into his bedroom.

I smiled.

"I have extra toothbrushes under the sink." He pointed to the bathroom and let go of me. "Let me grab a blanket and pillow off the bed, then I'll be out of your hair."

"Max…"

He stopped.

I looked down at my feet. "I don't want you to sleep on the couch. How about if we share the bed? If you don't try anything." When I looked up, he was still just watching me. "And if I could, could I borrow a pair of your shorts and a T-shirt."

"Are you sure you want me in here with you?"

"If you promise not to try anything. And let me warn you, waking me up out of a deep sleep is not a good idea. I like to punch." I made a fist and pretended to swing.

Max smiled. "One more time. Are you sure?"

I nodded. "Shorts and a T-shirt?"

With a light kiss on the lips, he headed for his dresser. "Now if I will be able to go to sleep with such a beautiful women lying next to me…" He muttered loud enough for me to hear on purpose. I could hear the smile in his voice.

Chapter 16

I came out of the shower the next day to find Max returning from a run. His sweaty shirt clung to his cut abs and sculpted chest. His breathing was just slowing and he looked hot, steamy, sexy hot. I plopped down on the stool, towel in hand drying my hair, all the while peeking from under it to watch him. He poured himself an orange juice while I fluffed my hair one last time. At his moan, I whipped the towel from in front of my face. "What?"

Max just shook his head setting his now empty glass on the counter. He walked past me and leaned in for a light kiss. "You're gorgeous."

I blushed. I had never heard anyone call me gorgeous, not even the rat bastard. "Not a little excited are we?" I asked noticing his growing excitement through his running shorts.

"Don't tease me, Mel. You're this close to being on the floor. My control goes only so far."

"Just out of curiosity, do you always get that excited by a woman drying her hair?"

He leaned close, whispering as though someone might hear. His soft breath on my neck gave me the shivers. "I can basically see everything through that shirt. I didn't even mean to pick an old, see-through one." With a quick kiss on the neck, he disappeared into his bedroom. As he exited with clothes in hand, he winked at me, headed into the bathroom and shut the door.

I blushed. I admit it. I rarely blush, but it seemed that Max somehow could get me to blush whenever he wanted. I had come out of the shower sans bra, still dressed in his shorts and T-shirt. I hadn't really thought about it. I blushed again.

I glanced at the bathroom door, hearing the shower start. I realized that I'd left my bra in there. So I hung my towel over my shoulders. It hung low enough to cover most everything. Pleased that I was now covered, I scavenged in his cabinets for food. He didn't have much in the way of food. I struck gold with a loaf of bread. *Soda and toast for breakfast.* I chuckled. *High school all over again.*

Shortly afterward, Max came out dressed in a pair of jeans and a dress shirt hanging open. His bare feet completed his relaxed, handsome look. I did a quick up and down on his body. *Oh man, he looks yummy.* Max caught me looking at him and he smiled.

"Right after lunch, I'll drop you by Degrad's office." He began buttoning up the shirt then rolled the sleeves up part way. "He's taking you to the hotel. I'll already be there, playing the upset boyfriend. In the meantime, I'll check in with Goins and Hambrick. Do you need anything while I'm gone this morning?"

"Food. There is no food here, Max. You do have grocery stores here in California, right?"

Max blushed. "Well, I didn't think I would need to house the overflow from the city jail." He moved past me and grabbed a soda from the fridge. Then he stood next to me as I was leaning on the counter.

"I'm going to get on your computer, okay?"

"Sure." Max glanced down at my chest. "You didn't have to cover up for my sake. I like the view." He gave me a kiss and was out of my reach before I could hit him. "See ya," he said. His laughter drifted back to me.

I washed the dirty dishes by hand. When I was done, I headed to the desk where the computer sat with Tada following me. There was something in the information that Rich found that was bothering me. I should see the connection. I frowned as the computer booted up. *What had I seen? It has to have been really small or it would be screaming at me. What is it?*

I worked most of the morning going over Rich's information and confirming several other facts. But still I felt I was missing something. Finally it seemed useless to beat the dead horse, so I shut down. A glance at my watch showed that Max would be coming home soon. Then the 'show' would begin.

I grabbed a glass of water and headed out on Max's steps for a breath of fresh air. It was a cool, clear morning. I still had on his shorts and top, but since he wasn't here I didn't feel the need to change, yet. I was quite comfortable. I studied the area. *Nice neighborhood.* There were a number of apartment buildings in the area and residential houses as far as I could see. It was quiet now since most of the people were off to work.

I noticed the green car was still parked down the street, but no one was in it. Probably a visitor to one of the other apartments. I stretched and sat down on his top step. My mind drifted to the murder investigation.

What am I missing? Is it something in Marsha's profile or Cynthia's? Is it one of the grant proposals that I've seen? I frowned. Taking a drink, I shook my head. *This is frustrating. Normal for me but frustrating.* I held the glass between my legs and looked into the water.

Then, there's Max and me. What did I want with Max? Am I looking for a casual relationship? Or do I want more? Why am I reluctant to sleep with him? Why am I hesitating so much? That is so unlike me. I saw what I liked and went after it. I knew I liked Max. I did. So why am I indecisive? What's holding me back? I knew I frustrated Max. I'd be if the situation were reversed.

I took another drink, then set the glass down next to me. I leaned back on both hands and looked up at the sky; wispy clouds floated across. The slight breeze lowered the temperatures into the high sixties and made me wish it was spring, especially back home where they were knee deep in snow. The morning sun shining on me made me feel sleepy and content.

The hair on my neck rose, and I suddenly felt someone watching me again. I jumped up looking around but saw no one looking suspicious. I studied the cars and roads close by. No one. *That's strange.* With a shake of the head, I went back inside the apartment. I could understand feeling like someone was watching me at the conference, but here at Max's house? It reminded me of how I felt back home.

As I walked past the couch, Tada jumped at me with a loud meow. She crouched, watching me. This time I merely chuckled. "Good try Tada, but I only fall for that trick once."

The cat followed me into the bedroom and hopped up on the bed. She tried to sit in my lap earlier as I worked on the computer, but I didn't let her. She meowed for my attention.

"You miss being babied, don't you?" I asked. I smiled, remembering Craig's cat. I didn't particularly like cats, I was more of a dog person. When I moved from Maryland after the accident, I gave his cat to Craig's parents. *Maybe I should get a dog when I get home.*

"Mel?"

The door to the apartment swung open. Max was home. I walked out to see him dripping mud inside the door. He was mud from head to toe, picture worthy. I chuckled. "Rough day at work?"

"Shut up. I had to tackle a suspect and ended up in mud," Max grumbled. "I need to clean up, then we'll head to Degrad's office. We'll probably be late as is."

I nodded, stepping out of his way as he walked to the bathroom. "You're cute all muddy."

Max leaned over and kissed me on the cheek. I could see his bad mood evaporate immediately. "I'm cute, period."

I chuckled again as he disappeared into the bedroom. After I cleaned my cheek, I sat down on the couch and flipped channels on his TV. Nothing interesting. Finally, Max finished his shower and walked out of the bathroom.

He had on a new pair of jeans. His T-shirt was draped over one shoulder as he fluffed his hair dry. Again, his bare feet accentuated his yummy look. He spoke as he came out. "We'll need to pick up something to eat on the way, if you don't mind."

"Not at all." My eyes followed him into the kitchen, tracing the outline of his body. His sleek body moved like a lion's. I had never seen him completely shirtless before and could see just how cut he was. He didn't have a body builder's physique, but had defined chest muscles and a hard stomach. His jeans hung on his hips in just the right way.

"Mel?"

I pulled my eyes and thoughts away from his body to see his Cheshire grin. I blushed.

"Like what you see?"

"Shut up."

He glanced at his watch. "I could call Degrad and tell him I had car trouble." His eyes were sparkling, even as his eyebrows lifted. He shifted his weight on his feet.

I grunted. "No. We need to get going."

"Sure?"

"Did you get a chance to talk with Goins or Hambrick? Anything new?" I stood up and joined him at the breakfast bar.

Max nodded as he tossed the towel on the counter. He slipped into his shirt, then quickly smoothed his short brown hair. "Yeah. The knife was wiped, but they still got two really good prints from it, neither of which was yours." He gave me a smirk. "It's definitely the one that killed Vernon. And there were some fibers on it. The lab's still working on the fibers." He grabbed socks out of his pocket and walked to the living room closet and pulled out a pair of running shoes. He sat and put them on as we spoke.

"Who do they suspect?"

"They're leaning toward Marsha."

"But how could she have planted it in my coat?"

Max shrugged. "The theory is that she somehow got Teresa, the waitress, to get house keeping's master key card or something. They're still working on it."

I looked away in thought.

"Now what is going through that mind of yours?" He crossed his arms.

"Something doesn't fit. I know something isn't right. I've been trying to figure it out all morning. Something I saw." I looked at Max.

He nodded, accepting my intuition. The serious expression stayed on his face. "Let it rest. It'll come to you."

I nodded as we both moved toward the door. As Max was locking up the apartment, I leaned on the railing of the small landing outside his door. I was still deep in thought.

Max pulled me into him. "Let it rest, Mel." He gave me a breath stopping, tongue-in-the-mouth kiss. When he finished, he looked me in the eyes. "I think you should stay here after Saturday, for a couple of days. What do you think?"

I had actually planned that, now that I can't head to Florida. "Maybe. I'll think about it."

Max winked. "Come on, you criminal." He took my hand as we walked down the steps.

"Hey, it wasn't a valid arrest. My record is still spotless."

He chuckled. "Somehow I doubt 'spotless' would be the way to describe your record."

I looked at him with fake hurt on my face. By this time we were standing near the Trooper.

He pushed me up against the truck, and as he unlocked the door, he held me in place with his body. "I heard several stories. I particularly like the Blair backyard story." He gave me a conspiratorial grin. "Really, half-naked jumping fences to avoid the police?"

I shook my head. "I was in my underwear. Butch never gets that part right. He's always exaggerating. And I wasn't trying to avoid the police, I was trying to get home before curfew from an impromptu swimming party in the Blair's pool. And although they weren't home, they'd given us permission to swim there while they were gone. It was the busy-body neighbor who reported us. Still, I did get grounded by my dad."

Max gave me a look of disbelief. "What about the Barryanne Park incident? A couple of patrolmen chasing two kids, one possibly a female, through the park after midnight?"

"Who told you that?"

The smile got bigger. "A source."

"It was Mitch, wasn't it?"

"I'll never tell." He gave me another kiss—this time just a smoochy one. He opened my door, then moved around the vehicle.

I climbed in and crossed my arms. Mitch was going to get an earful from me when I got home. He had promised that no one would ever hear about that, particularly because it was his best friend at the time who was running with me after daring me to set off fireworks in the park pavilion. And what a firework display it had been. Epic. I looked at Max who could hardly contain himself. I huffed at him, causing him to burst out laughing.

As we passed the green car, I noted the license plate and noticed that it was a rental. I looked at Max. He was still chuckling.

"When you get to the hotel, ask Rich to let you look at the paperwork he brought. Maybe you can pick out what I'm missing."

"I will, but you need to let it lie. You really are like a little pit bull." Max mimicked biting and shaking his head.

"I approach all my activities with the same zeal." I lifted my eyebrows twice.

Max's eyes got bigger. He mumbled something under his breath that I didn't hear.

Chapter 17

The afternoon was hard and seemed to never end. People kept staring and whispering around me. I knew that everyone was talking about my 'arrest'. Knowing that I was innocent, and that I would never see these people again, allowed me to get through the day without blowing my top. I continued to try to figure out who might have killed Vernon and to watch everyone watching me.

Winslow told me to ignore them. She said she knew I was innocent.

Max left right after our late supper. He whispered that he'd check in with his fellow cops about any breaks in the case and call me later with an update. Then with a quick kiss he was gone. John and Rich walked us to our room, and we planned to meet up with them in the morning at the restaurant.

With a sigh, I closed and locked the door. I was finally safe and away from prying eyes. I got a soda from the small fridge and sat down on the couch to relax. As I kicked off my shoes, Winslow came out of the bathroom. "Just one more day then we can fly home."

Winslow nodded. "Yeah. Thank goodness. This has definitely been a weird conference. One I hope to never repeat," she said with a full body shake.

I nodded. I knew it was hard to deal with death. I sat my can on the table and headed to the bathroom. Not only to go but to change into my sleeping clothes. I was tired; the night before I hadn't slept well in the new place and having Max so close. Twice during the night, I almost woke him up to make love, but I didn't. A good night's sleep was what I needed most.

I put the regular clothes in my suitcase and joined Winslow in the living room. Grabbing my soda, I sat on the couch. She had been typing on the computer when I entered the bathroom but was now on the phone.

"No, I'm sure. It's ours now. Go ahead and order those chemicals… Yes, I'm sure. Only one more issue to solve, and that'll be resolved by morning… It does feel good." Winslow smiled and finished off the candy bar she was munching on. It was a nightly routine of hers. How she stayed so thin and in shape eating that many calories was beyond me. "I know. Tell Bob to check in with the manager of the foundation first thing in the morning." She unwrapped another peppermint candy bar. "That's right… Yes. Bye." She hung up and continued to munch her candy bar.

I smiled. After taking a drink and swallowing, I asked, "How do you eat chocolate this late at night and still go to sleep?"

Winslow shrugged. "Habit. I used to eat them to stay awake in the lab. It became a sort of thing with me and my researchers. It's hard to break that habit. Do you want some?" Winslow broke off and held out part of the peppermint bar to me.

"No. I'd never be able to sleep." I sat down and we talked about inconsequential things. I took another large drink. It wasn't my usual soda since the machine was out of it. I thought it tasted funny, but it was probably just because I didn't drink this kind. Or maybe it was just warmer. It tasted the same as the soda I had had on my first night here. I mentally shrugged. The conversation turned to more important issues.

"Do the cops have any idea who killed Cynthia?"

"They think me."

"So, they've stopped looking for someone else?"

I yawned. "To be honest with you Kate, I wasn't really arrested. The case against me was flimsy from the beginning. The cops have another person that they suspect and used arresting me to get possession of the knife. It has some good finger prints on it, and now it's just a matter of time until they get the real murderer."

"You mean the murderer didn't wipe the knife of fingerprints? Anyone who watches TV knows to wipe it down. How stupid."

I nodded, suppressing another yawn. "Yeah, only that's TV. They still pulled two good prints. It's not as easy to wipe finger prints off things in real life as it is on TV. The forensics people are good."

"Uh, interesting," Winslow said softly. She wiped the corner of her mouth with her finger.

I finished off the can of soda. "Don't tell anyone that. Max and the others are working hard to wrap this up before everyone starts leaving the conference."

"Max?"

"He's a detective here in Mayfield. He used to live in Quincy. That's where I met him. He moved out here about six months ago."

"I didn't know that."

"He was here playing the boyfriend undercover to find the murderer."

"You two seem too friendly for him to be 'playing'."

"Yeah, actually I'm probably not flying back on Saturday. I think I'll be spending a couple of extra..." I drifted off watching her eat the chocolate bar. At the same time, I got woozy, I felt flushed. It sort of felt like I had slugged down a glass of whiskey. My head spun a little bit. I scrunched up my eyebrows as I considered the feeling. I'd never had this feeling drinking whiskey. But yet I knew that I had felt like this before. *Strange.* "Hmmm."

"What's wrong, Mel?" Winslow asked, looking at me oddly.

"I... I don't know." I leaned my head back. "Chocolate. Cynthia Vernon had chocolate right before... there was chocolate in her mouth when she was..." I stopped as a thought hit me. Even as my thoughts got spongy, the thing bothering me became crystal clear.

I had seen Winslow's grant list. It matched several that Cynthia and Marsha were vying for. And on the V&D list there was one major grant to the tune of one million dollars. I had read about that grant on Max's computer. If the number one applicant refused or somehow was disqualified, it passed to the number two applicant. It was for something that I knew both labs worked on. What if Vernon won, but her death would disqualify her lab? And I knew from my conversations with Winslow that she needed over five hundred thousand dollars to keep her doors open. Oh man! And I had just told her about the cops.

"Mel?" Winslow stood up.

"You! You were Cynthia's lover, weren't you? You ate chocolate with Cynthia Vernon... Did Cynthia get the grant for her lab for the one million and you were second? Her death means that..." It was as though I couldn't stop my mouth from speaking my thoughts.

"So you put it together. It doesn't matter. How do you feel?"

"I can't..." I pushed off the couch and fell to the floor. She moved toward me. "I feel..."

Winslow smiled with a crazy look in her eyes. "The drug won't show up in blood tests by morning. I put it in your soda. After it gets dark, we'll take a little trip to the top of the building and you're going to go flying."

"But..."

"You'll have left a note confessing to the crime and that you just couldn't take the guilt. I'll take a sleeping pill, one that will show up in tests, to confirm that you'd knocked me out." She stood over me.

She began to sway back and forth. The room was starting to spin too. I'd dealt with bed spins during my drinking years as a youth, so the spinning didn't bother me much. It was the waving of everything that was the worst. Between the two of them, my stomach was flip-flopping. And I knew I was in big trouble. My eyes glanced at the table near the couch. "You killed Cynthia." I reached for the cell phone, but Winslow grabbed it first. She tossed it across the room.

"Marsha's a mouse, and with Cynthia's death I am assured that my lab gets the grant." Winslow smiled again. "I injected the same drug into the chocolate bar. It took longer to work, but she finally didn't put up any resistance. Neither will you soon." She laughed.

Winslow's laugh caused shivers up and down my spine. Her eyes had a crazy gleam. My stomach dropped to the floor as dread sunk deep into my bones. I was in big trouble. Big trouble.

I scrambled across the floor trying to get to the door. Winslow took her time getting there before me. So, I pulled myself up using the chair and stumbled into the bathroom. I looked back to see Winslow slowly shaking her head with a grin.

"My plan is foolproof. I've already figured how to get in the bathroom, even with the door locked. That's okay, spend your last cognitive minutes alone."

I fumbled with the lock as she walked away from the door. I looked around. The walls seemed to ripple up and down. The toilet swelled and shimmered. The shower curtain waved in a serpentine fashion. My head started pounding in time to the billows of the shower curtain. I pulled my eyes away from it. This felt like a much heightened or enhanced version of my first night here. *Did she drug me then too? She must have in order to see Vernon.*

My eyes were drawn to the swelling toilet. It was expanding like an inflating balloon. Bigger. Bigger. *What if it burst? Ewwww.* The sink caught my attention next. It was vibrating like a washer that's off balance. I giggled. *Did I do that out loud?* My hand flew up to my mouth as I giggled again.

My hand. I held it out and studied it. It waved at me. *Am I controlling it?* I just had to find out. Clap. My hands came together. Clap. The sound boomed. Boom. Boom. I giggled again, but this time it sounded more like hiccups.

Hiccups. Funny things. Stop. Think. What am I doing in here? I could actually hear my brain working. *Wow! That's so cool. Stop. Think. Oh yeah! Winslow drugged me. Cool drug. Feels like the time I ate mushrooms with Bart. Bart had been so funny. Hiccups are fun. I'm hiccupping. No, giggling. Stop. Think. Drugged. Yeah, Winslow. Trying to kill me.*

I panicked for just a second, then calmed myself down. I needed to arrange my thoughts. *Stay focused.* I had no way of getting help. I needed to somehow let the guys know that Winslow had killed me because I knew I was going to die. I spotted her eye liner sitting on the back of the swelling toilet. *If I touched the toilet would it pop? Focus.* I grabbed the eye liner and tried to write on toilet paper. but it just tore.

The floor. It was undulating like a roller coaster. I giggled again. *Focus.* Write on the floor. Surely the cops would scour the hotel room with a fine tooth comb. A *fine tooth comb. Why comb your teeth? Nasty. Focus.* I needed to put it where she wouldn't see it as she came in. *Where?* I looked around but everything was spinning and moving. I barely held back the vomit.

I crawled over to the vibrating sink and wrote on the wall under it. *It was rubbery. Stretchy. Rubber. Rrrruuubbbbeeerrrr. Focus!* I shook my head to help focus. I concentrated hard on my hand. It wasn't cooperating very well, but I knew it was my only chance. It looked like I wrote 'Winslow killed Vernon'. I studied the writing. *Looks like a Parkinson's patient in an earth quake wrote it.* I dropped the eye liner. It bounced and the noise reverberated like a shot ricocheting.

Focus. Maybe if I drank some water or splashed it on my face, I might be able to stay awake for a while. Maybe I could fight her when she came to get me. All I had to do when we left the hotel room was make enough of a ruckus to get someone's attention.

I drank several handfuls. The water slid down my throat like snot. *Cherry snot. Snot. Ewwww. Sssssnnnnooooottt!* I giggled. My legs gave out. I fell back to the floor. None of my extremities appeared to be able to function. I tried yelling but that came out more of a gurgle. Gurgle. I made the sound in my throat. I heard Winslow laugh through the door.

"The drug affects the muscles first. And with the dose I gave you, you should be unresponsive in about five more minutes. Sorry, Mel. Sorry this has to happen to you. I like you, but I'm so close to a break through, that nothing is stopping me. Nothing."

I laid there with my head on the cool tile floor, watching the white walls pulsate like the room was breathing. *Funny. What does a bathroom smell as it breaths?* I giggled again.

I heard pounding on the door. Indian drums. Bass drums. Ominous drums. *Were Indians after me?* I giggled. *Focus!*

The door seemed to bend inward, and I moved toward the shower, trying to escape. It seemed like a lot longer than five minutes, and I was still awake and thinking. *Well, sort of awake and thinking.* I could still hear my thoughts moving and communicating with my body. Sandpaper scraped as I blinked. *Weird.* The door burst open in a splash of light. The pieces of the door spiraled into space like something off of a science fiction show.

A face appeared in front of me. "Mel, are you okay?" The words were drawn out and sounded funny, like a super slow recording.

I stared at the face, trying to move away from it. It was distorted and undulating in front of me. "Get away," I slurred. My words sounded like the face's words. I brought my hands up to ward off the face moving toward me. *Hey, my hands still obey me, shaky as they were. Maybe I can get away from Winslow!*

"Mel, look at me."

I studied the bulging eyes and large bulbous nose. It wasn't a female face at all.

"Get an ambulance. Find out what Winslow gave her. Get Rich here." The face had turned to another body that was waving in the doorway. That body looked like a stalk of corn blowing in the breeze. Of course the whole doorway was bending around too. *Weird.*

I turned my eyes back to the face in front of me. It was moving closer rather than farther way. It kept coming in waves.

"Mel, it's Max. You're going to be okay."

"Max?" I shook my head, slurring the words. I sounded like I was in a long tunnel. And it even looked that way, the face was beginning to go black at the edges. "Winslow…"

The face smiled at me, but it didn't look like a friendly smile, it looked like one in a carnival. It was a smile from the mirrors in a horror house.

"We know. She's taken care of. Just hold on, Mel. We have an ambulance on its way." The face moved in closer, concerned. "Mel, do you recognize me?"

I followed his lips moving and the words seemed to be waves too. I smiled at them as the waves hit me. "I'm…gonna…sick." My stomach heaved.

"Collect the vomit." A female voice waved in from the doorway.

A garbage can appeared at my face and turned from square to round and back again. I vomited. I could almost feel every molecule of the vile stuff moving up my throat. The muscles in my throat contracted, and I felt each and every fiber work. It was strange.

Then blackness enveloped the room. Only a small dot remained in the middle, and the bulbous nose was stuck in the hole. I reached out for the nose to hold into it. I didn't want to disappear into the dark hole.

"Max!"

I grabbed on as darkness swallowed me.

Chapter 18

Darkness was all around, so complete it seeped into every pore in my body. I couldn't see, I couldn't hear. But I could think and talk to myself. As long as I could hear myself talk, I was still alive. I kept up a constant banter. Yes, if I heard myself I was alive.

Unless I saw Robbie or Craig. In that case, I was dead. Dead and gone. But I didn't want to see either of them. Okay maybe Robbie, but I didn't want to die.

Time meant nothing to me as I kept talking to myself. *Stay alive. Keep talking.*

Slowly I became aware of sounds. Distant and weird sounds, and they weren't coming from me. I stopped talking briefly and listened. *Strange.* All of the words were running together. And they sounded really far away. I puzzled over that. Maybe a speaker. Yeah, it could be coming from a speaker.

And now that I was thinking about it, the darkness wasn't quite as dark, more of a thickening twilight. I tried to actually open my eyes. *No, not yet. Won't work.*

"Mel?"

That had come through loud and clear. I tried my mouth. *Would it work?* A gurgle was the closest I came to speech, I think.

"You're safe, Mel. Wake up."

I knew that voice. It was my brother. *What is Rich doing in my darkness? Why is he trying to wake me up?* Suddenly the memories came back. Winslow tried to kill me. The face and voices before the dot went away. I tried my arms, but they were held by something, same with my legs.

"Mel, calm down. You're safe. Open your eyes, Sis." His voice was calm. I knew that I could trust him. I was okay. I was safe.

I opened them to a bright light. It hurt. Oh man, my whole head pounded, worse than my worst hang over. I groaned.

Rich chuckled. "Too much light, uh? Hold on."

I heard him move away. The sounds were becoming clearer to me. I heard talking on an intercom system, and then the lightness went darker. I struggled again, I didn't want to go back to the darkness. It was lonely. "Rich?" *Where did he go?* "Rich!"

"I'm here."

I felt him grab my hand and rub it.

"Right here, Mel. I went to dim the lights for you. Try your eyes again." Then I heard a new voice. I didn't recognize it.

"Is she conscious?"

"Yeah. I think she's finally coming around," Rich said. "She tried to open her eyes. Apparently the light hurt." There was a slight pause. "Mel, try again with the eyes. The doctor wants to look at you."

Oh! A doctor. Great! I hate doctors. Now I remembered that Max had said an ambulance was coming. I was in the ER, I bet. I opened my eyes to find the room swaying, again. I immediately closed them.

"Ms. Addison, try again please."

"Moving. Sick." My words still slurred a little. I tried my hands again. *Why can't I move them?*

"Stop struggling. You're secured to the bed," Rich said gently. "Can we take the restraints off, Doctor?"

There was a long silence.

"Please?" Being polite had worked in the past.

The doctor chuckled. "Sounds like she's coming around fine. Yes, take them off, but I want someone at her side until she is more aware."

I could feel them removing the tight things from around my wrists and ankles.

"Try the eyes again," the doctor commanded. "I want you to look straight up at the ceiling. Concentrate on the sprinkler head right above you. I need to check your eyes."

"Kay." I tried again. This time I did what the doc said and it wasn't as bad. He flashed a light in both eyes.

"Ms. Addison, go ahead and close your eyes if you want. I want you to lay perfectly still. Any major movement and you'll get queasy. I can't give you anything until we are completely sure of how much of the drug made it into your system. We're waiting on blood tests." He paused and I heard him scratching on something. I guess he was writing something down. "Someone that you know will be here until we get you upstairs. I want you to talk to them. If you get sick, they have a pan for you to vomit in. That is a side effect of the drug. Do you understand?"

"Yeah," I mumbled. "My head hurts."

"Yes, I would imagine. The drug can initiate a major migraine, it's part of the sensitivity to light that you're experiencing. We'll keep the lights low for that reason. And you hit your head when you fell. There are no stitches, but you have a bump on the back of your head. It's nothing to worry about." He patted my arm. "I don't want her moving. If she becomes agitated, we'll have to put the restraints back on. Talk softly to her. I'll be back to check on you in a little bit, Ms. Addison." I heard him walk away.

"Rich?"

"Yeah?"

"I'm thirsty."

"Sorry no water. The doctor said it would make you throw up. As soon as you are more cognizant, I'm supposed to call Max and he and Goins or Hambrick will be by to take your statement. I think it's best to wait until you're upstairs."

"I have to stay?"

Rich chuckled. "Yes, and no arguing about it. You gave us a pretty good scare."

I sighed. I hated hospitals, hated them with a passion, especially since the accident and my long stay in one in Annapolis.

Rich chuckled again. "Too bad. You have to stay, but the good news is I haven't called Mom and Dad yet. I'll do that after you give your statement."

"Great. Just great."

***

It took them two hours before they had a regular hospital room for me, then the painful transfer. I could feel every scratch on the floor in my head. Even the noise of the elevator made my head feel worse than my worst hangover. And I couldn't take a pain killer for the migraine until I showed them that I was able to stay conscious for four hours. So far so good, although I'd spent most of the time with my eyes closed in a darkened room.

Finally I was able to keep my eyes open but only if the room was darkened. Movement didn't make me want to puke anymore, it just increased the loud rock band in my head.

Rich called Max and Mom and Dad. I said a few words to my parents to reassure them. Rich told them to wait until morning to hold any sort of conversation with me due to my migraine.

The time was peacefully quiet with either Rich or John sitting silently with me. That is until the cops showed up. Then I had the most painful half hour of my life, including the birth of my son and my car accident. With both of those, I was at least allowed drugs.

Goins finally left with my statement. Rich and John departed for the hotel for some sleep for what was left of the night. Only Max remained. We didn't talk for a long time while I tried to dial down the sound on the rock band in my head. I also watched the clock. Forty-five minutes until my first pain pill.

I cleared my throat softly, my eyes closed. "So… Did Winslow confess?"

"She didn't need too. We have more than enough evidence to convict. Fingerprints at the scene and on the knife are hers. Fibers from the knife match her briefcase. Shoe prints match. She's as good as convicted." He paused. "You did good staying conscious, but out of curiosity, why did you grab my nose?" It was asked with a smile in his voice.

I kept my eyes closed. "The room was turning black. Your nose was all that was left. I didn't want to disappear. Sounds funny now, but at the time it seemed logical." I smiled.

Max laughed. "You pinched really hard."

"Sorry."

"It's okay. The doctors said they suspected you had a lethal dose in you, but by vomiting, most of it came out because you hadn't absorbed it yet."

"Yeah. The big meal right before helped too. It's a good thing Winslow was answering all of those questions after the last session and we ate late."

"I'd like to know how she came to have that drug, but she's not answering any questions. The drug is rather exotic."

I chuckled. "Not really."

"Excuse me?" He leaned in closer to the bed. "Did you ever…"

"Once. The drug is a derivative of a mushroom. The doctor told me that. I uh, I tried a couple of them in the past."

There was quiet from the side of the bed.

"Don't tell Rich or John."

There was a soft sigh. "Hessor?"

"Yeah, when we were teens. His Aunt had just come back from a trip to South America a couple of months before. I don't remember where they were. Bart had been with her. This was before the big blow up with her and my Dad. Hmmm. I don't remember the reaction last time being this severe."

"The doctor said it was a concentrated amount."

I opened my eyes to look at Max. He was staring at the floor. "So, I'm not the little angel you thought."

Max looked up. "I never ever thought of you as an angel, not with the stories I've heard." His eyes were hard. "That was really stupid, Mel."

"I know that now."

"Did you know that the water you drank would make you vomit?"

"I would love to say yes, but in all honesty, I didn't know. I thought maybe I could dilute the drug so that I could maybe fight and get away from her when she came to get me."

Max just stared at me.

I closed my eyes. "Does this mean that I don't get to be introduced to the California way of life?"

He picked up my hand. "No. I still want you to stay." He kissed my hand. "I'm just amazed at your youthful stupidity."

"Isn't that the definition of a teenager? Young person doing stupid things and hopefully surviving them."

Max chuckled.

"How did you know it was Winslow?"

"Goins and Hambrick finally got through the security tapes. Both Dodington and Winslow made calls from that phone, weird because they both have cells. Anyway, when I showed up at the station with Rich's information, we poured over it. That was when they became more suspicious of Winslow."

"More suspicious?"

"Goins had told Hambrick that she thought it was Winslow due to the fact that she had the most access to you and your stuff. She could have borrowed your cell easily. And placing the knife... Anyway, we were coming to search her briefcase. On the side of the knife was a sliver of material, those fibers I mentioned. The lab thought it might be rawhide from a briefcase. I remember that she never went anywhere without it. We went to Dodington's room first. She let us in, and it turns out her briefcase is synthetic cowhide. She is a staunch proponent of animal rights. Marsha almost came unglued when we mentioned the leather. When we got to your door Winslow was evasive and didn't want to let us in. She said that you were sick. I knew something was wrong."

"Hmm."

"You know you kept up a constant mumbling the entire trip here to the ER and during the hour that you weren't responsive."

"Really? You could hear me?"

"Yeah."

"I knew that as long as I could hear myself, I wasn't dead, unless I saw Robbie or Craig. So I kept talking to myself to keep myself alive." I rubbed my face. "Could you understand me?"

"Not most of the time." Max chuckled. "Once you started laughing."

"I must've sounded like a freak."

"You're alive, that's all that counts." He paused. "The doctor says that most likely they'll release you in the morning. Are you going to the hotel or did you want to go to my place?"

"Why?"

"Because if you want to go to my house, I'll need to leave you keys. I need to work tomorrow."

"I don't know. Probably the hotel, I guess. It hurts too much to think. Talk with Rich or John."

"Do you want me to leave?" Max rubbed my hand gently, little more than a caress.

"No," I whispered and ran my thumb over his hand. His hand made me feel safe. We stayed that way until the door opened.

"Ms. Addison?" the nurse asked softly.

"Please call me Mel."

"Mel, how are we?"

"*We* are in pain."

"Has the pain diminished any?"

I felt Max rub my hand again. I quirked up the corners of my lips as I cocked an eye open. "It doesn't feel as bad when Max holds my hand."

Max blushed. He chuckled as he let go of my hand.

"What?" I asked him. "You want me in pain?"

"No. You are a pain." His smile belied his words.

The nurse laughed. "Well, I have something not as good as this handsome man's hand, but I bet it'll cut the pain better." She held up a plastic wrapped pill. She quickly popped it out of its holder into a small paper cup. She handed me a cup with water that had a straw in it.

I slurped down the pill as quickly as I could.

"Depending on how long it's been since you last slept, that pill might make you sleepy too." She tapped a few things on the computer in my room then left.

"So, I take your pain away?"

"One little comment and your head swells."

Max laughed.

I grabbed his hand. "Thanks for being here. Yes, holding your hand has been comforting."

Max leaned over and kissed me gently on the lips. "You're good at flirting."

I winked at him then grimaced in pain.

He laughed some more.

Within minutes, I was asleep.

***

The next morning I was staring at the muted TV because none of the channels had anything interesting to watch. I couldn't deal with the pain the sound caused, but the movement on the screen gave me something to look at.

The door opened and Max stuck his head in and smiled. "Good morning, Tiger."

I tried a smile back. "Yeah. Nothing good about it."

He walked over and took the chair next to the bed. "You're alive. That's good. How do you feel?"

"Like crap." I rubbed my eyes. "My head still hurts."

Max smiled again. "A migraine. The doctor said it should go away this morning. Is it better than last night?"

"Yeah." I closed my eyes after glancing at the clock. I felt best with my eyes closed. "What are you doing here this early?" It was almost seven in the morning. "Sorry to sound so grumpy. I didn't sleep well."

"You went out like a light last night."

"Yeah only for about four hours. I've been awake off and on since then. Between the nurses coming in and this headache..." I shrugged. "Not that I'm not happy to see you, but what are you doing here this early?"

"I just wanted to stop in before I went to work."

"Visiting hours aren't until nine." I cocked an eye open.

Max's grin lit his face. "Flashed my badge. It gets me in anywhere, anytime."

"Ah! Abusing your authority."

"Perks." He paused. "I spoke with Rich last night."

I yawned as I spoke, "Yeah?"

"He said he'd pick you up this morning when you get released and that you'll be going back to the hotel. Hambrick released the crime scene late last night."

I nodded and yawned again. My eyelids were heavy.

Max stood and gave me a full mouth kiss. "I'll let you go back to sleep."

"'Kay. Can you do me a favor?"

"Sure. What?"

"Can you call Rich and ask him to bring me a new set of clothes? Those have vomit on them, and I can smell it from here." I pointed to the bag of clothes on the chair.

"Not a problem. Go to sleep, Tiger." He kissed me once more then left.
***

Rich stuck his head into my hospital room just as I was finishing lunch. "Hey."

"You couldn't get here an hour earlier so I was spared this cardboard food?" I asked seriously.

Rich shrugged.

I smiled as he sat down and placed the bag of clothes on the foot of my bed.

"The doctor said he was releasing you after one o'clock. I figured you'd be sleeping most of the morning. He also said that you'd be overly tired for a couple of days." He smiled back. "Have you had any calls?"

"From everyone. Do you think they announced it on the radio back home?"

"You know Mom."

I shook my head.

Rich looked around the room. His eyes landed on a pot of dead flowers. "Nice arrangement. Don't tell me that Max is suddenly getting cheap? Or is he mad that you solved his case? Again."

"I don't know where they came from. I turned off the phone for a while. When I woke as they brought in lunch, they were sitting there. I don't think that they're for me. Anyway, the note says 'Long time no see, but I'll be seeing you soon.' It's signed DM. I hit the nurse's call button, but so far no one has checked in. You don't think it's some funny California thing, do you? People sending dead flowers?"

"They're weird out here, but I think it's probably something else. I wonder what the message means anyway."

"Kinda creepy."

Rich cocked his head and glanced at the flowers again. "Do you think it means something?" There was a tone to his voice, as if humoring me.

"Nah." I shook my head at him, dismissing the flowers from my mind. "Hey, I had a thought. Now that Winslow is in jail, how are we going to get paid?"

"You don't need to worry about that. We have a legally binding contract, so we'll get paid."

"But what if she refuses to pay?"

"First of all, her company works through regular accounting channels. Secondly, John and I will file papers against the company when we get home. Don't worry, Mel."

Shortly a nurse entered with papers. I had already gotten dressed and was waiting impatiently for her. I knew from experience that she carried my discharge papers and the 'what to do in case' papers.

I smiled at her as I sat on the side of the bed. My head was only aching a bit. "Do you know who or when these were delivered?" I pointed to the dead flowers drooping over the vase.

"Oh my!" she said, blushing. "This morning we were cleaning up dead flowers. Someone must have left them in here by accident on rounds or something. Sorry. I'll take care of them."

"Not a problem." I nodded. I wanted out of the hospital.

"Okay here are your orders, if you should start vomiting…"

Chapter 19

After getting back to the hotel, I slept most of the afternoon. Max took all of us out to a local remodeled diner that had excellent food. The meal was fun, with Rich and Max exchanging stories about funny police calls. When we returned to the hotel I was starting to get tired again. Max stayed and we lay on the bed, shoes off, watching TV.

"Mel?"

My head snapped up. "Sorry. I keep drifting off." My eyelids felt like mud filled shoes. I was leaning into Max's chest with his arm around me. I snuggled in closer.

I felt his chuckle in my head. "How about I go and let you sleep?" He rubbed my arm.

In answer, I snuggled even closer, rubbing my cheek on his chest. "You could stay."

"And have you fall asleep while we're making love?" I could hear the amusement in his voice.

"'Kay. Just to sleep then." I opened an eye and looked up at him. I felt sleepy and so comfortable.

He chuckled again. With a quick move we were both laying flat on the bed, my head still resting on his chest, his arm still holding me. Max tucked the blankets around us. His lips touched mine, just barely. "'Night, Tiger."

I mumbled good night and gave into the comfortable feeling. It was sweet.

Much later in the night, I woke to find myself sleeping on my left side with Max curled up, spooning me, also asleep. I smiled and relaxed. The feeling of having a man in bed with me made me feel loved, a feeling I hadn't had in a long time.

I laid there awake savoring the moment. I was just the right temperature and so relaxed. I sighed and tried to drift back to sleep. But I couldn't. *Why am I awake? It was a noise that woke me. Hmmm.* With a mental shrug, I sighed and wiggled to get comfortable.

Max shifted in his sleep too, moving closer and put his arm over me, but he didn't wake.

I smiled. Then I froze. *There's that noise again. A light footstep. A breath?* I sat up, waking Max up too.

"What?" he asked rubbing his eyes.

"I heard a noise."

He kissed me. "It's a hotel. Of course there are noises." He pulled me back to the bed and resumed spooning, snuggling in close.

I lay awake and alert.

He chuckled and kissed my neck. "Do you want me to look around the room?"

I didn't answer him right away. It was almost as though the room itself was waiting for an answer. "No."

"Relax. Go back to sleep. Unless?" The sleepy sound in his voice evaporated on the last word.

I slapped the hand that was draped over my side. With a sigh, I relaxed. "I'm being silly. Of course it's just hotel noises."

***

We met Rich and John downstairs the next morning and checked out of the hotel. Max drove us to IHOP for breakfast, then to the airport. After the guys were through security, Max and I headed to his apartment.

"Home," Max said, looking at me. "For at least a couple of days for you."

Getting out of the Trooper, I got a strange feeling that I was being watched. This happened every time I left the hotel room and worse, three times someone had called the hotel room this morning before we left. I looked around, but no one seemed to care about us.

"What?" Max asked as he rounded the Trooper to get my bag out of the trunk.

"Nothing."

"No, really." He looked around himself. "What?"

"Just a funny feeling that I'm being watched."

Max smiled at me as though I was a simpleton. "By whom?"

"I have no idea. It must be my imagination, probably left over from everything this week. Forget it."

He closed the trunk and grabbed my hand.

I reached out for the suitcase and he shook his head. "Stop babying me, Max. I'm fine. Just a little tired."

"I'm not babying you. I'm being a gentlemen." He winked. "Besides, you heard your brother. You're supposed to take it easy."

I sighed as we started up the steps. When we got to the top, Max paused. I looked around him to see what he was looking at. There was a dead bird sitting on his porch.

"I wonder what happened to it," Max asked rhetorically as he stepped around it.

I shrugged. "I think I'm a jinx on the bird population. That's the second bird that's died around me."

Max swung open the door and pulled me inside. "Have a seat, you little bird killer. I'll get it cleaned up before Tada sees it. She'll drive us nuts with her meowing if she sees it."

I chuckled as the cat walked out of the bedroom and stretched. It meowed once then hopped up on the couch heading for me. "No way, Tada." I stopped her from sitting on me.

Max was back inside shortly, watching me. "I never asked if you were okay with Tada here."

"Craig had a cat. It knew I wasn't fond of it and always bugged me. I swear cats know."

Max chuckled at me as he headed to the kitchen. "Are you hungry for lunch?"

I stood up and followed him into the kitchen. "What? You actually have food here? Did you win the lottery?"

He smirked. "I thought after lunch I could show you around the area. There are several historical sites and such."

"Sure."

"I wanted to go on the motorcycle, but I think it'll have to wait a day or two. I don't want you getting sick on my bike."

I nodded in agreement as I accepted the glass of water. "Vomiting in a helmet is no fun."

"The voice of experience?" Max paused in setting sandwich stuff on the counter.

"Yep."

Max shook his head with a grin. "You must have been one rough child to control."

"What control?"

***

The feeling of being watched was becoming normal, so it didn't bother me as much as I thought it would when we left Max's apartment. I kept my eyes opened and studied the cars parked near his apartment but couldn't see anyone suspicious. Finally after the first stop, I dismissed the feeling as a remnant from the murder investigation. I was going to enjoy myself.

Max drove us first to the coast. We travelled along the ocean, stopping occasionally to look at the beautiful shore line. Picturesque. We passed a sign to a historical mission site. I pointed it out. Since Max had never visited it either, we stopped and walked around.

The ambiance of the mission was great. Even though we were near other houses and buildings, the mission seemed to exude a feeling of calm and quiet. The Spanish architecture, with its arches and exposed wood rafters, made me feel as though I was back in time. The quiet of the chapel and surprising coolness made a romantic setting. Max and I sat on one of the benches staring at the altar area. We gazed up at pictures and statues while whispering quietly. His arm draped over my shoulder as we soaked in the history. The small garden, well-tended by the gardeners, allowed us to watch a multitude of humming birds buzzing around the flowers.

Max then took me to a state park near the coast. It was a long drive but well worth it, as he promised. The view of the ocean crashing against the cliffs was spectacular. There was a place in one of the rocks where the surf blew up in the air when the waves crashed in, sort of like a whale's blow hole or a geyser like Old Faithful in Yellowstone. Nature's show of force was amazing. We ventured down the steep path to the water and scrambled on the rocks, watching the breakers, tide pools, even seaweed on the beach.

We ate at a local hotel which was authentic from the 1880's. The lobby bar was elegantly carved. From the patina of the bar top and the way the wood looked and felt, it had to be hundreds of years old. The menu was excellent. And it had an absolutely beautiful stained glass dome over the bar.

Max was great company. I had such a great time that I totally ignored that nagging feeling of being followed. I refused to let it ruin the awesome day.

As we mounted the steps to Max's apartment, I looked around again. Nothing was out of the ordinary. I stopped behind Max who was intently looking at something on his porch.

"What?"

"Another dead animal. A mouse." He looked at me. "I didn't think I had mice. I'll have to call the landlord. I can't have mice in my house. I hate mice." Max slid the dead animal to the side of the porch with the toe of his shoe. He looked closely at me as I joined him on the small landing.

"What?"

"Maybe you are a jinx."

"Oh, and you'd like a live one better?"

Max laughed and pulled me into a kiss. "Hardly." He unlocked the door. As we walked in, Tada jumped out at us and we ignored her. That seemed to upset her and she hissed at me.

I turned to Max. "See what I mean. I didn't play her game and now she hates me."

Max laughed. "You feed her. She'll love you then. I'll play animal disposal again."

We had just snuggled up on the couch to watch something on TV when the phone rang. Since Max was on call he immediately picked it up. "Hello?... Hello? Stupid telemarketers. I thought I was on the don't call list." With a shake of his head, he hung up.

I cuddled into his arms as we watched a movie, he lounging on the couch with legs on the coffee table and I leaning on him. Max had his arm over my shoulder. It was so comfy. The phone rang again.

"Hello?... Hello?" Max hung up the phone, mad. He punched a few buttons on the phone. "And what good is caller ID?"

I chuckled as the phone rang again.

"Yes?" His tone was harsh, then he winced. "Oh hi. Sorry." Max smiled. "Sure. Hold on." He held out the phone to me. "It's your mom."

I took the phone, rolling my eyes and Max leaned over and kissed me on the lips. I smiled at him as I began talking with Mom. Thirty minutes later and two beeps on call waiting, which I ignored, I hung up.

The phone rang again, and this time he let the answering machine pick up. The phone disconnected right away.

"Enough," Max said and shut off the ringer. At my look, he smiled a lopsided grin. "The station has my cell number. They can call me on that or my pager." He pulled me in and kissed me.

As the passion intensified, he pulled me across him, now holding me in his arms. He placed butterfly kisses down my jaw, onto my neck then up to my ear. I moaned before he got there. He took his time though, breathing gently on my neck.

Capturing my earlobe in his lips, he tugged on it gently. Then took it by his teeth and massaged it. His tongue rubbed it in a leisurely manner.

My hands also began to move. I traced his chin with my fingertips, then ran them through his hair, along his neck, and back up into the hair behind his head.

His right hand moved along my back and massaged it in tiny circles. It moved to the back of my neck, as his tongue and mouth moved from my ear to the neck again and around to the front.

I tipped my head back letting him place those soft, butterfly, just barely-touching kisses on my neck. I was moaning very softly. It had been a long time since I felt like this. I missed it. Oh how I missed it.

His right hand moved down my arm and onto my flat belly. He caressed, then moved up along my side pulling me in tighter.

My hands were now on his tight chest, massaging, touching, unbuttoning his shirt. I savored running my hands over his bare chest.

His thoughts mirrored mine as he began unbuttoning my shirt, slowly and in the most tortuous, unhurried manner. He unbuttoned the last button

116

and was moving his hand to my face, his arm moving between my breasts, when his cell phone rang.

Max groaned. He kept kissing my neck even as he grabbed the cell off of his belt. It was still ringing as he brought it up to look at the screen when his pager went off.

He pulled away from my lips. "Someone better be dead." He flipped open his phone. "Bauer." He glanced down at my bra and chest. His eyes got a dreamy look. "Where again?" He kissed me on the lips. "Okay, I'll be there as soon as possible. Thanks."

I pulled out of his embrace.

He was breathing faster than normal, as was I. "Someone's dead. I have to go. I traded today off for being on call all weekend. Sorry."

I smiled but nodded at him. I went to button up my shirt but his hands stopped me. He leaned in for a quick kiss on the lips, then opened my blouse further. His eyes strayed to the right side of my chest. The still pink scar started under my breast and extended up into my bra.

He touched it gently, running his finger along it.

A shiver flickered along my spine.

"That was some injury, Mel." I could see his eyes change as he looked at it and touched it almost with awe.

I nodded.

"Much damage?"

Again I nodded.

He cupped the scar with his palm and looked deeply into my eyes. "I'm sorry."

"I lived." I pulled his hand away. "Almost didn't."

"How close?"

"For three days they didn't think I'd pull out of it." I looked away from him. "My family held a vigil over my bedside. Mitch was there when I woke up. I kept asking about Robbie and Craig. The doctors didn't want the family to tell me, but Mitch did." I buttoned the shirt and took a deep breath to get my thoughts away from my dead family. "You'd better get going."

Max pulled me into him, giving me a bear hug. "You'll be okay here?"

"What? Are you're asking me to come along and help you with a case?" I asked teasing. I knew there was no way he'd want me involved.

Max chuckled, then pulled me into him for an extremely passionate kiss, an 'I-don't-want-to-go' kind of kiss. "I might not make it back tonight. It depends."

"I understand. Get going."

He stood up and grabbed his keys off the coffee table. Max glanced back at me as he took a key off the ring. "Here." He held it out to me.

"What?"

"Motorcycle key. The helmet is there." He pointed at the closet in the living room. "In case you need to use it before I get back. Be careful with it." He turned to go. "Oh, there's an extra key to the apartment in the light right outside the door." He hurried back to me and gave me another kiss with a groan. "Sometimes I hate this job."

I chuckled as he left the apartment. Following him out onto the porch, I stopped and watched as he hurried to his Trooper. I waved as he drove away and saw him blow a kiss up to me. I leaned on the railing and looked the area over.

The stars were shining. It was a very romantic kind of night. I sighed. I had been quite willing to take this night to its logical conclusion. And from what I felt, it would have been a great night.

I sighed again and looked up at the night. A shooting star flew across the sky. I swallowed. Craig often used to take me out to see shooting stars when we were courting and first married. After he started his law practice, the tradition ended.

"Well Craig, is that a sign from you or what?" I shook my head. "Look at me. Now I'm talking to myself."

My cell phone rang. "Hello?"

"I just called to say good night," Max said with a soft tone.

I smiled, the warmth of his voice spreading through me. "Thanks. Have a fun evening."

He chuckled and hung up with a smoochy kiss.

I raised my eyes to the sky again. "Good bye, Craig. Rest in peace."

Chapter 20

I woke to darkness. Sounds drifted to me in the living room from the kitchen. I lifted my head off the couch, squinting past the counter to see a dim light. I sat up pushing a blanket off me. I hadn't fallen asleep with a light. It must be Max in the kitchen.

Sure enough, he was cooking, trying to be as quiet as possible. He still had his T-shirt and gun harness on. His back was to me, so I snuck up to the counter.

"You could have woken me."

Max jumped at the sound of my voice and turned. "Don't do that, woman."

I smiled. "Thanks for covering me."

He smiled back as he turned to the frying pan. "Are you hungry?"

"What time is it?"

"Around five in the morning."

"Are you done with the crime scene? No thanks on the breakfast."

Max smiled as he tossed eggs onto a plate and added toast. "Sure about breakfast?"

I nodded and leaned my head on my hand. I yawned.

As he walked past me to the other stool he kissed me on the lips. "The crime scene is finished. The perp is caught, and I'm on a break before I head in to do paperwork."

"My, my, but you do work fast here."

Max sat his food down in a hurry and grabbed me. With an animal growl, he kissed me. He pulled me up and backed me into the bedroom.

I pulled away from him. "Your food?"

"I'm not all that hungry for food." He grabbed my t-shirt and starting pulling it up. Soon it was off my head and on the floor. He stripped off his gun harness and let it drop to the floor too. His shirt followed mine. "I'm hungry for you."

We kissed with a fervor, moving slowly into his bedroom. His cell phone rang.

Max cursed under his breath. "I told them two hours." He grabbed it off his belt. Even as he did, he took a step away to look at my naked chest. "Bauer."

I shook my finger at him.

He licked his lips. "I said two hours." He grimaced. "Right now. Why?" His hand moved from my head, down my shoulder, and lightly touched my scar again. It was a crescent shaped scar the ran about three inches under my breast, around it, ending in a large mass of scar tissue near the top. He leaned down and kissed the top part of the scar as he listened.

"Now how did he get a judge at this time in the morning on a Sunday?… Yes, I'll be right in… No, don't take him out of the general lock up. Let him stay with the low-lifes. It might teach the rich brat a lesson," Max grunted a good bye.

I handed him back his shirt. "That's twice you've got me worked up and left."

"I know. I'm sorry." His eyes strayed back to my scar. "Does it still hurt?'

I shook my head. "And just so you know, I have no feeling around the scar."

"The whole breast is dead?"

"Dead?" I smiled at him as I put my shirt back on. "No." I lifted my shirt back up. "This here is still sensitive." Touching the area where I had feelings.

"Don't do that," he moaned. The look on his face was very much the universal look of a frustrated male.

I laughed and crawled into bed stealing a look at his alarm clock. Five-fifteen a.m. "Hurry back."

He swore as he put his gun harness back on. He leaned over and kissed me again.

I looked down to see his reaction to the brief interlude. I laughed at his 'manly pain.' "Can you even go into work like this?"

"Shut up." He looked around the bedroom. "I'm going to take the bike and leave you the Trooper. I feel safer with you in it. Where's the key?"

"On the coffee table where you laid it." I faked a yawn. "Guess I'll just have to take care of myself."

Max stared at me for a long minute. He cursed softly and was gone.

I sighed. It would take time to go back to sleep. So instead, I got up and ate Max's delicious breakfast. I cleaned his dishes and puttered around the apartment for a while.

Finally, I got dressed and grabbed the keys to the Trooper. I felt confined and decided to go for a drive. I took the same road we had driven the day before and headed toward the ocean. I parked the Trooper in a small parking lot near a beach and watched as the sun rose in a spectacular display of color playing against the clouds.

The beach was empty this time of day, so I hopped out of the Trooper and took off my shoes, deciding that a walk on the beach was just what I needed. It was very serene, with the waves making gentle sounds. I stood ankle deep in the surf relaxing, letting my mind wander.

It wasn't much longer when a man came walking down the beach. He appeared to be a beach comber. I glanced at him. Suddenly my sixth sense nagged at me. I peered at the man again. He was slowly making his way toward me. *Odd.* I turned and didn't see another car parked near Max's. *Where is his car? Maybe he lives nearby?* I studied him.

He wasn't a drifter. His clothes were in good shape. I looked up and down the beach, but no houses were visible. He wasn't necessarily headed right at me but just in my general direction. I wish I would have paid more attention to where he came from.

My gut was telling me this wasn't right. He kept his head down and away, so I never got a good look at his face. He was average height and weight. Maybe dark hair, the floppy hat hid most of his head. I headed back to the car. I turned at the Trooper to see where the guy was, but he had disappeared. *Not good.* I stood on the bumper of Max's truck to see if there were other cars parked along the road over the slight hill. *None. Now where did he go?* With a shiver, I climbed into the Trooper and headed back to the apartment.

As I drove, I watched for cars following me but didn't see any. Puzzled, I pulled into a local McDonalds and went inside to eat breakfast. I had already eaten once, but I was hungry again.

As I sat eating with my back to the wall as John taught me, I watched the parking lot. A green car pulled in. *Is that the car that was parked near Max's place? It sure looked like the same make and model.* It slowly drove around the building. The sun was shining just right, and I couldn't get a good look at the driver, except that he wore a ball cap pulled down tightly on his head. *Why does that remind me of someone? Do I know this guy? And how could I? I'm thousands of miles from home.* Suddenly he sped up and drove away fast enough that I didn't get a license plate.

I decided right then that if I got to Max's and the green car was parked there, I would call the guys to find out which rental car company owned it. I wanted to know who was in that car.

I got lost going back to Max's apartment. After several wrong turns, I finally recognized a street and made it back to Max's neighborhood. As I rounded the corner, I saw the green car parked where it had been. I slowed and wrote down the plate numbers. I called back home to Rich on his cell. It went to voice mail, so I left a message for him to call me.

An hour later he called back. "What's up? You okay, sis?"

"Yeah. Hey, can you run a plate for me? A California license."

"Okay. Why?"

"Call me paranoid, but I think it's following me."

"Have Max run it."

"He thinks I'm nuts. How hard is it to get me a name and address? I think it's actually a rental." I could almost hear Rich's frown over the phone. "Just humor me. Please."

"It'd be easier if... Let me get you the number of a friend, a private investigator, that lives nearby. His number is at the office. I'll call you in about an hour or so. Okay?"

"Thanks, Rich."

***

Lunch was a single affair again. Max called and told me that this case would take a good portion of the day, but he suggested that I meet him for supper at a local bar and grill where most of the cops hung out. I agreed and got there before him.

As it turned it out, it was reminiscent of the Full Moon, my Dad's bar, only with a more extensive menu. It was larger too, with about twenty tables in the bar and a separate dining area of what looked like another twenty tables. Half the tables were filled with people, all of them eating. Sitting at the bar, I just started on my second beer when three men walked in laughing and joking. I pegged them as cops. They sat down at a table on the far side of the room near the steel dart boards. They were still laughing but also talking in lowered tones.

A few minutes later one of the cops scooted onto the stool next to me. He was a bald, good looking black man. He ordered a soda then turned to me. "Hi. Haven't seen you here before." His smile was genuine.

"True."

He smiled widened, giving me a big, toothy grin. "Are you new to the area?"

"No. I'm just visiting a friend out here." I sipped at my beer. I was switching to soda after this. It would not be good to get a DUI in Max's vehicle.

The cop grabbed his soda and turned slightly on the stool, glancing back at his fellow officers.

Out of the corner of my eye I saw two of his companions giving him the thumbs up. I almost chuckled. When he turned back to me I smiled. "Got a bet going?"

"Excuse me?" His smile faded.

"A bet with your friends."

His eyes widened. "Sort of. How did you know?"

"I'm a very good read of people, and I know cops and how they treat each other." I smiled even bigger.

"How did you know we were…" He leaned his head on his hand. "So, I'm busted. Is this the big brush off?"

"What was the bet?"

"Twenty that I could get you to join us at the table."

"For what?"

"See the dark haired guy? He's getting married next week and he's so afraid to even talk to another lady. His fiancé is a real dragon lady. Anyway, we were going to ask you to well, dance with him or something."

I gave the black cop a dark look. "What? Do I look like a hooker?"

"No, no. Nothing like that." He patted my arm. "When we walked in, he about fell over when he saw you. I think he's infatuated." His dark brown eyes were looking intently at me. "We just want to embarrass him tonight. See, he's getting married on the East Coast and this is his last night in town. After we leave here, we're going to a have a bachelor party for him. We just want to embarrass him a bit, and, let me tell you, it's so easy to do."

I glanced the groom's way. He averted his gaze. I smiled at the cop sitting next to me. "Okay. First of all, what's his name and yours?"

"Ted. I'm Ray."

"Does Ted play darts?" I nodded toward the steel dart board in the corner.

"Yeah, he's pretty good."

"Okay, I'll come over so you win the bet, Ray. I'll challenge him to a game. I'll make his night, but I'm meeting someone and I don't know if he'll like me flirting with Ted." I drank the last of my beer. "So, you have to buy my date and me supper. Deal?"

"You drive a hard bargain, but deal." He held out his hand. His grip was soft yet strong. "What's your name?"

"Melissa."

He winked and walked away with a triumphant expression.

I smiled, knowing Max would love this. I ordered a soda from the bartender. As I waited, I noticed a guy walk into the place and sit at the far end of the bar. His head was down. He had a ball cap on. His face was trimmed with a beard and mustache. *Is this the same guy from the beach or driving the green car at McDonald's?* I covertly studied him. I wasn't certain though. I glanced at the three cops then back to the stranger. If he was following me for whatever reason, he wouldn't be dumb enough to try anything here.

I wanted to follow him when he left to see what kind of car he was driving though. I paid the bartender. "Do you know that guy at the end there?" I jerked my head toward the newcomer.

"Never seen him before. Why?"

"Nothing. Thanks." Grabbing my soda, I headed to the table with Ray, Ted and the other cop. Ray was the most fit of the three. Ted was your average guy: average height, weight, and looks. The third cop, who was older than the other two, had a crew cut and was slightly overweight. All wore jeans and t-shirts.

"Hi. Ted, right?"

"Uh, yeah."

For a cop, he sure wasn't very assertive. "My name is Melissa. Do you play darts? Ray said you were pretty good." I gave him my best flirty smile.

Ted gave a quick look at Ray then sort of puffed out his chest. "Yeah, but I don't like to brag."

"I'm waiting for someone and until he gets here, how about we play?"

"Sure." Ted stood. The older cop was introduced as Cliff, and he headed to the bar to retrieve the set of house darts. He and Ray seemed extremely pleased with the situation.

"Ted, do you know how to play Cricket?" I nodded my head to the dart board.

"Sure."

"Now, one thing though, I never play just for the fun of it." I gave him another flirty smile. "I always bet something."

"Like?"

"Well, usually money, but I'll make an exception this time, since you're cops and all." I winked. "How about sodas or beers for me and my friend due here any minute?"

"Done, but what if I win?" Ted said, getting into it.

"I'll give you a kiss."

Ray and Cliff busted out laughing.. Ted blushed a bright red. "Well, you see, I'm getting married…"

"Go for it, man," Ray said. "She's sweet!"

"Yeah man. Kisses from such a beauty," Cliff said slapping Ted on the back.

"Well Melissa…" Ted looked me up and down. "Okay. I guess a kiss or two won't hurt."

I leaned down and touched his chin. Getting right in his face, I said in a whisper, "If you win."

The other two cops hooted again. Ted blushed.

"Dibbles?" I held out a dart to him.

"What?" Ted asked.

"You've never heard of dibbles? It means both of us throw one dart at the board. The highest score throws first." I handed him one dart.

"Ladies first." Ted motioned for me to start.

With a nod I threw my first dart, purposely hitting a small number. Ted threw his dart and hit a twenty, which meant that he went first. And the game commenced. I purposely lost the first game, and with a comment that he was getting married, I gave him a peck on the cheek. The second game I toyed with him some and won by just one point.

It was during the third and last game that Max walked in. He stopped, seeing me flirting with Ted, but I gave him a smile. Ray called to him right away to come and sit with them. Cliff immediately invited Max to the bachelor party that night. Max declined saying he was busy, but his eyes had a puzzled look in them.

I turned to Ted as Max sat down. "Ted, who's the newcomer?"

Max almost smiled. He lowered his head to hide it. His eyes changed to a knowing look.

"That's Max. He's a detective. Ignore him, Melissa."

I looked at Max for a second, then went back to watching Ted throw the darts. He wasn't bad but not really in my league. I moved closer to Ray and lowered my voice so Ted couldn't hear me. "Hey Ray, my friend should be here soon. Don't forget your debt to me."

Ray nodded and as I moved away I heard him explain to Max, "I made a deal with her to pay for her and her date's meal if she played with Ted a bit. You know, embarrass him."

Max laughed, then turned to me with very amused eyes. I winked at him. He laughed even louder. He asked Ted while I started throwing darts, "What's the bet, Ted?"

"Sodas for her and her friend if she wins, kisses for me if I win," Ted said with a sly grin.

"But Ted aren't you…"

"Sheila will never find out. Besides, I think the next one will have to be on the lips, Melissa." He turned to me already puckering up. He was ahead of me in points.

"We'll see." I handed him the darts and checked out the bar. Sure enough 'my man' was still sitting at the end, nursing his drink. I turned my attention back to the game.

The other cops clapped at Ted's score. It looked hopeless for me. I needed to throw a triple fifteen and a double bulls-eye to win. Ted handed the darts over. "How about a preview?" He touched his lips.

I grunted at him, taking the darts and gave Max a quick glance. I purposely tossed the first dart away. It didn't even hit the board. "Do over!" I called out in my 'I'm a stupid girl' voice.

Ted shook his head. "No way." He began fingering his lips.

Max nudged Ray. "Twenty says she wins."

"Max, you're a sucker. In order to win, she has to hit a triple fifteen *and* a double bulls-eye. I'll take your bet."

Cliff chimed in. "Me too. I'm taking that bet too, Max."

"Done. Come on, *Melissa*. I've got a lot riding on this."

I chuckled. "Just how bad do you want your money?"

The others teased Max. He grinned. "Let's just say, I'll make it worth your while."

"Done." I turned to the board as I hefted the dart. I concentrated and tossed it into the triple fifteen ring which put me ahead point wise. Ray and the others were stunned into silence. The next dart made a hard thud as it jammed into the double bulls-eye ring. I won the game. They groaned.

Ted sighed in disappointment. Cliff's mouth was open, his drink half way to his mouth. Ray shook his head slowly.

I chuckled as I pulled the three darts out of the board, grabbed Ted's darts and headed to the bar to give them back to the bartender. He winked at me with a smile as he took them back. He'd been watching the game, as had several other people in the bar.

"We've been had gentlemen. We've been had." Ray threw his twenty at Max. "How did you know she was a shark?"

I saddled up to Max, smiling at the guys, and he put his arm around my waist. He gladly took the other twenty from Cliff. "This is Mel. I told you guys about her. Her dad owns a bar in Quincy, Illinois. When they're slow, all she does is throw darts. She can beat the pants off anyone."

Ray looked up at me. "He's your date?"

I nodded at Ray with a big smile on my face. Ray merely groaned and laid his head on the table, then rocked it back and forth. Cliff and Ted laughed at him.

Max patted him on the back. "I believe that you owe us dinner, Ray."

"And Ted owes us four beers or sodas." I sat on Max's lap with a little wiggle and gave him a kiss on the lips. "Are all of your fellow cops this gullible? I could make a lot of money ."

Chapter 21

Over the course of the next hour, seven more cops joined the group. Ray gave me a kiss on the cheek in thanks while we ate. They departed for the bachelor party. Ted was already toasted. I turned to Max. "You look tired."

"Yeah, but I have the night free." He raised his eyebrows twice.

"Sure and have you falling asleep in the middle?"

Max tossed his napkin on the plate. "I will not fall asleep, believe me. I had one of the guys drop me here since I didn't want to drive the bike this tired. But that means tomorrow you'll have to drive me to work. Is that okay?"

I nodded as I saw my guy at the end of the bar heading out. "Just a minute, Max." I followed the mysterious guy out the door to see him get into a red Chevette with a rusted bumper and huge dent in the right rear panel. I frowned, hoping it would be the green rental.

Max appeared at my elbow. His gaze followed mine. "Who is he?"

"I don't know."

"Then why... Do you think he's following you?"

"I don't know," I murmured. I wrote down his license as he took off away from us. I wanted to know who he was. By now, Rich's contact here in California should have the person who rented the green car.

"Mel, aren't you being a little paranoid?"

I turned to look at Max. "Someone is following me. I know it. I can feel it. I'm going to find out who it is and why."

"Okay. Okay," Max said holding his hands up to ward off my anger. He looked down the now empty street where the Chevette had gone. "If you are done playing detective, do you want to go home and finish where we left off?" He put his arm around my waist.

I huffed and turned to look down the street where the red car had disappeared. As we moved to the Trooper, I looked around. I knew someone was watching me.

Max fell asleep in the car as I drove us home. When we arrived, I made him go straight to bed and since it was only eight o'clock, I promised that maybe we'd play in the morning. I immediately called up Rich's friend, Hank.

"Find out anything?"

"Hi Mel. Yeah, the car was rented to a Burton Franks. California driver's license, address in the Valley."

"But?" There was a catch in his voice.

"I called the number on a whim. The phone was disconnected a while ago. I did a bit more checking and the license used to rent the car was fake. I notified the rental agency, but the car was already returned, last night. I have them faxing a copy of the license to me. I'll bring it over to you tomorrow, or you could stop by tonight."

"Hmmm."

"Does this help any?"

"Maybe."

"What's the story?"

"I think I'm being followed. I have another plate I'd like you to run, if you would." I gave it to him. "Let me know when you get the fax and the info on this plate."

"Hold on and I'll have the plate for you in…" He paused. "It's registered to a Enrique Martinez, in San Diego." He gave me the details.

"Enrique? Sounds Hispanic."

"From his address, I'd have to say that's a real strong possibility. I've had a couple of cases in that area and it's 98% Hispanic." There was a pause. "Was the guy you saw Hispanic?"

"About as much as I am."

"Let me call a cop friend to see if this has shown up on the hot sheets down there. I'll call you right back."

I hung up the phone and sat at Max's counter thinking. Several minutes passed when I had a sudden thought. I grabbed Max's cordless phone so that Hank could still call me. "Rich, hi, it's me. Sorry for calling so late and thanks for putting me in touch with Hank."

"Are you being followed like you thought?"

"I don't know. It's hard to tell. Whoever is doing it is really good. Hank's running another plate for me."

"Good. Does Max know about it?"

"Yeah. He still thinks I'm being paranoid."

"Are you?"

"No. Every time I go out, I feel like I'm being watched. When you were in my house and found my papers rifled through, did you notice any more hang ups on my phone?"

Rich didn't answer right away. "Maybe. To be honest, I didn't look too hard."

"I tried to get my messages remotely, but I must have changed the code or something. I couldn't retrieve them."

"I'll go over first thing in the morning and check. Anything else?"

"Yeah. Anymore damage to my car or any dead birds or messages left at the office since I left?"

"None." Rich paused again. "Maybe you aren't being paranoid, now that you point it out. John and I'll look into it first thing. Stay on your toes, Mel."

"Yeah."

"Is Max there? At his home with you?"

"Sleeping."

"Alone?" I could hear the smile in his voice.

"Yes! He's on call all weekend. He got called out early last night and has been awake since. I made him go to bed. I'm sure you remember how it was."

Rich chuckled. "Have him call me when he wakes up. Take care, Mel."

I hung up from Rich right as Hank called back.

"Bad news, Mel. The car hit the hot sheets yesterday evening."

"Where was the rental returned?"

"San Diego. Six blocks from the Martinez address."

I cursed softly.

"Do you want me to call Rich? I think he should know about this."

"I'll tell him."

"Okay. If you need anything Mel, you call. Day or night."

I smiled at the phone. "What is it about men that they think they need to protect and treat me like a sister?"

Hank laughed and said goodbye.

After shutting down the apartment and feeding the meowing white fur ball, I slipped out of the house and took a walk around the neighborhood. I walked slowly, checking cars in the dark. Sure enough around the corner was the dumpy, red Chevette. I quickly pulled out my cell and called it in to the police. Then I sat nearby and watched to see if the guy showed up.

When the cops arrived, I told them I had noticed the car cruising the area slowly and just wanted them to check it out. I pointed out a bumper sticker from the San Diego area. It wasn't long before the cops reported it as recovered to the police department there and called a tow truck.

As I waited with the cops, I kept a close watch on the crowd but didn't see the guy again. I gave the cops a description of him when they left and headed back to the apartment.

Max was sleeping hard, so I settled down on the couch to think some more. *Now, let who ever this is try and follow me!* I ended up falling asleep on the couch.

***

"Mommy watch!" Robbie grinned as he climbed up a pole onto the huge playground equipment. His light brown hair showed a touch of red highlights in the sun, just like mine did as a kid. His brown eyes were wide as he worked his way up the pole and twinkled as he kept looking at me to make sure I was watching. He was dressed in his favorite dinosaur t-shirt and jean shorts.

We called him 'Monkey-Boy' because he climbed on everything. It started the minute he could walk. I even caught him once climbing the walls in the hallway, bracing himself between the walls to climb. He had heard his dad talking about it with a couple of friends.

I clapped and laughed as he climbed. When he got to the top, he held up his arms like a gymnast.

"Way to go, Robbie. That's my boy!" Craig said, suddenly standing next to me.

My smile faded as I looked around. Yes, this was the park in Annapolis Maryland where I always took Robbie. It had a big playground area, four tennis courts off to one side, a huge flat green field where soccer teams practiced, a water fountain, a shelter house, and neighborhood houses surrounding all.

Robbie slid down the slide then ran up to me, launched himself and gave me a big hug. It was the type of hug he always gave when I picked him up from daycare or anytime I left him anywhere for more than an hour. It was his 'I'm-so-happy-to-see-you, love-you' hug.

I hugged back tightly. It felt so good to have my little boy in my arms again. I held on longer than normal and Robbie began squirming.

"Mommy, Daddy watch me run!" He wiggled free and ran across the nearby field.

"He sure is growing fast," Craig said turning to me with a smile. He was dressed as he always was during the week, suit and matching tie, Italian shoes and perfectly styled close cut blond hair. He was standing in what I called his model pose. Right hand in pocket. Left hand in a loose fist held mid stomach. He used this pose in court a lot, usually when he was trying to impress the jury or giving a closing statement.

I turned my attention back to Robbie who came barreling toward me at full speed. I caught him, swung him around and up into my arms in a hug. I could tell my smile was huge. He was breathing hard on my neck and laughing. My hug tightened and I kissed his cheek. Again he wiggled to be released. I reluctantly let him go.

He bounded away with a giggle and a wave. This time his hair was longer as though he needed a haircut, and he had on his second favorite t-shirt, his wolf shirt. He ran full speed for his bike, still with training wheels, parked on the sidewalk a short distance away.

"I still think he's too young to take off his training wheels. He's going to fall and hurt himself," Craig said. I turned and Craig was dressed in jeans and a ragged black t-shirt. *His* favorite shirt that I always threatened to throw away. And when I did throw it away, he'd retrieve it from the trash.

"Mommy. Mommy!" Robbie yelled from his bike.

I turned to see him riding toward us, peddling as fast as he could, his blue helmet on his head. Suddenly he wobbled as his training wheels disappeared. I started to move toward him but didn't make it in time before he fell.

Immediately he began crying as his knee and hands bled from scrapes and his little chin puffed up. I picked him up as I slid to the ground next to him, pulling him into my arms. I rocked him and wiped tears and made soft 'mommy noises'.

He cried for a bit, then his cries changed to giggles. He once again wiggled out of my arms, helmet and bike gone. This time he was dressed back in his favorite dinosaur t-shirt. He was jumping up and down, excited about something.

I stood up.

"Mommy did you see it? Did you see what Ms. Jen had? Did you see the snake? A snake, so cool! Can we get a snake? Please Mommy! Please!" He turned his 'puppy dog' eyes on me as he pleaded. Ms. Jen, Ms. Priscilla, and Ms. Laura were his favorite librarians. His last story time had been about snakes and lizards.

"Please Mommy!" His jumping suddenly slowed then stopped. Robbie began rubbing his eyes. His body slumped as he grew tired. "Love you, Mommy." His adorable sleepy voice tore at my heart.

Craig shifted several times on his feet. Again he was dressed in his business suit. His eye brimmed with tears. "I'm sorry, Mel. It was stupid. It was wrong. I love you, Mel. I love you."

There was a sad look on his face as he took Robbie by the hand and they both walked away. Robbie turned once to look back at me. There was blood running down his face.

Tears streamed down my face. I sobbed. My heart broke.

An alarm sounded in the bedroom and woke me up. I could feel tears on my cheeks and quickly wiped them with the back of my hands. I stretched. I was stiff and covered in white fur. Max strolled out rubbing his eyes. He was wearing only a pair of loose shorts that hung on his hips. He stretched and yawned.

"Why didn't you wake me earlier?" He walked over and knelt next to the couch. "And why didn't you come to bed?"

"I was thinking and fell asleep. I only just woke up myself."

Max leaned over and kissed me. He started getting into it, but I wasn't responding. He backed off. "What's the problem?" he asked glancing at the kitchen clock. "I still have an hour before I have to leave."

"I just don't feel like it right now." I sat up and looked down at the blanket. The dream was still vivid, vivid and visceral. And I knew why. A year ago today, they had been killed. *Change the subject. Change the subject.* I cleared my throat.

Max watched me.

"I did some checking…"

Max grimaced. "Here we go… the Snooping Sneak strikes again."

"The guy at the bar was driving a stolen car. And the green rental I mentioned the other day was returned six blocks from where that car was stolen. Also, I found the red Chevette just a block over on another street."

He cursed softly.

"Yeah. I turned it in to the cops. They came last night and took it away. Let him follow me now."

"Mel…"

"Don't start. Just don't." I stood up and walked away.

Max still knelt by the edge of the couch, staring at me. He finally followed me into the kitchen. He stood behind me as I faced the sink, getting a drink of water.

"What did I do? Why are you mad at me?"

I hesitated. "I'm not mad at you. Really. Just leave me alone right now."

Max stood there for a few more minutes. His stare burned like a laser. I refused to turn around. I could almost hear his puzzlement. Finally he turned and went into the bedroom to take a shower.

I grabbed a bagel off the counter and took my drink out onto the porch to sit on the steps. Not only was I keeping an eye on the area, but I was also contemplating my day. *What am I going to do with myself?* At least I wasn't home where everyone would want to see and talk to me. I knew before the day was out Mom would call, as would probably Craig's mom. I really didn't want to talk with anyone.

Max walked onto the porch and made his way past me on the narrow stairs. He stopped several steps down and just looked at me. In his hand was a bagel balanced on top of a coffee cup. He looked extremely handsome in his white shirt and blue tie, but I was too distressed for him to affect me. I refused to meet his gaze. I did not want to talk about it or really anything for that matter.

"You say that you aren't mad at me, but then what are you mad at?"

I shook my head.

"Because I slept all night?"

"Don't be stupid. You were tired."

"Because I got called out the other night?"

"No, it goes with the territory."

"Then?"

"I'm not mad at you." I looked up. "Ready to go to work?"

Max didn't answer me right away but stared into my eyes. I broke eye contact and looked away. Max followed my gaze around the area. "Anyone suspicious?"

I shook my head.

Max turned and walked down the stairs. I could tell he was confused by my actions, but I couldn't put into words what I was feeling. It was better to not say anything.

When we reached the Trooper, we stared at it. Someone had keyed the whole driver's side. Not once but twice. Two nice, deep, down-to-the-metal gouges. I took a deep breath and looked around the area again. I had definitely made someone mad.

Max set his food on top of the Trooper and looked closer at the deep gouges. He followed them the length of the vehicle. "How did the car look last night when you were out here?"

"Fine," I sighed. "It's my fault. I'll fix it for you."

Max turned to me, lips compressed in a hard line. "It's not your fault, but I think the guy should have been handled differently last night. I wish you would consult me about these things."

"You were sleeping."

"So someone is following you and now has damaged my truck. Any clue who?" He crossed his arms.

"None. John and Rich are looking into the incidents back home, but they've stopped back there."

"Of course, you're out here."

I looked at the side of the truck.

"This is not good."

"I know." I looked at him. "Do you want me to go home?"

Max sighed, his lips loosening a bit. "Of course not. Just be more careful who you piss off." He motioned to hop into the passenger side of the SUV, then retrieved his stuff off the top. As he drove he called it in to the station.

We were met in the parking lot by a uniformed cop who shook his head at Max and started filling out forms. I leaned on the patrol car we were parked next to and stared at me feet. As I was only half listening to the guys talk, my eyes panned to the SUV again. From my leaning angle, I saw something sticking out from under his rear bumper on the passenger side. I went to investigate.

I ran my hands under the bumper and felt a small box. Getting down on my hands and knees I took a better look at the little black box.

"What are you doing now?" Max asked. He and the cop walked around the car to stand behind me.

I looked up at Max with a grimace. "You might want to see this." I pointed at the object.

Max's face scrunched up in disgust as he got down on his hands and toes. He obviously didn't want to get his dress pants dirty. A curse escaped his lips. One of his knees went down on the pavement as he moved for a better look.

"What?" the other cop asked. He got down on his hands and knees. "What is that?"

We were all staring at the small device attached to Max's bumper. I locked eyes with Max. He cursed softly again then tore the item off. It had been attached by a strong magnet.

Standing up, he locked eyes with me. "You were right about being followed. And this is how he followed you."

I nodded, not wanting to go with 'I told you so.'

Max studied it then held it out to the uniformed cop. "It's a GPS sender unit."

Chapter 22

"Mel was right. Someone was tracking her." Max watched as the police officer turned it over.

I went back to lean on the police cruiser as they discussed the new development. My mind focused briefly on what this meant, but I quickly drifted back to my thoughts about my family. With hands in my pockets, my mind was not in California but in Maryland a year ago. It was at this time of the morning that I took Robbie to his last story time at the library. He loved them.

Robbie almost turned himself inside out that morning when he found out that the stories would be about snakes and lizards. He loved snakes and dinosaurs. Ms. Priscilla lead them in a song and dance. Ms. Laura read them two stories—one about a snake that was lonely and another about a lizard's first day at school. Then Ms. Jen brought out a six foot corn snake for the kids to touch and see. I don't think Robbie had ever seen a snake before. I had to admit the red and orange creature was beautiful.

I remember Robbie's eyes got the widest I'd ever seen them. He all but vibrated in excitement as he waited for his turn to see and touch the snake. He even got to study it longer in its cage after story time as I spoke with Jen about other matters. For the rest of the day it was all he talked about. He even recited to his daycare providers everything he learned about snakes that day.

And then, of course, when we got home we had to look up information on the internet about corn snakes. Robbie absorbed information like the best paper towel. As I drove him the babysitter later, I made the decision, if his enthusiasm continued longer than two weeks, to get him a snake or lizard for his birthday when he turned six and to…

"Mel?"

I looked up to find Max standing in front of me. He had obviously been studying me. The other cop was gone.

"Are you okay?"

"Yeah." I could feel my eyes were moister than usual. I rubbed my nose to bring my attention back to the present. "Done with the paperwork?" My phone rang. I unhooked it as Max nodded with a strange look in his eyes. "Hello?"

"And just when is Max going to call me?"

"Shut up. I forgot. He's standing right here." I held out the phone to Max. "You were supposed to call Rich. I forgot. Now he's mad. Here."

Max smiled, taking the phone. "Hi Rich… Yeah, she told me… Really? Well, isn't that strange, my truck got keyed this morning. And we found a GPS tracking unit on it… Yeah, okay. I will. You do the same… Do you think she'll let me lock her up in my apartment?" Max smiled at me.

I stuck my tongue out.

Max's face sobered. His expression changed. His face softened to a kinder look. He softly sighed as he cocked his head. His mouth lost the hard line that it had all morning. "I didn't realize that Rich. It explains things. Thanks for the heads up… I will. Thanks." He handed the folded phone back. "Why didn't you tell me that the accident was a year ago today? I would have understood."

I looked down, my eyes tearing up.

"Rich wants you to call him this afternoon. He's working on something regarding the intruder at your place." Max reached out and pulled me into a hug. "You can talk about anything with me, Mel. If I had known this morning, I wouldn't have pushed so hard."

I returned the hug then pushed him away. "It's just, I don't…"

"Wear your grief on your sleeve," Max interrupted. "Been there." Max took my hand. "Will you be okay today?"

"Yeah. I'll probably just hang out at the apartment."

"I could take emergency leave."

"I'm not going to be good company. Besides, I'd prefer to be alone. I know it sounds strange, but it's the way I am. Thanks for the offer."

Max leaned in for a light peck on the cheek. "Call if you want to talk. It's mostly an in-house day for me, go straight home, stay in the house. Do you understand, Mel? I'm serious about this."

With a nod, I hopped into Max's Trooper and headed away from the police station. Since the GPS unit was no longer attached, if whoever was still following me, he or she would have to do it the old fashioned way. Which gave me the possibility of discovering who they were.

I decided to pick up some toys for my niece and nephew. Not that being in a toy store would be easy today, but at least it would keep me busy

First I stopped and put gas in Max's vehicle. As I stood at the pump, I studied the surrounding cars. None seemed suspicious. Next I stopped at a coffee house and got a hot chocolate. I sat for a few minutes to watch cars. Nothing again. I drove around until I spotted a mall. I decided to head there. Once inside, I stood just inside the double doors to see if someone followed me. After five minutes and not seeing anyone, I headed to the toy store.

I walked up and down several aisles. Some of the toys I recognized as ones that Robbie had owned. As I touched them I teared up but didn't cry. After the accident, after I got out of the hospital, I donated all of his toys to a local woman's shelter. I think Robbie would have liked that. I'd seen him once give a neighbor kid one of his toys when their house was broken into.

With toys in hand for Rich's kids, I headed to the bookstore in the mall. There was a man with a ball cap walking down the mall toward me. He had a beard and mustache and was about the same height as the guy at the beach and the bar. My gut twisted when I realized he'd been in the toy store with me. I discretely set my bag of toys on the edge of the fountain in front of me. I turned and confronted him as he neared.

"Why are you following me?" I demanded, getting right in his face.

He took a step back, his hands went up in front of his chest, palms out.

I immediately moved into a ready stance.

"Easy, Lady." He smiled, holding up my sun glasses. "You dropped these in the toy store."

I relaxed a bit as I took my glasses back. "So, you aren't following me?"

He chuckled. "No, ma'am. Why would I do that?"

A lady walked up to him. "Ready to go, Hun? We're running late."

I relaxed even more. She was pushing a stroller with a toddler shoving crackers into his mouth. "Sorry, sir."

"That's okay. Have a good day." He hurried away with his family.

I took a deep breath to calm myself. As I looked around – everyone was looking at me. I gave a shrug and a smile. I grabbed my toy bag and headed to the book store only slightly embarrassed.

After leaving the mall, I stopped by the grocery store to pick up some essentials that were missing from Max's food supply and some extras for me. Then I decided I wanted steaks for supper, so bought a couple of good looking porterhouses.

Driving back to Max's apartment, I couldn't tell if anyone was following me, but it didn't feel like it. With a sigh, I pulled up to the apartment building and looked around. No one suspicious.

When I reached the landing carrying my packages, I stopped. Propped against his door was a dead raccoon. From the looks of it, the poor thing had been hit by a car.

I scooted it to the side and went in to get a garbage bag. After bagging it and dumping it in the dumpster, I stood looking over the area.

Someone was still after me.

But who, and why?

***

I was still on the phone when Max entered the apartment. I nodded in greeting, glancing at my watch. It was only early afternoon. He stripped off his tie and tossed it on the couch. As he walked nearer to me, he unbuttoned the collar of his shirt, then leaned over and gave me a kiss on the cheek. Rounding the counter, he removed his gun harness and laid it down. He grabbed a soda from the fridge and sat down next to me at the bar.

"I know. That's good to hear, Phyllis." I turned to Max and whispered, "I'll be done in a minute." I took another drink of the tall glass sitting in front of me. "Sure. I will. Thanks for the call, Phyllis. You take care and tell Harold hi for me... I will." I closed up the cell phone and took another big drink. "Craig's parents."

Max leaned over and looked in my glass. "Kool-Aid?"

I smiled. "In remembrance." I hefted it, drinking.

Max got a puzzled look on his face, grabbed the glass out of my hand and sniffed it. "What's it mixed with?"

"Vodka." I smiled again. My cell phone rang.

"Your phone has been going to voice mail all day."

I shook my head. "I turned it off most of the day. Everyone has tried calling." I checked who it was. "Mitch." I laid it back down, not wanting to talk to anyone else.

Max grabbed the cell off the counter. "Hi, Mitch... No, Mel's currently getting drunk." Max laughed. "No, Kool-Aid mixed with vodka..." He listened for a while, occasionally nodding. "I will. Thanks." He hung up and laid it down.

I shut it off. I didn't want to talk to anyone the rest of the night.

"Mitch said that everyone has tried calling you. He thought he might have better luck getting through." Max smiled. "Is that why you stayed out here, so you could hide?"

I gave Max a grin. "I planned on a trip away from home anyway. Of course, I had to get a refund on my other tickets."

"Where to?"

"Florida. The Keys. I've only been there once."

"Why?" He leaned his head on his hand and watched me take another big drink. There was a small smile playing at his lips the entire time.

"I don't like to talk about things. Not to change the subject but..." I told him about the incident with the raccoon.

"Why didn't you call me right away?" he asked, sitting up straighter.

I didn't answer, knowing it would just make him mad.

He sighed. "Let me guess, you didn't come straight home like I told you. Like you promised."

"I never agreed to come straight here."

"Fine. Where did you go and did you see anyone following you?" He wasn't mad, but he wasn't happy either.

"No one followed me."

"Sure?"

"None that I saw."

"But someone could have been."

"Jeez. Maybe but I…"

A knock on the open door interrupted us. Max hopped up with a guarded look, grabbed his weapon and walked to the door. "Yes?"

"My name's Hank McGrew. I have something for Mel. Is she here?" He was an older man, maybe late fifties but in great shape.

"Hey, Hank," I called from the bar. "Come on in."

Hank laughed. "Rich said you were getting tanked." He handed a piece of paper to Max who was still wary. "You must be Max Bauer. I'm Hank Gruber, a private investigator here in Mayfield." Hank held out his hand to Max. "Rich asked me to sit with Mel until you got off work." Hank glanced at his watch.

Max smiled. "I took a couple hours off. Thanks for coming over. Who is this?" He studied the paper.

"A copy of the license of the man who rented the green car. Did Mel tell you…"

"She did. Thanks."

"Sure. Mel, I'll call Rich and tell him your babysitter wasn't needed."

I flipped Hank off who laughed as he walked out the door.

Max sat down next to me and handed me the paper. "Is this the guy following you?"

I studied the photo. "It could be the guy at the beach and at the bar. This is a bad copy."

Max frowned. "The beach? When? What happened at the beach?"

I told him of that incident. Max cursed softly, his lips tightened into a hard thin line.

"You know, he sort of looks familiar, but I can't put my finger on it." I continued to study the photo.

"Maybe if you weren't drunk." Max smiled as he said it.

I shook my head. "This is only my third drink, and I'm out of vodka. I didn't buy that much. I'm feeling really good, but I'm not drunk. Okay, I'm legally drunk, that's for sure. But I'm not drunk drunk."

"Drunk, drunk?" Max chuckled. "You're cute when you're drunk."

I smiled. "I'm cute, period."

Max laughed at his own statement. "Touché. Are you hungry?"

"I'm getting there. I bought steaks for supper, but I didn't know when you'd be home. They're in the fridge."

"Sit back Ms. Addison and be prepared to be amazed. I specialize in steaks." He rubbed his hands together as he stood up. After checking out the steaks, he looked through his cabinets and cursed.

"What?"

"I'm missing a couple of special ingredients." He turned and looked at me. "I'm going to run to the store. Want to come with me?"

I thought about it. "Nah. I'm a little inebriated. Wouldn't be good to go out now, especially if something reminds me...." I shook my head. "I'll stay here." I saw him open his mouth, so I beat him to the punch. "With the door locked. I promise. And I promise I won't go anywhere, even for a walk around the block. And I promise I won't open the door for anyone or run with scissors either."

Max laughed, gave me a tongue in the mouth kiss, grabbed his stuff and left, of course, locking the door behind him.

The imp in me surfaced and after he drove away, I unlocked the door chuckling to myself. I returned to the couch and stared at my hands. My mind wandered to Robbie's birth, his first birthday, Mitch and Robbie playing Candyland one Christmas laying on the floor at Mom and Dad's and more.

I even thought of the good times with Craig. There were some, not near the end but earlier in our marriage. His last words to me. "I love you, Mel. I love you." All of the bad times with Craig came flooding back.

I wiped tears from my cheeks as Max's home phone rang. The answering machine picked up. Max's voice came over the speaker. "Mel, turn your cell on. I have a question for you. Call me."

I grabbed my phone, turned it on and dialed Max. "Yes?"

"First off, leave your cell on just in case. What I wanted to know... you're not allergic to anything are you? Like mushrooms or anything?"

"No."

"Good." His voice showed that he was smiling. "This is going to be good. Do you need anything from here?"

The warmth of Max's voice pushed away my negative feelings for Craig. A contentment filled me. "No. I'm good."

"I know you are. See you soon." He ended the call with a smooch.

I chuckled and relaxed into the couch. I noticed Tada still sitting on the window sill, sunning herself where she had been since I got back. She was staring at me but now closed her eyes.

More images of Robbie and Craig floated by until I heard footsteps and the screen door opened. Keys jingled in the lock. Max entered carrying two bags. "Why was that not locked?"

I grinned.

"Bad. Bad, Mel." He kissed me as he passed, then headed to the kitchen.

I stood and followed as Max set the bags on the counter. I moved to peek inside. Max playfully slapped my hand, and I crossed my arms in mock anger.

He grinned. "It's a surprise for after dinner."

Soon the sizzle of the steaks with mushrooms and onions filled the apartment. Corn on the cob was cooking on the stove and potatoes in the microwave. The smells made my stomach rumble. It was glorious.

We ate at the bar next to each other, mostly in silence. I continually made groans of ecstasy. Max's eyes crinkled in obvious pride. Tada meowed for food.

I burped. Max was a great cook. The steaks were cooked to perfection.

Max laughed. "I'll take that as a compliment."

"That was delicious. Thanks."

"I do know my steaks."

"Yeah." I stared into his deep blue eyes.

"I have a surprise for you." He stood up and headed to the bag still on the counter. He pulled out another bottle of vodka. "Just in case you want to continue drinking."

"Maybe, but now I'm out of Kool-Aid."

His smile grew as he pulled out a large container of cherry Kool-Aid. "Your favorite."

I stared at the container. The last time I bought one that big was for Robbie's fifth birthday party. I was immediately back at my house in Annapolis, Maryland with ten five year olds and all of the ensuring noise, confusion and fun.

"Mel?"

"Yeah?" I blinked away tears, looking at him. He was right in front of me. "What?"

"I'm sorry. I didn't mean to make you sad."

"It doesn't take much today. You didn't mean to." I hopped off the bar stool and headed to the couch. I could feel the roller coaster ride starting. I fiddled with the string hanging off the end of the blanket folded on the arm.

Max sat next to me and tossed Tada off the back of the couch. The cat sulked away to the bedroom. Max pulled me into a hug. "Do you want to talk about it?"

"No."

"I never did find out much about the accident."

I nodded.

"Even Mitch only had details from the police reports and what you told the insurance people." Max kissed the top of my head and leaned his head on mine.

"I... I can't talk about it." I sniffled.

"Why?"

I shook my head.

"Have you talked to anyone about it?"

Again I shook my head.

"Why?"

I shook my head once more.

Max suddenly moved me so he could look into my eyes. His eyes seemed to be searching my soul. "You're feeling guilty about something, aren't you?"

I looked away from him and fiddled with the edge of the blanket again. He pulled me back to the hug position and gave me a squeeze. We sat that way for several minutes. My thoughts ran in circles. I wanted to talk but I couldn't. I knew that I wouldn't fully heal until I let out what I was feeling but couldn't. Jason had said no. And I trusted Jason. I had to, he was my lawyer. But.

Max's comforting me felt so good, so natural. I leaned harder into him. "I've only talked to Jason Landry." It came out as a whisper.

"The Maryland lawyer partner of Craig's?"

I rubbed my face on his T-shirt. I snuggled in tight, just wanting to be held.

"Why?"

"There's a huge law suit pending, several actually. Jason said... Jason said not to tell anyone, especially my family. Besides, it's not like they would understand anyway," I whispered.

"Talk to me, Mel. I promise, I won't tell anyone. I can see that it's eating you up." Max matched my tone and sound level. He hugged me tighter.

I shook my head.

"Is it about Craig?"

I didn't answer.

We sat again for a few minutes, Max holding me as I relaxed in his arms. It felt nice to have someone hold and comfort me, someone who wasn't pressuring me to talk about anything or judge me. My circular thoughts continued.

I eventually went to the bathroom. When I came out, I headed to the kitchen to grab a soda. I didn't want to drink more alcohol. I knew it wasn't going to help. Instead of sitting on the couch, I walked over to the screen door. The sun was starting its downward arc. I glanced at my watch.

Max appeared at my side. He put his arm over my shoulder and stood there with me staring out the door. Softly, as though not wanting to break my mood, he said, "Do you want to head to the beach? I always find it soothing to walk the beach when something is bothering me."

"That would be nice." We grabbed light jackets and headed out.

Max didn't speak the entire trip. When we got there, we took off our shoes and headed to the surf. There were a few people playing in the sand but it wasn't crowded. Max took my hand and we walked for a while in the breakers, then turned and headed back.

Most of the people had already left the beach by the time the glorious sunset showed her finest. We returned to the beach area near the parking lot. I stared out at the water. Max put his arm around me. I glanced at my watch again.

"That's like the fourth time you've done that."

I nodded.

"Waiting for something?" he asked with a smile.

I looked one more time and waited for the hands to make another round before speaking. "One year ago, at almost this exact time, the tractor trailer hit my car."

Max squeezed my shoulder.

I sniffled back a tear, but it fell anyway. I had to tell someone. "The sun was shining toward the oncoming lane in which the truck was driving. The light turned green for us to go across Highway 301. Apparently the trucker didn't see the light turn or something. He hit us broadside on the driver's side." I sniffled again as the tears flowed. "The impact... It pushed us about one hundred feet down the roadway. The car was stuck under the front of the truck. All of us were trapped in the car. I was conscious all the way until I arrived at the ER. I remember the firefighters cutting us out and... I was told later that Robbie was killed instantly. He..." I stopped and wiped my tears.

Max pulled me into a hug, holding me tight.

"I knew. I just knew when we stopped moving that he was dead. I never asked at the scene they tell me. I asked about Craig but not Robbie. I just knew he was..." I hugged Max back, burying my face in his chest. "They told me he never felt a thing. Robbie had been tired, the babysitters. He fell asleep on the way home." I sniffled again. "So I guess... I guess it was a good thing. The last thing he said to me as he fell asleep was... He said, 'Mommy I love you.'"

Now the tears flowed uncontrollably. I couldn't stop them. I didn't even want to anymore. I had only cried this hard once in front of anyone and that was at the small memorial held after I was out of the hospital.

"Let it out," Max whispered.

"I never said... At least I don't remember saying that I loved him back."

"He knew, Mel. He did."

"I know." I pushed away from Max and walked farther down the beach toward the water. The sand was a fuzzy blur. I found a big rock and tossed it into the ocean. I squatted down in the sand, scooping up a handful. Slowly I let it run through my fingers.

Max squatted down next to me.

I glanced at him but he was staring out at the ocean. I saw him turn to me, and I looked down at the sand still running through my fingers. I picked up a shell and fingered it, then tossed it back into the ocean too. I wiped the tears with the back of my hand. "Craig and I had been arguing. Not something new. The witnesses at the scene all confirm that the trucker ran the red light, but…"

Max sat down next to me and waited.

"But if we hadn't had been arguing, maybe he would have seen the truck or something. I would have seen the truck. I know…" I sniffled again. "I know… I mean, I know I can't play what-if, but it was our fault that Robbie… Robbie died. We were arguing and weren't paying attention to the traffic. I should have waited to confront him. I should have waited."

"Is that what Landry doesn't want anyone to know?"

I nodded. "My family wouldn't understand anyway."

"Why?"

I sniffled. "I had filed for a divorce earlier that afternoon. That's just not done in my family, not my Catholic family." I wiped tears from my face. They weren't flowing very hard now. "Craig and I had been having trouble for over a year, an ongoing thing. I caught him one night at the office with… with the wife of the other partner. To say I blew my top is an understatement." I slightly smiled, remembering how loud and vicious I had been, then the smile faded. I picked up more sand. "I never told anyone that before, not even Jason."

The silence lengthened.

"Was it Jason's wife?" Max asked.

I looked over at him in surprise that he figured it out. "Yeah. She begged me not to tell Jason for days afterward." I looked out over the ocean and then sat next to Max. I pulled my legs up to hug them. "That incident was a couple of weeks before… before the accident." I rocked a little. I wiped my tears again. "Mitch was by my side when I woke. They say I kept asking about Robbie and Craig. I don't remember much until one day Mitch told me. He said it was the day after I woke up. He told me because I was insistent and he said me being me… My memories of those first couple of days are… Anyway, when I was finally conscious and thinking, I told Jason to call the lawyer I hired and stop the paperwork, since it wasn't necessary. Sebastian, my lawyer, wouldn't tell Jason why I filed. I think Mitch suspected that we were having trouble, but I never told anyone. Craig wanted to work through the problems. I just wanted out. That night we were arguing over the usual stuff." I stared at the waves hitting the beach in front of us. The sun was almost completely set. I glanced at Max and saw him looking around the beach. "Someone?"

"No. Just keeping my eye out though." Max patted my arm. "Does Jason suspect anything?"

"I don't think so. Wendy said she would get help if I didn't tell him. He's a good friend and I didn't want to hurt him, especially after the accident. I mean with Craig dead and all, what does it matter? Maybe I should have told him." I shrugged. "Anyway, if the other lawyers find out about us arguing, it might put a different spin on the lawsuit. I'm not in it for the money, but that trucker took my family from me, even if the rat bastard was cheating on me. I had been told by different doctors that I wasn't supposed to be able to have kids and there went my one shot at it."

Max rested his hand on my knee and squeezed.

"There was a big mess at the hospital when they brought Craig and me in." I rubbed my right leg as I stretched it in front of me. "The emergency room doctors didn't call for a consult fast enough and I almost died right there, then once again on the operating table. There were several other problems that occurred and..." I stopped and looked down at my feet. "One report said there was a medical question with Craig's death. We have a multimillion dollar lawsuit against the hospital in his death. Medical negligence. Jason is sure of winning that one. That's his specialty, medical malpractice. Nathaniel Brooks, the other partner, is handling Robbie and Craig's wrongful death suit against the trucker and the trucking company, along with the insurance company."

"Was he negligent?"

"Yeah, besides running the red light, he was driving on medication and medical advice to not operate heavy machinery. The cops charged him with vehicular manslaughter and he's already pleaded guilty. He's serving time in a work release program. The problem for them comes in the fact that he told his bosses about the medication. They needed this shipment delivered immediately and offered him a bonus to take the load anyway."

Max shook his head in disbelief. "This is all on record?"

"The offer and orders to take the load are from Jason's and Nathanial's inquiries. Of course, the trucking company is denying it." I grew silent.

Max broke the silence with a whisper. "I'm sorry."

"Thanks, but I'm so tired of hearing those words. Please don't say them again. I'm so tired of it. I feel like someone should scream at me that I killed my son."

"Mel, you didn't kill your son."

The tears were starting to flow again. "I did. I killed... I killed Robbie. If I hadn't had been selfish and... and waited until we got home to have the argument, we wouldn't have gotten in the accident. I started the argument that night. It's my fault."

"The accident was not your fault."

I nodded in agreement. Intellectually I knew that, but it didn't make the searing pain in my heart go away. Most days it was only a dull ache, since it had been so long since the accident, but some days it was almost unbearable. We sat there until it turned dark. The sound of the waves was the only noise.

"Can I ask you a question?" He spoke softly, just above a whisper.

"Sure." I had long ago stopped crying.

"It sounds to me like you've forgiven Craig, not only for his indiscretions but also for his part in the accident. Why can't you forgive yourself?"

I wiped my face. I didn't want to cry again but the tears welled up, threatening to fall again. "I can't. I'm his… I was his *mother*. I'm supposed to protect him. I failed. I wasn't vigilant and he died. It's my fault. The argument. The accident. His death. My fault."

Max stood up, pulling me with him. He tipped my head up to look at him. "The accident was not your fault. Forgive yourself. Beating yourself up over it won't bring him back. He's dead. He loved you. Robbie knows that if there was any way for you to have saved him, you would have. You know that too. Do you think he would want you to be in this much pain?"

"No." Tears began flowing down my cheeks.

"Forgive yourself. There was nothing you could do. It's over. It was an accident. Not your fault. None of this is your fault." Max shook me. "It's time to let go of this quilt and forgive yourself."

I looked into his blue eyes. They were illuminated by the bright moonlight. I burst out crying, crying harder than I have ever cried before.

Max drew me into his arms and held on. "That's it, Mel." He hugged and patted and rubbed my back.

Chapter 23

It was late by the time we got back to Max's apartment. We hadn't spoken much after my crying incident. I liked that about Max. I really didn't like small talk when I wanted to be quiet. He seemed to know that, even when we first met.

I felt like a burden had been lifted. My heart didn't hurt quite as bad, and I felt like I walked with a little lighter step. I was still sad to be sure, and Robbie's death still left an ache deep down, but it wasn't as bad as normal.

I crawled into bed next to Max. He was already in shorts, no shirt, hands behind his head relaxed. I crawled into bed in my sleeping shorts and nightshirt. He pulled me into a hug. I cuddled in his embrace and got comfortable. His warm skin was nice under my face. I could hear the steady rhythm of his heart.

"Thanks Max. Thanks for, well, for being here and listening."

"Anytime, Tiger." He paused. "Feel better?"

"Definitely better. Talking about it did help, but I still feel sad, hurt… it's hard to describe…"

"Mel, Robbie's death will always be painful. That's normal. I meant, how do *you* feel?"

I shrugged. "Better."

"Good."

I smiled. His hand was lightly stroking my arm. It sent shivers up and down my spine. A warm feeling settled in my groin then spread. It had been a while since I had had this whole body feeling, even when kissing Max the last couple of times.

With a quick wiggle, I sat up, looking at Max.

"What?"

I smiled.

He got a strange look on his face. "What? What's going on now?"

I gave him a grin and stripped off my t-shirt. In the moonlight coming in from the window, I saw him look down at my chest. I raised my eyebrows at him.

Max shook his head. "Not tonight. This is wrong."

I grinned. "I know what you're thinking, but it's after midnight, Bauer." His eyes met mine as I wiggled out of my shorts. I had on my lucky-duck underwear.

Max chuckled. "I still think this is wrong."

I leaned over and whispered, "Then let it be wrong." I began kissing him with a passion I hadn't felt for many a long year. He returned the passion as I crawled on top of him.

Max pushed me away and sat up, holding me at arm's length. He was breathing faster than normal. Max shook his head. "I have to warn you, it's getting to a point where I won't want to stop." His blue eyes were a dreamy sky color in the moonlight. He caught his breath. "I don't think we should do this tonight."

"Stop being a gentlemen," I said, also catching my breath. "I want... no, I need this."

"Are you sure?"

I ran my hand over his chest and felt his muscles tighten and relax with my touch. His breathing picked up again.

"Yes."

Max scooted closer to me. His eyes locked with mine and I could see desire erupt in them. His right hand touched my face and he traced my chin with his fingertips, barely touching.

Fire raced down my body. His touch was like small electrical shocks on my skin. I moved to get closer to him to kiss but Max shook his head.

"I've waited a long time for this night. I intend on fully exploring you." Max smiled at me as his hand moved from my jaw-line down onto my neck, his left hand barely caressing the skin on my arm.

The sensations were some I don't think I have ever felt. I took a deep breath, enjoying the feeling of a man touching me again.

His right hand moved back up to my chin and then to my lips. Max's eyes followed his hand. His left hand caressed my right arm in small circles. The fingers moved back and forth on my lips, barely touching. This butterfly touch was so erotic. No one had ever used it on me before. His index finger slightly parted my lips, and I tongued his finger with the tip. Max smiled at me.

"I have to warn you before we go too far that I'm not the biggest instrument in the orchestra."

"So?"

His smile increased. "But I play it like a pro."

I smiled back. "Let's see how 'musically inclined' you are then."

He chuckled. Giving me a peck on the lips, he pulled away again. "I want to pleasure you."

His fingertips made their way down my chin and neck again. His other hand came up my arm and across my shoulder. Max's eyes locked with mine. "One last time, are you sure you want to do this tonight?"

"Shut up and get busy." I pulled his head in for a heart stopping, panty wetting kiss.

He pushed me away after a minute. "Then enjoy." He laid me back on the bed. His hands continued their slow, tortuous movements along my body. Caressing. Touching. Rubbing. Playing.

I felt that I couldn't get my breath after several minutes. My senses were reeling. I had never felt this way with any man. My arms and legs were trembling even though I was lying down, and my nerves were on fire. "Stop. Max, Stop," I gasped, grabbing his right hand. "Stop, you're killing me."

Max leaned up on his elbow, the smile disappearing as he stared into my eyes, a serious look taking over. When he saw that I had regained control of my breathing, he shook his head. "No, not killing. I'm bringing you back alive."

I took a deep breath. I had never felt like this before, so maybe he was right. I swallowed another deep breath.

"Trust me." His blue eyes were shimmering with an emotion I couldn't recognize.

Not trusting my voice, I nodded.

His lopsided smile returned as his hands began where they had left off. He leaned up and kissed me, a slow tortuous kiss. Aggressive, yet gentle. Possessive, yet freeing.

I felt the cat jump up on the bed and without breaking the kiss, Max swept Tada off the bed with an arc of his arm. She hissed at us and disappeared.

Max finally finished the kiss. He smiled, his eyes a dusky blue. Then he began kissing my neck and shoulders.

Within seconds, I couldn't believe that I had this many nerve endings in my body. I arched and jerked in pleasure. My hands gripped and un-gripped the side of the bed.

A loud meow sounded from the living room. A hiss followed.

I lifted my head. My dreamy, almost unseeing eyes trying to focus on the dark doorway that led into the living room.

"Forget her," Max whispered in a husky voice.

"But..."

Then he made me totally forget her.

***

Max munched on a piece of toast, fully dressed, standing at the counter the next morning as I walked out of the bedroom after my shower. He smiled at me. His eyes ran up and down my body and he let out a groan. "You're so sexy in those cutoffs."

I glanced down at myself. These were actually one of my oldest pair of shorts, the most comfortable pair that I owned. I walked into the kitchen and grabbed a bagel. As I leaned on the counter across from Max, he sipped his coffee. His eyes held me with a look of pure joy.

"I knew you'd be good, but it was better than I fantasized about."

"You did everything, and ditto back at you." I paused then grinned. "Never let it be said that you aren't first chair in that orchestra, Max."

Max laughed. His eyes crinkled with joy and what was probably pride.

"Hey, did you move my ducky underwear?"

Max shook his head as he took another drink. "Check the blankets, maybe I didn't get them all the way to the floor."

"I checked everywhere."

Max looked at me puzzled then sighed. His attention centered on the cat sitting on the counter near him. "Tada, are you hiding things again?" The cat had either a totally pissed off look or one of total indifference. For me it was hard to tell. Max looked at me. "She's been known to hide things when she's gets mad. I don't think she appreciated it when I tossed her off the bed."

"Underwear?"

Max laughed with a nod. "It's happened before, not underwear but socks. Don't worry, it'll turn up when she gets tired of playing her games." He finished his coffee, placed the cup on the counter and crossed his arms. "What's on your schedule today?"

"Why?"

"Someone is following you. We've established that. I want to know that you're safe."

"I'll be fine. I might go shopping again. I saw a computer store I'd like to check out and ask some questions." I took a bite of bagel. "I'll have my cell phone with me, don't worry. I'll stay in public places. No dark alleys for me."

Max stood up with a glance at his watch. "I'd rather you stay here inside where you'll be safe, but..." He sighed. "I need to get going." He tightened his tie and smoothed his shirt. As he passed me, he pulled me into him for a kiss, a passionate, 'I-don't-want-to-go-to-work' kind of kiss.

I chuckled and turned to watch him leave. He opened the door and froze. Puzzled, I headed to see what the problem was.

There was another dead animal on the porch. A fat, bloated dog.

Max turned to look at me. His eyes narrowed in anger. "Just who is this person and why is he mad at you, Mel? This is getting serious."

I cursed softly. While Max headed back inside to get stuff to dispose of the animal, I looked the area in front of the apartment building over again. *Who is it? And more importantly, why?* My eyes swept the parking lot cataloging cars and came to rest on his Trooper. "Max, forget about the animal."

"What?" He was already headed my way.

"Someone left a present on the Trooper." I pointed out the door. I glanced at Max who was now standing next to me.

Max grabbed my arm as I started out. "I'll get it." There was an envelope under the windshield wiper. A large manila envelope. "Stay inside."

"Bauer."

Max turned to me with a hard, 'don't-mess-with-me' kind of look. "Stay here." He handed me the garbage bag, pointed at me and with caution headed down the steps.

I watched him. Max was in no actual hurry to get the envelope, I could tell. He stopped at the bottom of the stairs and checked the area before leaving the relative security of the building. His head moved slowly in all directions checking out cars and buildings. I stepped onto the porch.

"Get back inside."

"Just go get it."

"Back inside," his tone was brittle and authoritative.

"Sure." I stepped inside but remained at the door. When I saw him move toward the Trooper, I opened the door, stepped over the dead dog and moved back onto the porch. My eyes kept moving, checking everywhere. No one seemed to care about the car or us. I noticed several people heading to their cars, but they were people I had seen before, and I knew they lived in the other apartments.

Max quickly retrieved the envelope using a plastic baggie on his hand. He hurried back up the steps. I quickly put the dead dog in the garbage bag but left it on the porch. I held the door open for him. "Close and lock the door."

I did as requested, then returned to the counter. By this time, he had opened it cautiously. I watched as he checked out the inside first.

Max looked up. "Photos."

"Of?"

With another glance at me, he pulled them out. "Don't touch anything."

I nodded as he pulled out a pile of eight by ten photos, grimacing as he did so. The top photo was of me sitting on the steps with my bagel and drink yesterday morning. I cursed under my breath.

Max flipped to the next photo.

It was of me walking on the beach by myself. From the direction of the shot, the man on the beach had to have taken the picture. The next photo was of Max and me in bed together in the hotel. Then the two of us hugging on the beach from last night.

Our eyes met in silent understanding. Someone was seriously stalking me.

The next photo was of me sleeping in the hospital. I swallowed, trying to settle the anger quickly building inside of me. Someone had been continually violating my life. I bet the dead flowers were from whoever took the picture of me. *But the message made no sense. D.M. Who is D.M.?* Even as I thought that, Max flipped through the next two photos.

The next photo was of me sitting in my car back home doing surveillance for the guys. A flip revealed the next photo to be pictures of documents. I leaned in closer. A really foul curse slipped out of my mouth. This was too much.

Max leaned in for a closer look too. He grimaced. It was a photo of the death certificates of Robbie and Craig. Even more disturbing, was a death certificate next to the other two, blank except for my name. Max reached for his cell phone. "Get me Captain Thomas, now. This is Bauer."

I flipped with Max's plastic bag to the last photo. It was a funeral scene. "Oh God!" My stomach dropped into the apartment below us.

"Is that Craig and Robbie's funeral?"

I shook my head. "I was in the hospital for weeks. They were buried while I was…" I reached for my cell phone and quickly dialed a number. "John, hi. Get Rich. Max and I just figured out who is following me… No, we just received a bunch of photos from him. And I need the number to that cop in Oregon. Devon Miles is after me."

Now the note with the dead flowers made sense.

Chapter 24

"Who is Devon Miles?" Max asked when he figured out that I was on hold.

"He's..."

Max held up his hand. "No, tell him this is important... Yes, I'll wait." He looked at me to continue.

"He..." I paused then returned my attention to my phone.

"Devon Miles? Are you sure?" Rich asked, his voice raised in fear.

"Yes I'm sure. He sent me a bunch of photos of me, including one from Roma's funeral."

"Where's Max?"

"He's right here next to me on the phone with his captain."

Rich cursed. "This is serious. Miles is a career criminal. Are you ready for Yardley's number?"

I wrote it down.

"I want to talk with Max."

"He's on the phone with his captain."

"Have him call me right away. Don't leave his side, Mel."

"Yeah, yeah. Later." I hung up and dialed Oregon.

"So, who is Devon Miles?" Max asked still holding the phone to his head.

"He's... Detective Yardley, please. Thanks." I turned to Max. "He's..."

Max held up his hand again. "Captain, the situation I told you about yesterday... Right. I just found a pile of photos establishing that a Devon Miles had been following her... Yes, she recognized that they came from him... I'm still trying to figure that out... Several dead animals, and she told me that she had several dead animals in Illinois too. One of the photos is of death certificates of her husband and son along with a blank one with her name filled in… I don't know, something to do with Oregon…" Max turned to me. "Who is Devon Miles?"

"He's…"

"Detective Yardley." A deep bass voice sounded from my phone.

"Detective, Melissa Addison from Security Investigations in Quincy Illinois."

"I remember you." There was a smile in his voice. "What can I do for you?"

"Devon Miles has shown up."

"Where? How?"

"He's currently stalking me. We think he has been for at least a week."

"In Quincy?"

"No, I'm in California right now. Mayfield, California."

"California?" The puzzlement was obvious in his voice.

"It's a long story, but he sent pictures of me at various times, including Roma's funeral."

"Are you in a safe location?"

"Yes." I smiled at Max. "The person I'm staying with is a police officer." I noticed Max was motioning for me to get on with it. "Look, Detective, it appears that Detective Max Bauer needs me to answer questions for him."

Yardley's hand covered the phone. "What? Can I put you on hold, Ms. Addison?"

"Sure." I turned to Max. "I'm on hold."

"Don't say 'he's' again. Who is this Miles?"

"Devon Miles was the stalker in a case of Rich's at home. We were helping Roma Tronlowski to get rid of him, legally. When she went to visit her family in Oregon, he killed her." I screwed up my face at him. "Sorry, is suspected of killing her."

"And?"

"He's also an ex-con from Texas, where Roma had been living before…"

"Ms. Addison?"

I turned my attention back to the phone in my hand. "Can you hold for just a minute, Detective? Thanks. As I was saying…" I paused to take a breath and figure out who I was supposed to be talking to. "She hired us to track him. He followed her to Illinois. We were in the process of helping her, when bam, he killed Roma and now he's got an arrest warrant in Oregon… Detective Yardley back to you. It's still in force correct?"

"Yes."

I nodded at Max.

"Can I speak with this Detective Bauer?"

"Sure. I'll put you on Bauer's call back list right after my brother."

"Tell him my captain will be calling him in a minute," Max leaned closer to me.

"Did you get that, Detective Yardley?"

"Yes, I did. Has Rich changed his number, I have it as…" Yardley read back the number to the office.

"That's it."

"I'll wait on Bauer's Captain's call, then I'll call Rich. You be careful, Ms. Addison. Miles is dangerous and smart. Stay close to this police officer."

I sighed. "Of course, Detective. Thanks." I hung up and turned to Max. "Anything else?"

"Both Detective Yardley's and Rich's number?"

I told him Rich's office number, then pushed the paper I'd written Yardley's number on. Max repeated Rich's into the phone then read Yardley's off my paper to his captain. "Right… Just give us a call… Trust me, she's not going anywhere." Max nodded and hung up the phone. His cop mask was on and on tight. "Now that we won't get any interruptions for a few minutes, tell me about Devon Miles." Max stripped off his tie and got comfortable.

I told him about Roma hiring us to find Devon, the man stalking her. How we had deceived him into thinking I was Roma so she could visit her family before going into hiding until the cops caught him. And how he had figured where she was and killed her. When I finished, Max just shook his head. "Have you ever thought about going into a different profession?"

I made a face. "You're supposed to call Rich and Detective Theodore Yardley in Oregon. Both want to talk to you."

Max nodded as he dialed Rich's number. "This is bad. If he's killed once already…" He shook his head at the situation. "John, it's Max. Rich wanted me to call." He listened for a few seconds. "My thought exactly." He looked thoughtfully at me. "I can try, but you know Mel… Reassure Rich and family that she won't be left alone. The Captain has already assigned me to protect her. After he talks with Yardley in Oregon, he'll decide the course of action… No, Mel just told me all about it." Max smiled, then chuckled. "Even if I have to cuff her to me."

"Bite me," I said softly, once more looking over the photos. I was not going into protective custody. For a short time after Dad arrested Madeline Hessor, the family had been put in protective custody while Dad was in the hospital. Twice I skipped out on the police watchers, much to my father's dismay and disgust. After 'recapturing' me, they proceeded to take me to the hospital to 'talk' with Dad. Needless to say, I was not only grounded but given a severe punishment.

"We'll be here at my apartment or you can call my cell. Do you still have the numbers?… Good. See you then." Max hung up his cell.

"John's coming out?"

"Tomorrow, unless he can book an earlier flight."

"Why?"

"Protection." Max shook his head at me as I opened my mouth to speak. "Don't even go there, Mel. You're being protected by someone until this Miles is caught. Period. No argument."

***

Several hours later we were sitting at the counter eating a late lunch. It had been a busy morning. Phone calls back and forth between everyone kept one of us on the phone almost the entire time.

Captain Thomas sent a plain clothes detective over for the photographs. They were going to dust them for prints, but he wasn't hopeful. From all the information that he'd received from Yardley, Miles was going to be hard to catch. Thomas also informed us of a new development in the Miles saga. It would seem that he was also wanted by San Diego police in connection with an unsolved murder. That was before he started stalking Roma. Max was extremely unhappy.

Now there was a blessed silence for a while.

"Mel, those hang ups… Do you think they were Miles?"

"Undoubtedly. He used to call Roma all the time. She said he called hundreds of times a night."

Max stared at the answering machine. "Maybe I should have a trace on my phone, in case he calls again."

"Wouldn't be a bad idea." I still hadn't looked at him since sitting down to eat. I was deep in thought. *Why me? Why did he pick on me? Now my life will be turned upside down. I'll be forever looking over my shoulder for him.*

Max called his boss and instituted the trace for his phone. So far we had no indication that Miles knew our cell numbers. *But how hard could that be? Or how long?*

Again silence reigned for a few minutes. The house phone rang. We looked at each other. Max immediately called a number on his cell to start tracing. After four rings the answering machine picked up.

Max spoke into his phone. "Where? Paris? As in France?" He looked at me. I shrugged back and so did he. "No, I don't…"

The person on the phone began speaking, "Maximillian…"

"Never mind. It's only my Mom. Thanks." Max hung up his cell.

Max's mom continued, "I guess you are not at home. You must be at work…"

I smiled. The tone in which she said 'at work' indicated that she didn't really like Max's choice of professions. Max shook his head as he grabbed the phone. The disgusted look was priceless.

"Mom, I'm home and I can't talk long. What do you want?… No. For the hundredth time no…" Max rolled his eyes at no one. "I've already sent Grandma's birthday present… Yes… I see that you're in Paris, again."

I mouthed 'again' to Max.

He grimaced with a nod. "You saw Clare…. Yes, I know she's on her honeymoon… That's nice, Mom…" Max held out the phone to me then laid it on the counter. He stood up and got another soda out of the fridge. I could hear her still talking, rattling on about something. When he returned, he picked up the phone. "She's still going on," he said not even trying to be quiet about it. "Mom?… Mom! Look, I have to go… Yes, I'm always careful, Mom… It's what I do… Goodbye." Max hung up the phone.

"Family troubles?" I asked with a grin. So I wasn't the oddity who didn't get along with their mom.

Max shook his head. "And then some. Too long of a story."

"Since I'm stuck with you as my personal shadow, I think we have time, *Maximillian*."

Max grabbed me by the head and put me in a head lock. Then with a chuckle he let up to kiss me on the lips. "I hate my full name, *Melissa*."

"Touché."

"Let's just say my parents didn't like it when I became a cop. They haven't liked anything I've done. We've been at odds for years." He grabbed the dishes and moved into the kitchen to the sink.

"And?"

"And nothing. I went my own way." He shrugged.

"So, they're in Paris?"

"Yeah."

"Do they go there often?"

"Occasionally."

"Bauer, you sure are closed-lipped about your life." I smiled at him as I rounded the counter. I picked up the dish towel and began drying plates.

"It's not something I like to talk about. My family." Max looked at me. "I think you can understand that."

"Absolutely. Still, I am a detective in training."

Max smiled. "Insatiably curious?"

"That's me." I put the plates away and started on the glasses he had just finished washing. "So, have you been to Paris?"

"A couple of times. It's not what it's cracked up to be."

"Really? Not romantic?"

"Smelly."

"Okay, Bauer. Where's your favorite place in the whole world?"

"For?"

"Anything. Just your favorite."

Max stopped washing the utensils and looked at the water for a few seconds. "The whole world, huh?" He frowned. "I would have to say Heathrow Airport."

"Excuse me? An airport?" I leaned on the counter and crossed my arms. The place he liked best was an international airport. "This I have to hear."

Max chuckled. "Not that bizarre actually. They have the best fish and chips, assuming the kiosk is still there."

"Fish and chips are the reason that you like that place over everywhere else?"

Max shrugged. "Sort of like your Maid Rites. Greasy and bad for you but, man, were they good."

I started laughing.

Max flicked water at me.

With an evil look in my eye, I began to roll the towel between my hands in the air. I was holding it by two diagonal corners. It was wet enough to make a really good smack.

His eyes widened. "You wouldn't."

"Towel fights were one of the fun things about doing dishes in my house. And I did a lot of dishes." I continued to roll the towel with an evil chuckle as Max backed up a step.

"It's so... so...."

"The word you're looking for is childish and yes, but I think a good hard smack..."

Max pointed in warning. At the same time, we spotted the other towel on the counter. We both lunged at it, but Max got there a split second ahead of me. Now with a wicked look in his eye and smile on his face, he also rolled a towel. "You're no match, Addison. Locker room towel fights were legendary where I went to school."

"I thought California schools would be more about would be self-esteem and good self-image and stuff."

We were standing ready to do battle.

"I didn't go to high school in California. I went to college here." His evil grin grew. "I went to a private all boy's school. No girlie girls to mess up a really good towel battle." He raised his eyebrows at me several times. "Give in, Girl. You won't win this battle. Trust me."

I considered. He did have a wicked spin to the towel, and I knew that my brothers could always smack harder than me. Against other girls I had been the queen, but against *some* boys, well that was another matter.

"Good idea, Mel. I was captain of my towel team. And I'm not kidding. Give in or prepare to feel the sting." He flicked it in the air. A good whizz and crack followed.

I lowered my towel. "Okay, okay." I still held it in my hands.

Max smiled with a head shake. "Drop the towel, Addison. I've used that trick many times myself. Fake giving in, then give a quick flick. Naha. Towel down."

I laid the towel on the counter. Surrender being the best course here.

Max, in a quick move, looped his towel over my head and pulled me into him. "I accept your surrender, Ms. Addison. As for my terms…" He kissed me and as he did he lowered the towel to bring my hips into his. "Never declare war against a better opponent."

I grinned. "And what are your other terms?"

"Well," he began, then backed up against the counter as my hand made contact with his crotch. "Mel?"

I was holding on tight, not enough to hurt, but enough to get his attention. "As Al Pacino in the Godfather said, 'Keep your friends close, but your enemies even closer.'"

Max chuckled. "Ah! I see." His face changed as I leaned forward for a kiss, still holding on. "Okay," he stopped kissing for a second. "Maybe we could come to a mutual understanding of…"

I licked my other finger and put it in his mouth. Then I pinned him against the counter and unbuttoned his shirt. He wiggled against me then pulled me in tight.

I unbuttoned his jeans with a quick flip of my fingers.

"You seem awfully experienced at that."

I grinned. "I was a *very* popular girl in high school."

"I wouldn't have pegged you as slutty."

"Not slutty. Even then I knew what I liked. For your information, I lost my virginity when I was twenty. So you see, I didn't mess around in high school." My hands were still busy.

"Mmmm," Max said softly as he began to enjoy himself.

"And you?"

"What?"

"Virginity?"

"Sixteen with Clare." He closed his eyes, then blew out his breath. "Back seat of my corvette."

"Corvette? My, my. You must have been a rich kid."

"Yeah. True."

I chuckled and leaned in to kiss him. His hands gripped my head and the kiss became aggressive again. Now he was the one moaning at what I was doing to him. This went on for a few minutes.

When I was done, I broke off the kiss and looked him in the eye. I laughed and backed off. "So, what else are we doing today?"

His blue eyes had that dusty, sultry look.

"Not that." I scrunched up my face. "At least not now." I needed to get his mind back to important issues. "How are we going to catch Miles?"

Max crossed his arms after re-buttoning. "*You* are doing nothing."

"Excuse me?"

"Captain Thomas wants you in a secure environment. Safe. At least until we get a better feel for Miles and his actions. The safe house isn't available until tomorrow. And until John gets here to help guard you, you're not leaving the apartment." Max's face was set in stone. "No matter what you say."

"So, I'm captive either way. If I get past you, Miles will get me. If I stay here, I'm a prisoner." I shook my head at Max. "This is unacceptable. I will not live my life this way."

"If you don't, you won't live."

"That's not a given."

"You're staying, Mel. Period."

I stared into his eyes for a brief moment then walked away. *I won't accept this situation for long. No way, no how. Let Miles come at me. I like it better that way. Get it over with.*

Max left me alone. We didn't speak for over an hour. Even then I debated not joining him. Slowly I walked out and sat near him on the couch.

He flipped off the TV and turned to me. He had on his cop face. "What would be your solution?"

"Go out. Find him or let him find me. He wants to play with me, taunt me, before he kills me. That's how he gets his thrills."

"Bait?"

I nodded.

Max's lips tightened. "Too dangerous." He shook his head. "We actually discussed it. That will be used only as a last resort. You're safe here."

"Fine."

"Fine." He turned the TV back on. A knock sounded at the door. He hurried to answer it.

I turned off the TV and joined him. He was talking softly to someone standing on his porch. Too softly for me to hear until I moved behind him.

"...it wasn't there on the last patrol around," the man said. From the looks of him he was probably a police officer.

Max looked out the door then turned and saw me standing there. "There's another envelope on the Trooper."

"I told you he wants to play with me."

"Mel, this is Detective Triscon. Bruce, this is Mel."

Bruce Triscon nodded. "Max, do you want me to get it? He might want to take you out too, since you're guarding her."

Max shook his head. "Stay with Mel. Keep her inside." He took the pair of gloves Triscon handed him and walked out the door.

Triscon stood his ground at the door with a serious look at me, then turned and watched Max. I walked up behind him and looked out the door. "We've been making regular rounds hoping to find this guy. So far nothing. This last time around we saw the envelope."

Shortly Max was back in the apartment. He laid the envelope on the counter. It didn't contain photos this time, I could tell. There was something bulky in there.

With a sharp knife, Max slit open the opposite end. A loud curse escaped his lips. He glanced at us.

Max pulled out my ducky underwear.

Chapter 25

"He was here last night," Max's voice sounded far away, like in a tunnel.

I stared at the underwear. I went from upset to overload in about half a second. Not only had Miles stolen my underwear, but he had done it while we were making love. And he had *watched* us.

"Mel?"

I could feel my nails digging into my palms. My arms twitched. The next thing I knew I was sitting on Max's bed. I took deep breaths. *In and out. In and out. Calm. Calm.* My heart beat loudly in my ears. And even though I was in the bedroom, all I saw was my underwear. My breathing was ragged and uneven. I could feel myself beginning to shake. With a whole body shake I clenched and unclenched my fist. I had only been this mad once and I had lost it then.

Calm down. Calm down. Calm down.

When I finally looked up, Max was leaning on the post watching me. I glanced at the clock on the head board to see that it was over half an hour since he opened the package. I took another deep breath and shook myself.

"Now what?"

Max shrugged. "Triscon took the package and is talking to the Captain."

I stared at Max's feet.

"One thing is sure. We aren't staying here," his voice was determined.

"If he found his way in here, he can find his way in anywhere."

"Not a hotel. I'll make sure we aren't followed."

"So that I have to look over my shoulder the rest of my life? I think not. You tell your Captain that." I watched as Max's eyes got hard. "I'll refuse police help soon. Let him come and let's get it over with one way or the other."

"A death wish? That's not you."

"I didn't say I wanted to die, I just want to confront him. He needs to be stopped."

"Not at the expense of your life." Max stood up and moved into the living room.

I sat on the bed for a while then joined Max in the living room. "How long is it going to take your Captain to figure this out?"

Max shrugged.

For the first time, I noticed that Max put his shoulder harness on and had his gun strapped to his side. Before he just made sure it was within easy reach. I swallowed. He was as serious about this as I was.

"Do you have an extra gun in the house?"

His head snapped to me. "Of course."

"Where?"

"You're not wearing it. That's illegal."

"I know. I just want it within reach."

Max contemplated my request. He stood and walked into the bedroom, returning with a handgun, a Beretta nine millimeter, like the one he used. He showed me that it was empty and handed it to me.

I looked closely at it. I was familiar with the Beretta. I checked out the various parts.

Max sat near me and watched. He handed me the clip when I was ready. "You've handled guns before."

I didn't answer. Instead, I shoved the clip in and worked the slide. It was now armed.

"Yes. Safety off, then pull the trigger."

I sighted down the barrel, then shoved the gun between the cushion and the arm of the couch. Max picked up the remote and turned on the TV. "I called Rich when you wouldn't talk to me."

"When?"

"After I pulled out the duckies."

"And?"

"He said when you go silent, stay out of your way and let you work through it." Max looked closely at me. "That is one hell of an anger streak, Mel."

I just looked at him.

"I watched you. Have you ever thought of getting counseling for it?"

"California stuff. I can control my anger. I have never let it control me. I get angry, yes. It's the way I am." I crossed my arms and stared back at him.

Max lifted one shoulder and went back to watching the show. His cell rang and after answering it, he merely listened. Whatever was being said did not make him happy. "I disagree Captain, but if that's how you want to do it, that's what we'll do until Huddleston gets here." He tapped his hand on the arm of the couch. "Fine. Have them do rounds every hour and check in every two… I will." He hung up. "Jerk."

I smiled. "Have you ever thought of getting counseling for your anger?"

He stood up quickly and paced the room, ignoring me. He checked the locked door then moved into the kitchen and stood there tapping his finger on the counter. I could see his eyes stop on each window and measure its vulnerability.

I followed and sat at the bar watching him. "Hey Bauer, are you going to tell me what's up?"

Max looked at me with hard, blue eyes. "We stay here the night. Tomorrow after John is here, we'll move you to a hotel until the safe house is available. Rich said as soon as he can wrap up his case, he'd be out the next day. But for tonight, we stay here."

The house phone rang.

I glanced at Max. Everyone had been using our cells. He moved to the counter and picked up the phone knowing that a trace was already in progress. "Hello?… Who may I say is calling?… Hold on." Max's face relaxed. "It's Jason Landry from Maryland." He handed me the phone.

I scrunched up my face in surprise. *Why would Jason call me from the Caribbean? And how did he get Max's number?* I cautiously took the phone. "Yes, Jason?"

"Hi, Mel."

I sucked in a silent breath and immediately hit the record button on the answering machine. I motioned to Max. "Devon Miles, I presume?"

Max put his head next to mine so he could hear him too. He glanced at the answering machine to make sure it was recording.

Miles chuckled. "Yes. I'm glad you recognize my voice."

"What do you want and why are you stalking me?"

"Stalking is such an ugly word." He paused. "It was inevitable, you know. You forced me into killing Roma. She should never have tried to slip away from me. And you should never have tried to pretend to be her. What kind of reaction did you expect? Now Roma is gone, thanks to you. You'll pay for forcing my hand so soon. And what I want is for you to die. Nothing more. And you will. Soon. And if need be, I'll take out that cop lover too. Bang. Bang."

"You won't get away with it, Devon."

He laughed. "Yes, I will. You aren't the first, neither was Roma, and you won't be the last. By the way, you looked so beautiful making love, at least what I saw. I couldn't stick around to see it all." He hung up laughing.

I slowly put the phone back in its cradle. My anger hit explode again, but soon dissipated. Max had shut off the recorder and was on the phone.

He looked at me. "They got the trace and the Captain dispatched two units to check it out. He's sending a unit by to get the recording."

I merely nodded.

"Call me as soon as you know. Thanks, Captain." Max hung up and immediately moved into his bedroom. I could hear him rummaging around in his closet. Finally he came walking out with a bullet proof vest. He tried to hand it to me. "Wear it."

I shook my head.

"Mel, put it on or so help me God, I'll strip you and do it myself." His eyes were rock hard. "Now!"

"I will not…"

"You will. And you will wear it day and night. He's going to shoot you. This will give you an edge. It's the best money can buy. I ought to know, my parents bought it for me." He tossed it to me.

I caught it, but didn't move.

"Put it on." Max jammed his hands onto his hips. His face hard as stone. The look in his eye was a strange one, one I hadn't seen before. "Now Mel." His eyes softened just a tad. "Do it. Please. For me."

I hesitated. Okay, it was the smart thing to do as much as I hated admitting that he was right. I looked down at it. I had never worn a vest before.

Max sighed softly and sat next to me. With a smile he took it out of my hands, probably realizing that I'd never used one before. I stripped off my T-shirt and he helped put it on. He adjusted it so that it fit just right. I put the shirt back on to find him staring at me.

"Thanks."

"Sure." I looked down at it again. It felt odd, bulky. Although, as thin as it was, I was skeptical it would actually stop a bullet.

Max leaned over and kissed me on the lips. "Don't leave my side tonight."

I tilted my head in question.

Max blushed. "I finally have you and now I might lose you. I can't let it happen." His cell rang. "Yes?" Another curse word escaped. "Okay thanks. Did the unit coming this way pick up a… Good. Thanks, Captain… I will."

I felt very conscious of the vest. I patted it again. The bulkiness seemed weird but then again, it also gave me a feeling of security. I smoothed out the shirt again, feeling Max's stare. "Yes?" I looked up catching an odd expression on his face.

"Nothing."

His expression changed as my head came up. It was a soft, tender look. A look of caring. I caught it out of the corner of my eye. "No, what?"

He shook his head and gave me another kiss on the lips. "Just so you know, I'm wearing a vest too."

"Good. I'd hate to think that I might have to leap in front of you to save your life, Bauer."

Max laughed and pulled me into a deeper embrace. He kissed me on top of my head. "The trace was to a hotel room. He used some sort of remote calling device. The Captain didn't understand the tech guy, but something about he called into the room and it dialed out or something like that. Miles rented the room this morning and left immediately. They haven't seen him since. He's a sneaky bastard."

"Now, now Max, that's no way to talk about my stalker."

Max chuckled, squeezing me tight. He just held me. "I don't want to lose you."

"Then when he shows up, don't miss."

Chapter 26

It was three in the morning and we were lounging together on the bed. Neither of us were sleeping tonight. We cuddled under the covers, entwined. We hadn't spoken much either. The units checked in every two hours on schedule, coming up would be the third time.

A knock sounded at the door. Max looked at his watch in the subdued night light in the bedroom. "They're early," he announced as he made his way out of my arms and toward the living room.

I stayed in bed, partially covered with the blanket. I sighed. If only this night would end so I wouldn't feel so confined. I heard a soft thump. My heart stopped beating. "Max?"

Footsteps. A meow, then a hiss. My heart beat accelerated.

Footsteps. Time seemed to have slowed to a snail's pace.

Footsteps.

A figure appeared at the doorway. "He can't help you now."

Miles.

I sat up, my hand snaking under the blanket for the gun. As I moved, so did he. He brought his gun up and fired. Time slowed even more. I could almost see the bullet headed my way. My arm didn't want to move. Then the pressure on my chest. Getting hit with a sledge hammer on the right side of my body. Air blew out of my lungs like a balloon deflating. I slammed backward into the head board. My head rebounded and hit again.

I stared up at him. He stalked closer. Miles' eyes slightly narrowed. I could see the creepy, crazy look, bat shit crazy. The evil grin grew. He started to raise the gun again.

Instinctively, I raised the Beretta. This time I was faster. A surprised expression filled Miles' face as I pulled the trigger. Once, then twice.

In slow motion, he flung backward against the wall, arms flying out from his sides. Still he held the gun. Blood spurted. The body thudded against the wall. It slowly slumped down into a heap on the floor, leaving a trail of blood on the wall. The right hand holding the gun twitched once. His eyes were vacant, open but unseeing.

My hand fell to the bed. I gasped for a breath as I stared at him. The smell of cordite filled my nose. I heard only silence behind the ringing in my ears, my heart beating, my breath shallow.

Pain. A tight clenching in my chest. Hard to breathe. Feeling like I was swimming in molasses, I released the Beretta, pain as I breathed. I couldn't pull my eyes away from Miles.

He stared straight ahead. His face seemed to be draining of color. A pool of dark liquid spread around him. The air took on a coppery smell. The air thick with death.

What have I done? He's dead. No more fear. I'm free.

I heard movement from the living room, but I couldn't peel my eyes away from the lifeless body slumped against the wall. The next thing I saw out of the corner of my eye was a uniformed cop peaking around the door frame, gun out. He swept the room and his attention rested on Devon Miles.

"Shooter is down." He moved into the room, gun pointed at the suspect, never taking his eyes off the stalker. Reaching down, he felt for a pulse. Then he stood up and looked at me. "Ma'am, are you okay?"

The voice sounded far away. I didn't answer. It was all I could do to breathe. Miles's unseeing eyes still captivated me.

"Get an ambulance." He leaned closer to me, blocking my view of Miles. "Mel, are you okay?"

I finally nodded to him as I struggled to breathe. My hand found the Berretta and grabbing it by the warm barrel, I handed it to him. Finally I looked up at the police officer. It was Ray from Max's bar.

Ray nodded, taking the weapon, unloaded it and stuck it in his waist band. "An ambulance is on its way. Are you having trouble breathing?" He squatted down to look me in the eyes. "Are you shot?" He peaked under the blanket which was only partially covering me.

I stared at him, focusing on his face. Suddenly it hit me. "Max? Is Max... Okay?" I tried a deep breath to fill up my seemingly empty lungs, but it hurt more than ever.

At that instant, the lights flashed on as another police officer came shuffling in supporting Max. With Ray's help, the two police officers sat Max on the bed next to me.

"Are you okay?" Max finally spoke after staring at me for a second. His attention turned to Miles' body then back to me.

"I… hurt." I rubbed my chest, especially the right side. "You?" Touching my chest sent lightning strikes across my body. Lights flashed in my eyes. I gasped again.

"Taser'd me," Max said and sort of collapsed on the bed next to me. "Luckily, they were coming early anyway, heard the shots fired."

Suddenly I couldn't breathe. I opened my mouth but nothing happened. I remembered this feeling of not being able to breathe from the accident. The crushing weight. The suffocating feeling. The panic. I gasped for breath, my mouth wide open. Body arching.

Max immediately sat up and ripped my shirt off. He stared at the bullet proof vest. Gently, he peaked under it but left it in place. "It didn't penetrate, but you've got a huge red area." He looked up at Ray who was watching both of us. "Get an ambulance."

"Already on its way."

The breaths finally came. The panic eased. I grimaced in pain. It hurt. It hurt so bad. I rolled onto my side in a ball, trying to hug the pain away.

"Mel?" Max sat down and pulled me into him, holding me tight, his strong arms around me, comforting as best he could.

I continued to gasp for air as we heard other sirens approaching. "Right side… Accident… Hurts… Can't breathe."

"Hold on. The ambulance is almost here." Max began rocking slightly. We could hear the sirens. Within minutes the paramedics hurried into the room.

They took a quick look at the dead body, but Ray was already directing them to me. An oxygen mask appeared over my head, then they manhandled me onto a stretcher. Ray took control, giving them information about the incident. Max followed me into the ambulance. Before we left the scene, Max leaned over and kissed me on the lips.

"I'll see you at the hospital later. I need to stick around here." He kissed me once more then looked at the two paramedics. "Take good care of her." One more kiss. "Love you. I'll call Rich."

Chapter 27

The emergency room was a busy place this early morning. I sat upright with an oxygen mask on. My chest still hurt, but I was no longer struggling for breath. My cell phone rang deep in my jeans pocket. I almost laughed. I had totally forgotten about it. I pulled it out and looked at the display. Rich.

"Hey."

"Max just called. Are you okay?"

"ER. Waiting on x-rays."

"What's that noise? Why are you talking funny?"

"Oxygen mask. I think I messed up my ribs again." I grimaced in pain. As the doctors said, talking hurt.

"The right side again?"

"Yeah."

A radiologist technician walked into the room.

"Rich, x-rays. Gotta go."

"See ya. By the way, good shot."

I gave half a chuckle and grimaced in pain as I shut off the phone. I knew I wasn't supposed to be talking on my cell in the hospital. "Hi."

She smiled. "Ready to get some pictures taken?" She was already releasing the brakes on the bed and getting me switched from the wall oxygen to a portable on the bed.

"Snap away Ansel Adams."

The lady laughed as she began pushing me out the door. I was in a great mood. I wasn't dead. Devon Miles was no longer after me, and except for this nasty pain in my side, I felt wonderful.

***

"Sure. Thanks, Doctor," I said as the doctor left. A new person appeared at my curtain. Max.

He smiled that lopsided, all in the face grin. "You're looking better than the last time I saw you. Are you okay?"

I was no longer on oxygen. And now the pain killers were starting to take effect. "Broken rib. Bruised a couple others." I pointed to the right side.

"What about the breathing thing?" He stood next to the bed and gave me another kiss on the lips. His hand caressed my shoulder.

"Muscle spasms. The shock of the impact and everything. Because of my right lung injury from the accident, I couldn't exchange enough air right away. My muscles tried to over-compensate and bingo, a spasm. I should have remembered what they felt like."

"What do you mean?"

"Been there, done that. So I'm back on muscle relaxants for my chest for a couple of days. My back will probably kink up tomorrow. I'll look like a pretzel." I smiled. "I'm being released. Are you here to take me home?"

"Uh, not home but to a hotel. They're still processing the scene." Max smiled back. This time he moved in and laid a kiss on me that almost took my breath away again. "I was so relieved to find you still alive. I heard the shots and, well, as I lay there, I about had a heart attack." His hand was on his heart. "I thought you were dead." He gave me another panty-wetting kiss.

"I thought you were dead when he showed up at the door." I took a very deep breath. "Thank God that's over."

"Yeah." Max hitched a hip on the gurney. "Before we go, you need to give a statement. Triscon is outside."

"Sorry for messing up your bedroom."

Max smiled as he traced my chin with his finger. "Not a problem. And just so you know, both shots were dead center. You took out his heart, completely gone. I think we need to call you Annie Oakley."

I smiled.

"I talked to Rich after he called you. He said just to let him know when you are headed home, and someone will be there to pick you up. I'll get Triscon and then we'll head to the hotel." He stretched as he moved out of the room. His butt looked so good from here.

Triscon walked into the room smiling.

"Hi Bruce."

"The benefits of the second amendment strike again."

I chuckled. "Yep. God help us if the criminals are the only ones armed someday."

Triscon pulled out his notebook and sat down in the chair next to my bed. "Okay. Start with after the phone call…"

***

We were in bed relaxing as the sun came up. It had been a very long day and I was exhausted. On top of that, the pain killers and muscle relaxants were really doing their job. I barely made it into the room and lay down before my eyes lids were doing the dip thing.

Max snuggled next to me. He leaned over and gave me a kiss, then pulled me into his arms. "Relax Mel. Go to sleep. You're safe. I'm here."

"Mmmm. Yeah." I drifted off.

"I love you, Mel. I love you."

***

I woke later to find Max sitting at the table in the room drinking coffee and reading the paper. His feet were on the other chair. His shirt was on the chair next to him. I studied him. His muscles were relaxed, but his chest and abs were so sexy.

Max looked up to see me watching him, a smile lit his face. "Good afternoon, Tiger."

"Yeah. It's afternoon?"

"Three-thirty," he said with a glance at his watch. "Hungry?"

I shook my head. "Not really." I frowned. Suddenly my gut twisted. Panic hit me. Hard. *What is going on? Why did I feel the sudden need to get out of here?*

"What?" Max laid the paper down. "What's wrong?"

"How long do I need to stay here to clean up this mess?"

"Everything is taken care of. It's pretty much been put to rest, some minor things. Yardley was not extremely happy, he wanted to catch Miles to face charges, but he was relieved that his case can be put to rest." Max leaned back in his chair. He studied me. "Why?"

I shrugged. "Just wondering how long I am required to stay?" The knot in my gut was twisting harder. *Why?*

There was a long minute of silence. "You can go anytime."

Our eyes stayed locked.

"I hope that you'll stay longer."

I stared at the wall behind him, the anxiety building. *Miles is dead. He is no longer out there watching me. So why am I so anxious?*

I got out of bed, gingerly. I took my time standing upright, testing the side. It hurt. Not as bad as last night but still painful. I grimaced, reaching full height.

"Are you okay?"

I nodded. "Just takes a while to straighten up. I'm used to it. I thought I'd never have to worry about this again." I rubbed the lower side of my chest. "The doc said that because of the accident, this side of my chest is weaker, especially the muscles. Guess it's back to physical therapy for me." I padded into the bathroom to do my business and maybe figure out why I felt this way.

The entire time on the toilet, I couldn't figure out why I was worried, tense, scared, panicked, even a little tinge of anger too.

Still holding my side I returned to the main room. Max was now sitting staring at the bed. He looked up at me as I entered.

"I'm taking a shower. Will you help me into my shirt and stuff when I get done?"

Max nodded.

I returned to the bathroom puzzled. There was a tension in the room that I didn't understand. And the knot continued to tighten. As I was showering I realized what might be part of the problem. *Max said he loved me. Twice. Why did he say that?* I stopped and let the water run over me, thinking.

I flashed back to sitting in my car. Craig pleading with me. *I love you, Mel. We can work this out. I love you, Mel. I love you.* Then the crash, the horrible sound of silence, of sobbing, me sobbing, death, Robbie dead.

No, I can't do this. I can't. I can't. The rat bastard. He cheated on me. He...

I sobbed then realized that the water was still flowing over me. I stood up, grimacing in pain again. Wiping my tears was useless.

"I can't do this," I said. "I can't. I need... I can't." I shut off the shower and stepped out. Drying the front was easy. It was bending over to do the legs and back that hurt. I shook hard. My hands trembled. I cursed. I needed help and Max was my only help right now.

I grabbed the extra towel and wrapped it around my body as best I could. Pausing before opening the door, I made sure that my hands were steady. Okay, as steady as I could keep them.

Max sat staring at the floor in the very same position I had left him.

"Hey, could you help me dry off?"

Max jumped like I had interrupted deep thoughts. He smiled but it seemed forced. "Sure. Could be fun."

I didn't respond but just moved toward the bed. I handed him the towel and he dried off my back and my legs. When he was doing the lower calves he kissed each one.

"Max, stop." I pushed him away in anger. The Rat Bastard had a calf and foot fetish. The anger was building. I painfully worked my right arm into my shirt. He offered to help, but I shook my head. I wanted to do this alone.

He stood watching me.

"Do you mind?"

"Not at all." He crossed his arms with a slight grin on his face. "Go ahead. I'll just stand here and watch."

I grabbed my stuff and headed to the bathroom with a disgusted look. It was hard getting the pants on. The bra was impossible, so I left it off, not to mention the elastic binder for my ribs. I grimaced in pain as it tightened. But the pain inside was worse, fear, betrayal, anger. He isn't the rat bastard. *It's Max, but still...* With a deep breath I exited the bathroom.

Max smiled. "Hungry?"

What am I going to do? The knot twisted again. I trembled. The gut twisted tighter. Any tighter and it could make diamonds.

Max gently hugged me from behind and kissed my neck. "What's the problem? You're too tense." He turned me around. "You're trembling."

I didn't look at him. I couldn't. "Max, I'm not staying. I want to go home." *Yes, getting away would make me feel better. I need space. I need to escape. Getting away would make this trembling go away and this twisting. And the new pain in my chest. I needed to think. I need to be alone. Get away.*

He pulled back. "When?"

"Now."

"I see."

"No. I don't think you do, Max."

This time he didn't speak.

I took a deep breath to try and relax the knot. "I just need to get home. I have things there… I want to… I need to go."

Max lifted my chin. "Look at me." He was unreadable for once. He studied me. "I know what you're thinking. You're scared. I understand. It was a traumatic thing that happened. I've shot and killed someone too. I know…"

"No." I clenched my fist to stop the trembling. "It's not that. I… yes, I've thought about killing Miles, but I'm okay with it. It was self-defense. He shot first. I'm okay with it." *I am, aren't I?*

"Then what?"

I didn't answer or look at him. I couldn't. I tried to relax my stomach muscles but they continued to twist and bunch. My legs started shaking.

"I don't get it. Is it me?"

I shook my head.

He scrunched up his face. "Talk to me, Mel. What did I do? Why are you leaving?"

"I just need to go. I can't… I can't… You said… I can't…"

Max shifted the weight on his feet. He shook his head. Then suddenly a new light came into his eyes. I looked away.

"I said I love you. Is that it?"

I gave a slight shake of my head. "I can't… You can't do this…" I cursed softly. With another grimace, now the twisting was working its way up my back too.

Max took me by both arms and made me look at him. "I love you. Yes, I said it. I do love you."

"Max, the sex was great and I do like you…"

"But?"

I sighed to relieve the new pain in the chest. "I don't… I can't do this."

"I see." Our eyes stayed locked. Max finally nodded. "Okay, if that's what you want. I'll call the station and tell them that you're headed home. I'll find out if you're needed for anything else."

I sighed as Max left the hotel room, but the anxiety didn't go away. I knew I had hurt him. I picked up my cell and called the airlines. Sure enough, there was a flight leaving in four hours. I slowly packed my clothes in the bag that Max brought from his house. I put his change of clothes in the hotel bag and locked the room.

We met out by his Trooper.

I ran my hand down the scrape on his truck. "Send me the bill for the Trooper."

"The insurance will take care of it. Don't worry." Max climbed into the truck.

I painfully got into the passenger's side, hoping the pain killer would start working. "What did your Captain say?"

"It was clearly self-defense. If we need anything we know where to find you," Max said before starting the engine. After it was running he turned to me. "Out to eat or did you book a flight?"

"My flight leaves in three and a half hours."

"To the airport then."

He accompanied me to the security gates. His hands were in his pockets and he wasn't looking at me. He hadn't looked at me the entire drive. Or spoke.

I turned to him. "I had a good time, Max. Thanks." Now I was nervous and anxious. *What is going on with me? I thought that once I was headed home I would feel better, relaxed. But it felt worse, much worse, anger, fear, and something else, but what?*

He didn't answer and the uncomfortable silence grew.

Max looked me in the eyes. "I do love you, Mel. I won't deny it, I fell in love. But it's obvious you don't feel the same."

His proclamation tightened the knot to its breaking point. I swear he could see my stomach moving and hear it gurgling. I just wanted to be alone. I needed to think. I needed to figure out what was going on. The panic was building again like flood gates had opened.

Max said nothing but shifted his weight. He stuck his hands deeper into his pockets. "Look at me." He waited until I did. "You're alive now, Mel. Live."

I rubbed my side in pain. I needed a muscle relaxer. I figured I'd take one on the plane and sleep for the flight.

"You're afraid." His blue eyes held mine.

I stared at him in disbelief. *How dare you! How dare you presume to know anything about me and what I'm thinking! How dare you impose your love on me! Just like the Rat Bastard. No, but...*

Max stared at me. His blue eyes unreadable. "Okay." He walked away.

"Max?"

He walked a few steps before turning partly around. Max paused then turned and continued on his way

"Max. Max?" But he kept walking.

What have I done?